The Telford Redemption

Alan Butters

Also by Alan Butters

The Factory

ST IVES MEDIA

ISBN: 978-0-9922675-3-7

PROLOGUE

Blundeston Moor, Southern Scotland – 1910

The boy stops, squinting against the wet fog that dances around him under the gentle push of the ocean breeze. He wipes his eyes, clearing tiny drops of moisture from his eyelashes. He listens. The sound of waves pounding on rock carries to him and he experiences a momentary stab of fear as he imagines that perhaps he's strayed too far this time. The boy had come to St Abb's with his father who found a job on a fishing boat working out of the small harbour. He loves these rocky hills but he hasn't entirely mastered their geography. Pushing negative thoughts from his mind, he calls out once again, his young voice at odds with the harsh and ancient landscape.

He hears a sharp bark but can't pinpoint its location. As he moves toward the ocean, the sides of the gully begin to rise around him and the craggy outcrops force him to pick his way carefully. The ground is slippery underfoot. Through the mist he sees that the gully leads nowhere. His feet are cold and wet from the holes in his boots and he's about to turn back when he hears another yelp, this time almost at his feet, startling him. His heart rate accelerates and a wave of goose bumps ripple down his arms.

He crouches, wiping his dripping nose against the back of his hand. The boy becomes aware of a cave behind a large and jagged boulder that has forced its way out of the wall of the gully. His young face is pulled into a frown as he asks himself why he didn't see it before now. How he could have been looking so intently but not seeing it. He examines the edge of the protruding boulder and the mystery deepens. Up close, its edges appear to have been chiselled into their current shape. Puzzled, he runs his hand over the cold surface of the rock, his small fingers tracing ancient tool marks. He stands and glances about him. All is nature, with the exception of this rock and the cave that it conceals.

The boy's curiosity about the rock is banished as the sound of his dog comes to him from deep inside the cave. As he bends to peer under the boulder he's amazed to see that it's not as dark underneath as he expected. Again he stands, looking for the source of the light but there are no holes in the gully's side that he can see. Bending forward he peers into the dim light, curious but hesitant to proceed. The dog barks, encouraging him on. The boy is unsure and a little apprehensive but he can't leave his dog behind. He stuffs his cap into the rope around his waist serving as a belt. Pulling his old jacket tightly around his bony shoulders and sliding on his knees through the wet moss, he slips under the rock and emerges into a small chamber.

The walls are stone but smooth, obviously this chamber too, is not a product of nature. He can't see the ceiling but light filters in from somewhere above. The floor is covered with a fine grey dust like powdered bone and in it he can see the dog's tiny footprints. A slight breeze caresses his face and carries with it the smell of the sea. His young mind grapples with the possibilities.

This place has obviously been fashioned by someone he reasons, and the fact that the entrance was so hard to see can only mean that they don't want anyone to find it. Pirates maybe. Obviously he shouldn't be here. As he rotates in the tiny space, taking it in, he's intrigued to discover that one wall finishes at an abrupt edge as though there might be a passage behind it. The boy's eyes are wide and he feels tiny and vulnerable in this secret place. His anxiety builds as he struggles to make sense of what he has found. He fights down the urge to simply turn and run. The boy wipes his nose against the incessant drip, hitches up his ragged trousers and steps forward.

As his gaze penetrates the gloom beyond the edge of the wall, a face abruptly materialises. Grotesque and malformed, it's like nothing he's ever seen and more hideous than anything he's ever imagined. In a panic he screams and pushes himself back, terrified by his discovery, desperate to get outside. He spins around and hits his head on a stone ledge protruding from the wall. His vision blurs and he staggers. Suddenly his feet are no longer touching the ground and he feels himself falling. With a sound like sticks splintering underfoot his leg fractures as he crashes awkwardly to the ground. For a few seconds the boy loses consciousness.

As his vision clears he at first imagines he's looking at a bright red light. Wiping away the blood trickling into his eyes he finds himself lying on cold stone stairs with his chin on the top step. His head is level with the hole through which he crawled only minutes before and he can see the feet of his dog waiting expectantly for him outside. He tries to move and a blast of pain is fired from his leg to his brain. For a moment he almost faints again. Only the sheer terror flooding into his mind from his memory of the face behind the wall keeps him conscious.

He doesn't want to think about what horrors might lurk in the darkness at the bottom of the stone steps but unwelcome images flash through his mind. A bony hand, the dead skin peeling back from dry knuckles, reaching out from the blackness below him, grabbing his leg, ignoring his screams as it drags him down the steps into the darkness. Fighting to control his breathing he hauls himself up onto the cavern floor and through the hole into the weak daylight. One side of the boy's face is ghostly white from the ancient dust blanketing the floor of the chamber. He rests his head against the cold wet moss before pulling himself up into a sitting position. He can hear the sound of his own heart beating.

Dreading what his fingers might reveal, he slides his hand down the injured leg, relieved not to find jagged bones bursting through the skin. Using the side of the gully for support he pulls himself upright and leans back against the damp rock. A wave of nausea washes over him and his vision begins to close down. With sweat streaming down his face, the boy manages to limp and crawl for almost a mile before collapsing from exhaustion. The last sound he remembers as the blackness embraces him is the dog barking. When the boy wakes he's lying in his own bed and his mother's face swims into focus, stern but concerned. Her mouth is moving but he hears no sound as he slips back into unconsciousness.

As time passes his young bones heal and the boy is no worse for wear save for a tiny scar above his left eye. Many times he has tried to find that place again, not at least to put an end to the constant banter from his father and his siblings regarding the outrageous story of the face in the rock. Secretly he is pleased never to have found it. He's by no means sure that he could go back into that cave and look at those cold stone steps leading down into the darkness.

Eventually he moves away but the experience stays forever etched into his memory. Even as an adult he has a nagging feeling of unfinished business. As though he failed in some way, didn't find something he was meant to find. Six decades later, the story has entered into the lore of the family and has become a favourite of his many grandchildren who beg him to tell it and then listen wide eyed and open mouthed at his tale of caverns and gargoyle faces. As the children grow, the story loses its power to frighten and eventually it becomes an amusing and treasured memory that, as adults, triggers with fondness images of the old man.

Except in the case of one curiously intense child. He grows up with no doubt that the old man's story is real and in his heart he knows that he will go back and face what his grandfather could not.

CHAPTER 1

"Prick!" Yells Sarah Nelson as the tears course down her face. "He's such a prick!"

A tiny drop of spittle flies across the room. Outside, the wind thrashes rain against her bedroom window in a harsh reminder that in the north of England, winter is here to stay. Maria, her friend of twenty years lets go of Sarah's hands and sits back, the chair groaning under her considerable bulk.

"Aye, he's that all right, and more." She replies, her Scottish accent thick with emotion at her friend's distress. "You know what the problem is with that wee bugger?"

"Tell me." Replied Sarah, looking up.

"The man has no class." With that, Maria leans back luxuriously and lets go such an extraordinarily thunderous fart that Sarah imagines the neighbours must have heard it above the storm outside. Unable to contain herself, Sarah explodes with laughter, spraying more spittle around the room before she can get her handkerchief in place.

"Maria! You're disgusting!" She exclaims, her tears turning to tears of laughter. "You really are."

"Better the shame than the pain I say. If I got ma hands on that randy bugger I'd sit on his thick head and gas him to death. It'd be good riddance to the midget."

"Eric isn't *that* short."

"Aye, ma Aunt Fannie." Maria snorted. "If his wee legs were any shorter his arse would rub out his own footprints. Don't *you* be defending him now, he got his leg over and then buggered off like rat up a drainpipe."

"Maria!"

"Well he did, didn't he. That's fuckin' men for ye, all they want is to get into yer knickers and then piss off for some other bit of fluff. Away tae fuck wi' em all."

Sarah shakes her head and smiles at her friend. "You've such a way with words, do you know that?"

"Aye, it's a gift."

"Oh God." Said Sarah blowing her nose and becoming serious again. "I have to get some new digs. At least get out of this place for a while."

"Why not come and stay with me the night?" Asks Maria. "We can order a huge pizza and get pished watchin' the telly. Mibee start a list of things to look for in the next guy so you don't end up wi' another big girl's blouse."

"I wouldn't know where to start right now." Replies Sarah shaking her head.

"Wi' a big tadger, that's first on the list!"

"Right. Like that'll guarantee me a long term relationship!"

"You think too much lassie. Come on get yousel' together and let's be away."

* * *

Dark grey clouds edged with black rumble across the sky above the Bedlington Police Station in Northumberland. The structure has the look of a schoolhouse or perhaps even a modern church building. Located on the A696 not far from the Scottish border, the building also serves as Area Command Headquarters for Northumbria.

Detective Inspector David Orbost sits at his desk staring into the middle distance, his mood only marginally brighter than the weather outside. As the rain taps at the window he wonders not for the first time what the hell he's doing in the north of England. His memory teases him with images of Melbourne Australia where he's spent the largest portion of his life so far. Despite the jokes that Australians level against his hometown, it *never* gets as cold as Northumberland and it's hard to forget this fact as the northern hemisphere's winter settles in.

David is one of the many Aussie kids born to British parents who had emigrated to find a better life and a warmer climate. To his parents, it probably seemed like a good idea at the time but David had been exasperated because as soon as the pair retired they began making plans to move back "home." Following a difficult separation from a long relationship, David thought what the hell, I may as well join them, they're not getting any younger and the change might be good. Within three months he landed a senior role with the local force and, eighteen months out, he still has misgivings about whether it was the right thing to do.

It's on grey days like this that David can't help feeling a little resentment toward his parents for dragging him and his sister around the world. As far as he's concerned the net effect of their emigration and subsequent return has been to split the family down the middle with his sister still in Australia together with her husband and kids and him forced to choose between living in the same country as his parents or his nieces and nephew. With hindsight they would have been better staying in England in the first place. He shakes his head as hail begins to strike the window. The sound of the hail always reminds him of his mother making popcorn in a steel pan when he was a kid. He stuffs his hands deeper into his pockets. The weather is worse up here by the Scottish border but the crimes had remained pretty much the same as down under. Until now.

His daydreaming is interrupted by his co-investigator, Walter Pembroke, who somehow manages to arrive each morning looking dapper regardless of the prevailing weather. 'Bright-eyed and bushy-tailed' the Aussies would say. Walter's almost burlesque English tweediness often provoked others to underestimate him – a fact that he has exploited to their chagrin on more than one occasion.

"Morning, David, looks like we might have ourselves another unfortunate young woman."

David's head snaps up. "What?"

The cross-border task force that the two senior detectives have been assigned to for the last three months is proving to be a tougher undertaking than he expected, particularly as the English investigators appear to have the burden of work to themselves. Two dead women have been found, several weeks apart. Both women are English but one was found in Northumberland and the other across the border in Scotland. Certain similarities between the murders, the details of which haven't been released to the public are too striking to be coincidental.

"Absolutely, old man," Walter continued, "I got the call on the way in. White female, mid twenties, found by a pair of lads who were fishing off the rocks this morning up at Rumbling Kern. Gave them somewhat of a shock methinks."

"Rumbling Kern, that's about, what – forty five kilometres north? A bit south of Craster?"

"Absolutely correct. I must say, David, you continue to impress me with your encyclopaedic grip of the local geography. Well done."

"Well, I'm still learning." David says, stuffing the few papers on his desk into a drawer. "So you're thinking it's linked?"

"I expect we'll make that determination presently. Unfortunately the body has spent some time in the water which obviously doesn't suit our purposes overmuch but it was clearly undernourished and our man at the scene spotted the ligature marks on the wrists immediately."

"Bingo!" said David grabbing his jacket from the back of his chair, his dark mood instantly dispelled at the prospect of activity. "So what are we waiting for?"

"That's the spirit! I have the keys to the motor in my possession - let us make haste before the scene becomes further degraded by the weather."

* * *

The man slips under the dripping rock and emerges into the dry of the chamber. He strokes the carving gently, almost lovingly, It's a pig's head, nailed by its ears to the wall. Its mouth bulges open and its eyes are wide with fear. A cat's head protrudes from the pig's mouth, its face deformed as if by a stroke. One side of the cat's face sags and it appears to be missing an eye. On the other side its mouth is drawn into a snarl, revealing a row of wickedly sharp teeth. Driven through the cat's neck is a heavy steel ring with ornamental carvings snaking around its perimeter. The cat's eye is made of amber; it blazes with an inner light of fury and animosity, a warning for anyone who dares to come within striking distance.

The man turns on his heel and steps lightly down the stone steps into the darkness, a contended smile on his face. The gentle sea breeze rises to greet him carrying with it a tiny whimper, a woman's sob from somewhere deep underground.

* * *

A bolt of pain shoots through Sarah's forehead as she swings her legs over the edge of the bed. Her mouth tastes like something has died in it overnight and her eyeballs feel too big for their sockets. Head in hands, she rests her elbows on her knees and takes several deep breaths. As she stands up on the cold wooden floor of Maria's spare room she becomes acutely aware that her bladder is about to burst and has to dash to the toilet before she further compounds the miserable way she feels by pissing in her pants.

Downstairs cooking breakfast, Maria hears the toilet flushing and yells up the stairs. "Five minutes to go! Should I crack open an Irn Bru?"

Sarah groans. She's in constant amazement at Maria's almost superhuman powers of recovery. They had both drunk like fish the night before but whereas Sarah wants to die, Maria seems entirely unaffected by the night's carousing.

"Bugger the Irn Bru, I'll just have coffee." Sarah calls back, the effort sending new bolts of pain through her head. "And aspirin. Definitely aspirin." She adds.

"You'll no' have aspirin for breakfast in my house, Hen." Maria calls up the stairs. "What you need is some food in yer wee belly."

Sarah knows it's hopeless to argue and she shuffles out of the bathroom. Settling for the first thing that swims into her bleary vision, she pulls on a pilled and shapeless tracksuit covered in cat hairs. After treading cautiously down the wooden steps lest she sets off the jackhammers inside her head, she slumps into the closest kitchen chair.

Maria turned around from the stove, hands on hips. "My God, Sarah. I tell you, if I was a lesbian you'd be in moral danger comin' doon the stars looking like that. I'm a sucker for that tussled 'I just woke up wi' mi' head stuck up a cow's arse' look."

Sarah simply hangs her head and groans. Maria places two aspirin and a glass of water by Sarah's elbow, leans forward and kisses her lightly on the head.

"I've made some toast, pet, eat what you can while I shower."

"Thanks." Sarah replies without looking up.

Fifteen minutes later, enveloped in a cloud of steam, a pink faced Maria emerges from the bathroom. The aspirin is beginning to blunt the edges of Sarah's headache and she has even managed a slice of toast.

"Ah see you've been piggin' out on ma toast." Maria says, a mischievous twinkle in her eye.

"Sorry, Maria, I did the best I could. Honestly."

"Aye, ma Aunt Fannie. At this rate you'll be as fat as me in no time."

Sarah smiles. "Thanks Maria. No, really, thanks for everything. You're my best…"

Abruptly Sarah's eyes began to fill with tears. Annoyed, she wipes them away with her sleeve.

"Did ye call in sick this morning?" Maria asks.

Sarah nods, a pained look flitting across her face. "I feel so guilty ringing up on a Monday morning and telling them I'm sick. They're such nice people, they always say it's okay but it must be a pain for them to be short handed in the shop."

"Aye, they're nice folk alright." Mariah said.

Sarah fishes around in her tracksuit pocket for a tissue before blowing her nose.

"I have to do something about my life, Maria. I drink too much, I go out with absolute tossers, I let people down. I'm thirty four years old for God's sake and I have my mum on my case all the time wanting grandkids and there's no prospect of that happening anytime soon."

"Ach. If yer mam had wanted grandkids she shoulda had more wains!" Maria replies. "It's no good stopping at one and then expecting a brood of grandkids. It's too much to put on a person."

Sarah smiles at her old friend. "Thanks for sticking up for me. You know my mum, she means well. And another thing she's always reminding me of, I have a damned arts degree, the only one in my dad's family to go to university and I end up working in a craft shop in Ashington! How does that happen?"

"Tell you what." Maria said, filling the kettle. "I've been invited out on Wednesday night to a party. You remember Eileen?"

"The one with hairy boyfriend who drives that noisy motorbike?"

"Aye, she's the one. Anyway she's having one of those knickers parties where you can buy wee panties made of rice crispies and giant rubber willies that glow in the dark. I promised her I'd go over there early and help her set up."

Sarah groans. "Come on, Maria, I hate that sort of thing. You know that. And Wednesday night's a bugger of a night for a party with work the next day."

"Don't be wet. You'll have a great time. It's just a laugh, you don't need to buy anything. I'll call Eileen and tell her we'll both go. It'll be good for you to get your skinny arse out of the house."

Once again Sarah knows that resistance is useless in the face of Maria's determination.

"There won't be any of those men with the oiled muscles and socks on their thingys will there?"

"We can only live in hope, hen." Maria replied.

* * *

David and Walter thread their way through the slippery moss-covered rocks toward the small group huddled at the water's edge. Gusts of cold wind steal the warmth from their bodies as they probe at clothing seams and exposed flesh. Walter of course has remembered his wellingtons whereas David's are sitting in the boot of his car back at the station. So far David figures that six months wear has disappeared from the sides of his new shoes and he's already managed to put one foot into the glacial water of a rock pool.

A barrier of plastic sheeting shields the dead woman from prying eyes and a uniformed constable stands with his face turned away from the wind, contributing a suitably official atmosphere to the site. David spots the police photographer packing his equipment into a large silver case, his lips pressed into a thin line. Tony Davis, a Scenes of Crime Officer is speaking quietly to him as he works. The Home Office pathologist, Trevor Norwich, is standing next to the body making notes, his head and shoulders visible above the opaque screen. As they approach the scene, David feels a familiar sensation coursing through his body. Part fear, part excitement, part guilt at the ease with which he's able to separate the wretched tragedy that lays before him from the academic and clinical process of detective work.

The blue plastic sheeting flaps and strains against its supporting poles as they step behind it and gain their first glimpse of the dead woman. The shock isn't as bad as David feared. The girl's skin is loose and grey like an old towel from which all the colour has been washed out. Her eyes, although open and staring, are milky and one looks as though it might have been pecked by a seagull. David shivers at the thought.

"What have we got, Trevor?" He asks.

The pathologist takes a deep breath, hands thrust deep into his pockets against the biting wind.

"So far as I can tell from my initial examination, white female obviously, probably early to mid twenties. Blue jeans, T-shirt, pullover, no shoes. No obvious signs of trauma other than pronounced ligature marks on both wrists and skin missing from bony prominences of the hands and arms. She has some other cuts and abrasions but they could have been caused by contact with the rocks. Birds or crabs have had a bit of a go at her face I'd guess. I'd also say she's quite a bit underweight but then lots of girls are these days I suppose. No identification."

"Any thoughts on the marks around the poor girl's wrists?" Walter asks.

Trevor waggles his head as if to indicate ambiguity. "I'll need to look more closely when we get her inside but my first impression is that she'd been tied up for a while. It looks like we have bruising and abrasions of various ages."

"Where are the young men who found the body?"

Trevor inclines his head toward the road. "They're sitting with a female PC. The SOCO reckons they're a bit rattled. Understandable."

"We'll have a chat with them in a minute. What did they say, do you know?" David asks.

"They told Tony that as the sun started to come up they saw something floating. Washing up against the rocks. They were hoping that it might be something valuable from a passing cargo ship but when they got closer they saw it was a person. To give them their due, in the dim light they weren't sure she was dead at first and so they took an arm each and dragged her up onto the rocks. One of the lads said he nearly pissed his pants when he touched her hand."

"I'll bet he did." Replied David. "Any idea how long she'd been out there?"

"Can't be sure yet but I'd say not long. Maybe overnight, maybe a bit longer."

Walter nodded. "Certainly long enough for her to have drifted many miles from where she was dumped though."

"Afraid so. If she was tossed in the water from the shore she could have drifted twenty or thirty miles down here. If she came from a boat, God only knows."

David looks at Walter and something passes between them. Walter nods.

"Same as the others, Certainly."

"Let's hope the bastard has left us something this time." David replies, turning to look out across the oily grey sea, the stinging wind driving tears to his eyes.

CHAPTER 2

Above the discreet whisper of the ocean the woman hears another sound. Someone humming a tune. She shakes her head in an attempt to release her mind from the grip of fear that clutches at her greedily during most of her waking hours. The woman's wrists are raw and bleeding from her futile struggle against the ropes, the knuckles bruised from contact with the cold stone wall. The humming sound is so totally out of place it's almost surreal.

Her mind grapples with the possibilities. Should she shout for help? If it's the man returning, she could be punished for calling out. If it's someone else, they might never find her down here if she doesn't make herself known. She decides to wait and see. A few minutes later she hears purposeful footsteps along the long stone corridor and she has to turn away from the bright light of the torch as it pierces the total blackness of her world. Dazzlingly bright shapes dance around the ancient walls as the man approaches. He had always switched off the torch before and existed only in her mind as a disembodied voice. Her mind races trying to determine if this change in his pattern is good or bad.

"Hello Amanda. How are you feeling?"

The voice is gentle, caring even. She doesn't reply, her eyes dart around the room, hungrily drinking in the details of her surroundings after the numbing blackness. She discovers a large room with exquisitely ornate carving around the walls. The light doesn't penetrate into the corners but she sees what could be passages with vaulted ceilings leading off into the darkness. Directly opposite her, sunk into the wall is an arch with intricate details around its edge. Faces, snakes, exotic fruits and scrollwork adorn its underside. Lying across the base of the arch and on top of a stone casket is a life size carving of a man. On his back, his hands are clasped in a penitent manner above his chest. At his feet, a small stone dog with the head of a lion waits patiently. Kneeling on the floor in front of the casket in a supplicant's position are two children, their faces intricately detailed and frighteningly lifelike. Their stone eyes are closed, their heads slightly bowed.

Suddenly the tumblers in her mind fall into place and she realises that she's imprisoned in a tomb. In fact she is lying on top of a large casket. Gasping at the realisation, her head jerks back and she bangs it hard on the stone wall causing lights to float before her eyes. Swivelling her head she sees that her wrists are secured to the wall with course rope tied to what appear to be very new and substantial metal hoops. Tears well in her eyes as she's presented with visual confirmation of the absolute hopelessness of her position.

Without speaking the man leans across and begins to untie her hands. She breathes in his smell, clean cotton, soap, perhaps a hint of cologne. She feels the warmth from his body near her own and strangely for an instant she finds comfort in it. His hands are large and powerful, his skin smooth. As the ropes fall away her hands drop to her sides and she cries out in pain as the muscles in her shoulders immediately cramp.

The man removes his backpack and begins to take out a thermos flask and sandwiches wrapped in greaseproof paper. She notices that his hiking boots and the bottoms of his trousers are wet and imagines that it must be raining outside. It's a painful reminder of how insulated she is from everything in this place. Day, night, sun, rain. It's all the same down here. As the man unwraps the sandwiches, the smell of the bread fills her nose and her stomach momentarily spasms with hunger.

"They do smell good don't they?" Asks the man as though he can read her thoughts. "I made them for you, Amanda. Please, eat."

Placing the thermos and food next to her, the man steps away and sits on a stone block at the other side of the chamber. She is conscious of his eyes on her as she eats. Despite her ravenous hunger she eats slowly and deliberately, savouring this partial freedom and not wanting to overload her desperate stomach. Her gaze takes in the elaborately carved walls, the inscriptions in languages she doesn't recognise. To her left a row of tiny figures study her every move from a stone shelf set just above head height. A cluster of tree-men, some with branches growing out of their ears and mouths, others with leaves sprouting from their eyes appraise her in silence. Tiny sentinels, their vigilance never wavering as centuries arrive brimming with promise and then retire, for the most part without distinction.

She surprises herself by managing to drink all of the strong black tea in the thermos. As she drains the last cup the man walks over and gently takes her wrist in his hand and begins to retie her to the wall. He isn't rough but her instinct warns her that to resist would be very dangerous. Suddenly the thought of being alone again in the darkness swamps her previous resolve to show no fear. She begins to cry. Ignoring her tears the man steps back, checks his work.

"Have you seen anything Amanda? While you were in the dark alone? Anything that you would like to tell me about?"

"Where am I?" She asks through her tears. "Why are you doing this to me?"

"You're in a very special place. Very special and very old. Many anchorites have come here. As for why I'm doing this to you, I had a feeling that you might be special. Are you special Amanda?"

"I don't know what you mean!" She sobs. "Please let me go. Please."

The man sighed. "Perhaps you're not special after all. That would be disappointing. We'll speak again soon. Goodbye Amanda."

The woman's eyes plead desperately for him to stay.

"Please don't leave me in here. Please, I can be special, just tell me what you want."

Without a word the man turns, collects his pack, and walks away. The light flashes around the walls as he retreats and then the absolute blackness returns. Her body is wracked with giant sobs and she feels as though her chest might burst. After a while, lulled by the far away sounds of the ocean and exhausted by grief, she slips into a restless sleep that not even the pain in her shoulders and back can prevent.

* * *

"God, I'm knackered." Detective Inspector David Orbost slumps into his desk chair on Tuesday morning.

"You didn't sleep well?" Asks Walter, looking irritatingly as though he'd just returned from two weeks holiday.

"I'm not actually sure I slept at all! By the time we left here last night it would have been, what? Midnight? When I hit the sack my head was just spinning. What time are we seeing the pathologist?"

"Unless I'm very much mistaken, that's our man getting out of his motor as we speak." Walter replies, looking out of the upper floor window.

David's head turns to follow Walter's gaze. "I'm glad he had business over this way, I didn't fancy going out to the mortuary today, that place gives me the willies."

"Murder itself is past all expiation the greatest crime, which nature doth abhor."

David raised an eyebrow.

"Goeffe." Walter added.

Their conversation is interrupted by the phone on Walter's desk announcing, somewhat redundantly, the arrival of the pathologist from the Forensic Science Service. The three meet in the reception area downstairs.

"Let us repair to the conference room and see what pearls you have for us." Says Walter, indicating the way with an expansive sweep of his arm.

When the three men are settled around one end of the long conference room table, cups of coffee at their elbows, David is the first to speak.

"Thanks for coming out, Trevor, you look about as tired as I feel.

What have you got for us mate?"

"Well," replies Trevor, selecting an A4 notepad from his impeccable leather briefcase, "I think we might have a couple more pieces of the puzzle. You gents will have to work out where they fit of course."

"Pray continue, my dear chap." Walter says.

"There are a couple of points to be made. As with the previous two women, victim number three did not drown. However, I think that in this case we have a cause of death."

David leans forward in his chair, his hunger for new facts written large on his face.

"You'll recall the ambiguities of the previous two victims where asphyxiation was indicated."

"Yes, you said respiratory failure but there was no sign of strangulation or suffocation." David said.

"Correct. I would suggest that victim number three died from a very subtle stable neck fracture."

"Meaning precisely what, old boy?" asked Walter.

Straightening his pad on the table, Trevor carefully aligns his pen parallel to the edge of the pages before continuing. David notes this little idiosyncrasy but knows better than to hurry the pathologist.

"If the vertebrae of the neck were to slide sideways in relation to each other, then we have a dislocation. This may take many forms and can be accompanied by torn ligaments, bone fragments etcetera. When the dislocation takes place, the spinal cord can be pinched by the shearing action of the vertebrae, resulting in paralysis. Of course, in the human frame there are massive front and rear ligaments protecting the vertebral bodies as well as shorter ligaments between the bony projections on the vertebrae. One of these ligaments was torn in the neck of victim three. A close inspection revealed damage to the spinal cord, which could have been sufficient to cause instant paralysis below the neck. Ergo, caseation of respiration and subsequent asphyxiation."

The room is silent for a few moments as the two detectives consider this new information. Walter is the first to reply.

"I don't suppose you've had time to check the first two victims for similar injuries?"

Clearly a little discomfited, Trevor corrects a miniscule misalignment of his pen and pad before continuing.

Actually I did re-examine the first victims, which, as you will be aware, are being kept by us pending further developments. They had no such torn ligaments."

"Bugger" David exclaims.

"However." Trevor continues, frowning at the interruption. "I examined the spinal columns in the same area and the damage was consistent in each case."

"So you're saying that the cause of death was in fact the paralysis in all three even though only one had the ligament damage?"

"Well, the cause of death was asphyxiation due to the paralysis but you are essentially correct, yes."

"Well I'll be." David said.

"How does this happen, Trevor?" Walter asked.

"We see this sort of injury, although usually less severe, most often in motor vehicle accidents. Whiplash is the legal term in most jurisdictions. It involves the neck bending forward and then a sudden hyperextension backwards."

David blinks a couple of times, his mind racing with possibilities. "But these girls didn't die in a car crash and then end up in the water."

"Quite so. I guess this is where you chaps come in."

"So, let's assume that you wanted to create this hyper whatever…"

"Hyperextension."

"Right. Hyperextension. Let's suppose you wanted to create this hyperextension deliberately. How difficult would it be and what sort of experience would you need to do it? Are we looking for a doctor here?"

"My goodness no!" Exclaimed Trevor. "A medical practitioner

would certainly know the mechanics of the injury but certainly not be trained to inflict it."

"Trained to inflict it." David repeated thoughtfully. "So someone in the business of killing then. A soldier or assassin of some sort maybe."

"I think that's much more likely. This would be a relatively quick and silent way to kill without a weapon. There may be others trained in this method of killing, secret service personnel, those sorts of chaps. I don't know, you would have to do your own research, it's not really within my purview."

A glance passes between the two detectives, both understanding the significance of this new information.

"You mentioned a couple of points to be made." Walter said.

"Yes, the other observation concerned some material found under the victim's belt."

"Material?" Asks David.

"Yes, there was a sliver of stone lodged between the victim's jeans and shirt. We had to go looking for it in her clothes after I noticed a mark in the small of the victim's back."

"What sort of stone?" Asks Walter.

"It appears to be marble. Now, this stone is quite small but under examination, one can detect tool marks on one edge and a very smooth surface."

"Like a headstone you mean?" asked David.

"Precisely. Perhaps some sort of ornamental masonry. From its location I'd say she was laying on or was dragged over some stonework."

David leans back in his chair and folds his hands behind his head. "So, we need to find a retired army bloke who has taken up stone masonry in his spare time."

"I think not." Replied Trevor. "The small piece of rock had obviously once been part of something larger but it wasn't chipped off."

"It wasn't?"

"No. Its edges were eroded. I suspect it broke away due to age. Whoever chiselled that particular piece of marble might have been dead for a thousand years."

* * *

Sarah sits at the breakfast table staring into her morning coffee. Her mother, Dorothy, bustles around in the kitchen preparing breakfast for her husband George and making more noise than usual. Since her father retired, Sarah couldn't help noticing the change in their relationship. It was as though George had upset the natural order of things by being in the house so much. Sarah has the distinct feeling that her mother resents him because her time is no longer her own. George has tried to interest her mother in playing tennis or golf, going abroad for a holiday, anything that they could do together now he's no longer constrained by work. None of his ideas have won any support. Sarah realises her mum would prefer to sit back and complain about him being under her feet all the time rather than put effort into changing anything. Not that Sarah herself is much better when it came to pulling her finger out, she thinks.

"What's on your mind, Mum?" Sarah said, sensing the tension in her mother's movements, her eyes not leaving her coffee cup.

"Oh nothing." She says. "It's just that Connie from next door told me you weren't at work again yesterday."

"Ah yes." Sarah said. "Connie the spy. Actually I stayed the night at Maria's."

"She's not a spy, Sarah, she simply made an observation. And you know what I think of that Scots woman that you seem so fond of."

"It's Maria. She has a name, Mum. You know that."

"Whatever. I don't think she does any good for you, she never has. Your father and I didn't scrimp and save to put you thorough university so you could fritter your life away drinking and carousing with her to the extent that you can't even go to work. You're a smart girl Sarah, top in your class for goodness sake!"

Here we go again, thinks Sarah. At that moment her father George walks into the kitchen, his face glowing from the shower. On his way to his customary seat at the table he plants a kiss on the top of Sarah's head.

"What did we scrimp and save for, Dot?" He said.

"You keep out of this George. You know you always take Sarah's side. I was just mentioning that Connie informed me Sarah wasn't at work yesterday."

Sarah catches the eye of her father and she suppresses a smile as he mimes the act of Connie peering through a slit in the curtains.

"All I'm saying, George, is that Sarah can do much better for herself but it's not going to just fall out of the sky and into her lap. I mean, thirty four years old, still living at home and not even a steady boyfriend. Spends all her time hanging around with that Maria woman who's just as bad. Fat chance we'll have of ever having grandkids!"

"Dorothy…" George started.

"Don't you 'Dorothy' me, George Nelson. It's time she did something with her life. Pulled her finger out before it's too late. And you're no shining example! Could have been a postmaster but no, you had to be a postman for thirty-five years because you didn't want a management job. We could have been sitting pretty!"

"We do okay, Dorothy. Don't be dragging up the past."

"You asked me to come and live here Mum. After I got sick, remember?"

Dorothy turns to face her daughter, her finger, encased in a fluorescent-pink rubber glove stabbing the air.

"I remember that very well, Sarah. And you are always welcome in this house. That's not the point. Your father and I want what's best for you, that's all."

"I know. And you're right, I am stuck in a rut but I'm determined to pull myself out. I went and saw Doctor Baxter yesterday afternoon."

"Oh yes?" Said Dorothy. "What did he have to say?"

"He's changing my medication. He's given me a prescription for a new drug that he reckons will not sap my energy like the current stuff."

"That's wonderful!" George exclaims putting his arm around his daughter and giving her a hug. His expression suddenly turns serious as the memory of his daughter's illness pains him.

"You haven't been hearing those voices again have you, darling?" He asks.

Sarah looks into his face and sees such love and concern that tears well in her eyes. She puts her hand over his and gives it a squeeze.

"Of course not, Dad. Doctor Baxter's just fine tuning things, that's all."

Dorothy tosses the bread knife into the sink with a clatter that makes Sarah jump. She folds her arms across her pinafore.

"Well, let's hope it gives you a bit more gumption." She says.

* * *

The rain hammers on the roof of the car and runs down the windscreen in tiny rivulets as Walter and David sit eating fish and chips. The view of the tiny harbour in the fishing village of Craster is all but obscured by the rain and the steamed-up glass. Using a drooping chip as a pointer, Walter attempts to impart some of the local history of the small village renowned for its kippers.

"I have a picture of you in my head as a lad, Walter." David says. "A keen cyclist. Off every weekend on your ten-speed with your little tent crammed into panniers on the back of the bike. Well-thumbed guidebook at the ready, ticking off these little historical villages up and down the country like a train spotter. Am I right?"

"Far from it, old man. I'm not actually sure I've ever been in possession of a bicycle. When one's father is a history Don and one's mother a schoolteacher, well, one's holiday activities do tend to veer toward the intellectual."

"Sounds like a riot. I'm amazed you ever got to be a copper with parents like that. Aren't you supposed to be toiling in the groves of academia or something?"

"Didn't work for me unfortunately. I did try it but I'm just not cut out for those hallowed halls I suppose."

"Black sheep of the Pembroke family?" David asks with a smile.

"Oh, it's not as bad as all that. I'm sure my father never understood why I wanted to get into police work but my mother was an enlightened woman. She pushed me to do what I wanted and then ran interference with my father. I owe her a debt of thanks for that, no mistake."

David smiles. His mind returns to the case that is never far from his thoughts. The pair had pulled on their raincoats to stand once again on the shore at Rumbling Kern where the third victim had been found, looking for inspiration but leaving without it.

"You know, I'm not sure how much farther we've progressed in reality." Said David, screwing up the newspaper around the remainder of his chips. "I mean, let's assume we're dealing with someone trained to kill in hand to hand combat. Let's also assume that the stone chip came from a graveyard or a church or a museum or whatever. That still doesn't really help us. There are still too many bloody variables."

"Quite so." Replied Walter. "Methinks that we'll need a couple more elements before a real picture starts to take shape."

"What pisses me off," continued David, "is that it's almost like we have to wait for him to give us more information, which means another dead girl. I reckon if he just disappeared now, he'd never be caught. No connection between the victims that we can find, practically no physical evidence, and no apparent motive."

"God made man to go by motives, and he will not go without them, any more than a boat without steam, or a balloon without gas."

"Disraeli?" Asks David.

"Beecher, Henry Ward."

"Well maybe he was right but discovering what that motive *is* can be a bugger."

"As you say, my handsome antipodean friend, it can indeed be a bugger."

"So, let's go back to first principles, making a couple of assumptions along the way. Let's assume that our man, and incidentally I think we're pretty much okay in assuming we're not chasing a woman here."

"Agreed. Although not impossible, a female perpetrator would be very unlikely in this instance. Pray continue."

"So, a man trained to kill. Let's go for the most likely explanation of a soldier, remembering that he might not have necessarily served in a British force."

"Absolutely. God forbid he might even be an Australian!"

"Not a chance mate. He'd have buggered off back home when this winter set in if he had any sense. Anyway, I think we need to put the stone fragment aside for the minute and concentrate on the soldier angle. Speak with the friends and relatives of the victims yet again to try to find if this soldier bloke is known to anyone. You have a better idea?"

"I'm afraid I don't, old chap. Let's get to it. You drive and I'll man the telephone."

* * *

Amanda's mind is clear. She couldn't remember at what point she'd come to this realisation but she is now certain. She will never be released from this tomb. She doesn't even know his real name but this one thing she knows beyond all doubt: this man means to kill her. After he'd allowed her to see his face, which he'd always been careful to hide before now, she became sure. Of course she's heard about the missing girls on the television. She knows in her heart that the man holding her captive is the one responsible for the disappearance of the other women. Strangely, rather than feeling a sense of despair and hopelessness, she feels somehow galvanised as though a certain clarity has come to her plight. She experiences a kind of intense solidarity with the dead women. She will do something, for them and for herself. Before she becomes any weaker she will fight for her life and if she fails, she will ensure that she leaves some sort of sign pointing to this place. She will not die without inflicting pain and she will not die in vain.

She thinks about her life of a few days ago, about her boyfriend, her parents who by now must be climbing the walls with worry. She thinks about the plans and dreams that she had. Travel, a wedding, a house, children. Anger begins to escalate inside her that a stranger could, without any reason that she can fathom, simply steal all this away. She experiences a lucidity that has been totally absent since she first woke in this tomb. Lying in total darkness on her cold hard bed of stone, she starts to plan.

CHAPTER 3

Maria pulls on the handbrake and turns off the engine. "Well, here we are, hen."

Sarah gazes up at the municipally styled block of flats, wet grey concrete with rows of symmetrical windows, their very uniformity depressing. "I don't know how I let you talk me into this. You know I hate these stupid parties!"

"Ach, quit bumpin yer gums and gi' me a hand with this stuff."

Together they wrestle with shopping bags loaded with potato crisps, French bread sticks, dips, pretzels and other assorted party treats that Maria has promised to bring. Finally, after several flights of stairs they arrive at the flat with Maria puffing and blowing like a train. Sarah dumps the bags on the floor, straightens up and stretches the kink out of her back while Maria catches her breath. After a minute, Maria nods and Sarah rings the doorbell. What happens next will forever remain unclear in Sarah's mind.

Instead of Eileen opening the door to the flat, a man is revealed. The expression as-handsome-as-the-devil flashes into Sarah's mind as her gaze settles on his face which hovers at least twelve inches above her own. The man takes the shopping bags from Maria's hands, effortlessly hooking them over one finger and then he turns to Sarah. For a moment their eyes meet. The man's eyes are the most wonderfully clear shade of light blue set against olive skin and framed by coal black hair. Sarah's breath momentarily catches in her throat.

The man smiles, revealing perfect white teeth and then something remarkable occurs. Abruptly Sarah feels as though an electrical connection has been made through the air between them. An invisible pathway between their eyes. She has the sensation of a burst of energy flowing from the centre of her being out through this invisible connection and then ricocheting back into her soul, only stronger. As if his energy has been added to hers. The last thing she remembers is the look of astonishment on his face and the realisation that he felt it too. Then her vision simply shuts down.

When Sarah comes to she is lying on a double bed and gazing up at the flaking paint of the ceiling. Momentarily, she's confused about where she is. She doesn't recognise this bedroom. Panic flares when she recalls the feeling as the lights were extinguished and then, moments later, curiosity as she remembers the face of the beautiful man in the doorway. She struggles to sit up, wincing at the pain in her neck and becoming aware of a lump like an egg on the side of her head.

"There ye are." Said a familiar voice. Maria's bulk blots out the light from the hall as she steps through the doorway.

"What happened?" Sarah asks.

"I was gonnae ask you the same thing!" Replies Maria. "You nearly frightened the bejeesus out of that poor boy. When he left his face was whiter than my arse."

"He's gone?" Asks Sarah, her disappointment obvious.

"Aye, he was just dropin' some stuff off for Eileen and leaving when you rang the bell. You made quite an impression though, he wouldna' leave before I gave him your name an' phone number."

"You did what?" Sarah cried.

"Ach, calm down. I saw that look in your eyes, you were ready to drop yer knickers right on the doorstep!

Sarah rubs the side of her head. "I must have fallen down."

"Aye you did all right. Cracked your heed on the door frame before he could catch ye."

"He caught me?"

"He did that. Moved like greased lightning. One second yer headin' for the floor, the next second he's got you in his arms. Carried you through to the bedroom like you were a just a wean in his arms."

"Oh God. How embarrassing."

"Don't be wet, lassies have been fainting into the arms of men since Adam was a wee boy. They love it, the bastards. Musta been that long slog up the stairs with the shoppin.' Anyway, his name is Mathias and he's gonnae call ye."

* * *

Amanda isn't sure how many hours have passed since the man left; it's difficult to keep track of time when all external clues have been removed. The only sensation she experiences from the outside world is the distant sound of the ocean and the merest suggestion of a breeze that carries with it a hint of seaweed and rock pools. It represents her only connection to the world outside. Her mind returns to what she had seen in the light of his torch. She is somewhere inside a very ancient world and death is nothing new to these stone walls. It's life that's the exception here.

A fine layer of dust covered every surface like sheets tossed over furniture in a house to which the owner would never return. She guesses that this place has lain undisturbed for a very long time. She'd seen passageways leading off into darkness, their arches adorned with carvings only glimpsed in the weak light but which were immediately both alien and unsettling. That she can be left here alone suggests that this tomb is not known, perhaps her eyes would be among the last to see it for God knows how long. She felt surprisingly calm, knowing that it would end soon. One way or another it would end soon. She hears a sound from somewhere far away. The muscles in her neck and shoulders are too sore for her to risk moving her head. The light from his torch begins darting around the walls, picking out faces from the many who watch in silence, growing brighter as he approaches. Her heart starts to beat a little faster.

* * *

Detective Inspector David Orbost, arms folded across his chest, stands before the window and stares out at another grey day. The traffic below passes the station building heading north and south, headlights on and wipers slapping at the persistent drizzle. It occurs to him that both he and Walter had already been at work when the drivers in the cars below were dragging themselves from their beds. Lucky buggers. David had been aggravated to wake up with a headache following his second restless night. Leaning forward, he rests his forehead against the cold glass. Closing his eyes, he asks himself the same question that he'd struggled with during the night, as he lay awake staring at the frame of light around his bedroom window created by the street lamp outside. What am I missing from this case?

He strolls to the evidence board they've set up showing the locations where the dead women were found and photographs of each scene. By comparing the lists of missing persons with the physical profile of victim three, they now have a name for the newest set of photographs. Jamie Anderson. David thinks back to her father as he identified the body. How old the weight of grief had made him appear. He feels his anger spike as he contemplates a repeat of the experience if they don't make some progress soon. The images on the board are indelibly set in his memory but he studies them again, hoping that he's missed some small detail, a connection or an anomaly.

"See anything old man?" Walter asks from across the room.

"I'll be buggered if I can find anything we haven't seen before." David replies, continuing to stare at the photographs. "Why do you suppose there was a gap between the first two victims and this latest one? Between bodies one and two we have about three weeks. Then two months go by with nothing. Now another. Why the wait? From the research, these guys tend to shorten the space between murders as they go on."

"There is one other possibility, you know." Said Walter.

"What's that?"

"That there are more victims but we just haven't found them yet."

"I suppose it's possible but somehow I don't think so. Our man doesn't appear to try very hard to hide the bodies, I mean, tossing number three into the sea to wash up wherever. That doesn't sound like someone who gives a stuff about the victims being found. Why do you reckon that is?"

"Perhaps he knows that we'll have nothing to go on." Suggested Walter. "There's no evidence of sexual assault so no bodily fluids. In fact apart from the restraints, no evidence of physical abuse at all. All of the victims have had food in their systems so he's not starving them to death although they have all been underweight to some extent."

"Maybe this sicko just likes his women thin. Or maybe he's just toying with us, demonstrating how smart he is, knowing we're getting nowhere." Said David. "Anyway, it will be interesting when the shrink shows up. I hope she can give us something to go on although I'm not getting my hopes up. What's her name again?"

Walter rustles through the pages in his diary. "I have her card somewhere here. Yes, Natalie Braithewaite. *Doctor* Braithewaite to you, University of Edinburgh, Lecturer at the School of Philosophy, Psychology, and Language Sciences. And she's a forensic psychologist actually. A profiler, as our American colleagues would have it."

"Is she any good?" Asked David.

"Oh yes, she worked with us once before, some time ago. A case concerning missing children if my memory serves me correctly. She's one smart lady, that one. And not at all difficult on the eyes, old man."

"As long as she can help with this case she could be a fat one-legged Russian potato farmer for all I care."

"Insofar as I recall, her CV was conspicuously silent on the topic of her agricultural accomplishments but I'm sure that you will find her contribution agreeable nonetheless."

* * *

Amanda's pulse is racing now and she's terrified that the man will notice something unusual. He places his pack in the exact location he used on his last visit as though it was some kind of ritual and then walks toward her, careful not to shine the torch into her eyes.

"Hello again Amanda."

"Please, I'm absolutely busting. I need to use the pot."

She hopes that her agitation over her full bladder (which isn't in any way faked) will mask the nervousness that she is experiencing now the time has come for her plan to become action. He seems to have a way of seeing into her head, reading her thoughts. Raw fear floods Amanda's body, forcibly reminding her that to imagine is easy but to act, to actually do it, is almost impossibly hard. Her fear is like a sedative, slowing down her thinking, causing her to delay, sapping her will. She bites down hard on the edge of her tongue producing a searing flash of agony. The pain shifts her focus allowing her to momentarily side-step the terror that threatens to sap her resolve. She blinks back tears as the metallic taste of blood fills her mouth.

"Of course. We can't have you wetting your pants."

As the man leans over to untie her wrists, she sees once again the strong hands and the tendons in his wrist that disappear into his shirt sleeve, senses the animal warmth from his body, his smell. She also catches sight of a strange pattern on the inside of his wrist. An odd sort of skin discolouration. She hadn't noticed it last time, it's quite unique and she makes a last minute change to her plan. His fingers work economically and without redundant effort as though the action of every muscle had been scripted. Amanda is mesmerised.

"You don't seem yourself today, Amanda. Do you have something to tell me?"

Her mind snaps back and she struggles to come up with the right answer. She has no idea what he wants from her, he gave her no clue as to his purpose. She decides to stick with the original story.

"No, I'm just dying to go to the toilet. I can't hang on much longer."

The man undoes the second restraint and steps away. He turns his back to fetch the metal bucket that she is forced to use as her toilet and for one crazy instant she contemplates attacking him immediately, leaping onto his back, sinking her teeth into his neck, ripping a mouthful of flesh away. Unconsciously, her hands clench into fists. The analytical part of her mind fights to regain control as she reminds herself that she has one final thing to do.

With a probing look in his eyes, the man turns and hands her the bucket. God, he knows something's up, she thinks. His look is one of inquisitiveness rather than concern. A look which spoke of total certainty that regardless of whatever plan she might conceive, he could control the situation. Absolute confidence that could never be threatened or breached by her. That one look so demoralises her that for a second she almost buckles, almost abandons the plan before even trying. She carries the bucket to the opposite corner of the chamber and places it in the shadows, all the while fighting against the fear and despair that clutches at her mind. She stands facing the man across the room.

"I need a little privacy." She says.

"Of course. Take your time"

He turns around and sits on the stone block with his back to her, humming to himself. Amanda clenches her jaw, steeling herself for what is to follow. This is it, she thinks. She undoes the button and the zipper on her jeans. Just before she pulls them down she slips a hand into her pocket and pulls out a small silver paper clip that she'd squirrelled away at the post office, moments before she saw the man for the first time. Seeing it laying there in her hand, her plan suddenly seems stupid and impotent. She struggles to banish the negative voice from her head and quickly straightens out one end of the paperclip. Her efforts result in a slender two-inch wire. It will have to do she tells herself. Pulling down her jeans and underpants together she sits uncomfortably on top of the bucket. She is gambling on the sound of her urination in the tin bucket covering what she has to do next.

Tears spring to her eyes as the end of the paperclip rips into the soft flesh of her inner thigh. It's all she can do not to scream as she works quickly, mercilessly. The feeling of the wire in her hand as she mutilates herself is sickening. It's as though she can hear the blunt wire tearing into her flesh. Her leg is on fire, the pain sending flares into her brain as beads of sweat stand out from her forehead. When she is done she pulls up her jeans, wipes her eyes with the back of her hand and palms the paperclip, taking care to wipe her own blood from the end. The man turns as she walks toward him, the bucket in her outstretched hand. She feels a trickle of blood dribble down the inside of her leg and tries to blot it with her jeans, praying that it won't show. She hands him the bucket.

"Feeling better now?" He asks.

She simply nods her head, not trusting her voice. The man turns to place the bucket next to his pack as a reminder to empty it before leaving. As he begins to turn back he starts to speak.

"We need to have a little chat, Amanda, something has come up in…"

As his face turns toward her she strikes with all the pent up energy and anger that boils inside her, aiming to plunge the paperclip into his eyeball. To ram it in as far as she can and then run before he's able to recover. She sees her arm moving in slow motion, sees the surprised look ripple across his face and, with terrible speed, sees his hand moving to intercept her blow. He catches her arm while the paperclip is still six inches from his face. She feels the bones in her wrist grind together under the pressure of his grip. She tries to pull free but her arm could just as easily have been embedded in concrete for all the difference it makes.

The paper clip slides from her grip and lands on the stone floor with a tiny sound. For a moment she thinks she sees sorrow in the man's eyes. Employing a move that almost makes it appear they are dancing together, he spins her around so her back presses against his chest. One of his powerful arms now encircles her body and effectively pins both of her arms. Her heart pounds and she has to remind herself to breath.

"I don't think we need to talk after all Amanda." His voice soothing, not a trace of anxiety or anger.

She feels his grip loosen and she's about to speak when one of his smooth hands cups her chin. For one second she thinks he might turn her face to kiss him but then she feels her neck twist sharply, the crackle of bones and ligaments popping inside her head. Lights roar in front of her eyes before the world simply appears to shut down; everything around her shrinking to a tiny bright spot like an old television being switched off. Then the spot is extinguished.

* * *

Doctor Natalie Braithewaite sits opposite David and Walter in a room used primarily for suspect interviews. A whiteboard has been set up at the front of the room and Walter has sneaked a jug of water and a glass from the conference room and placed it at Natalie's elbow. It brings a smile to David's face to see how he makes a special effort for academic types. Several other officers assigned to the case drag their chairs into the small room to hear what the psychologist has to say. Support for her role in the case is mixed with some among the team quite vocal in their view that the whole profiling exercise was simply Hollywood inspired bullshit. Most have never been involved in a case concerning a serial killer so neither David or Walter listen too closely to the dissenters. It wasn't David's idea to bring her in but when it was suggested to him by Chief Superintendent Wallace he was smart enough not to disagree. At least it made them look like they were pursuing every avenue and who knows, David had thought, it might throw something up.

Despite the nagging awareness that his thinking is not politically correct, David had to agree with Walter that she was very easy on the eyes. And she wasn't wearing a wedding ring, a thing he had become adept at spotting since the breakup of his last relationship.

"I'm sorry for the less than salubrious environment my dear but this room was all we could get our hands on today." Walter said.

A guffaw came from the back of the room and Walter responded with a frown. Natalie glanced around seeming to notice the room for the first time.

"This place is fine, Walter."

She leans forward to study her papers and a tiny wisp of dark hair escapes, falling over one lens of her delicately framed glasses. Absently she tucks it behind her ear. David, studying her face, observes this unconscious gesture. His mind begins to wander and it occurs to him that he's been living alone now for over two years. Looking at this attractive woman he finds himself imagining what it would feel like to touch her skin. At that instant she lifts her head and looks directly into David's eyes, a small smile playing at the corner of her mouth, one eyebrow raised in question.

"Yes?" she said.

David blushes deeply. "I'm sorry, I was staring. Christ. How rude of me."

"Keep your mind on the job, Guv!" said a wag from the rear, adding to David's embarrassment. Walter flashed his stare again.

She sat back in her chair, studying him. "Australian?" She asked.

"Yes, well spotted." David said, glad of the distraction. "Born in Melbourne of English parents and back in the old country for the last couple of years."

"Interesting." Natalie Said.

"Woooo!" from the back of the room.

"Give it a rest lads, you've had your fun." David said.

"Yes, to business." Natalie said, shooting David a look of mock seriousness. "I've read through the files and of course spoken to Walter on the phone so I think I've been briefed reasonably thoroughly. I'd be misleading you if I said that I have anything startling to communicate as yet. I know that people in my profession are supposed to be able to describe these perpetrators to a tee but as you might guess, it's not that easy. But I can say some things today and I should be able to help you narrow things down as we move forward. If I'm to be useful though we will need to work closely on this and I would like to see everything you have as the case progresses. Please allow me to decide what information is or isn't relevant. Is that okay?"

"Of course." Walter replied. "You're the expert my dear."

"Thank you. I like to get that clear at the outset as without that understanding my role can be compromised. One other thing I should make clear. In the absence of data, I will be making assumptions. As new data emerges from your investigations those assumptions will be tested and some may be discarded. What I'm saying is that the process is dynamic and you mustn't attach too much to what I say in the early days if doing so might limit your investigation."

Natalie smiled at the men in the room. "That's the fine print out of the way. Let's get down to business."

She stood and moved to the whiteboard and David found himself appraising her body as she wrote. His imagination began to wander again. Get a grip, son, he tells himself. Natalie turned to face the room.

"DI Pembroke has told me that a few of you are new to cases involving serial murderers. Not surprising really, there aren't that many of them. I know you probably covered this stuff in your training but I'm going to start from first principles so that we're all on the same page. Move from the general to the specific. Apologies if I tell you something you already know. Okay?"

A couple of heads nod in the room and Natalie continued.

"First. I'm sure you don't need me to tell you that we're almost certainly looking for a male. Likely white, particularly as the victims so far have been white. Statistically he's probably between eighteen and thirty five years old."

"Are we talking about a psychopath?" Asked a junior officer.

"It's quite possible and until we see any contraindicating data, I'm assuming we're dealing with such a disorder. There has been a great body of work completed in this area over the last few decades and not all of the conclusions are in alignment. A few points can be made however."

Natalie turned back to the whiteboard where she had written a list of traits:

* No Conscience – Amoral

* Deceitful – Lies

* Fails to conform to social norms or laws

* Rationalises own behaviour

* No guilt for behaviour or poor treatment of others

* Nonconformist – ignores conventions

* Dislikes and resents authority

* Easily charming and makes good first impression

* Can be violent if thwarted

* History of irresponsible behaviour in school, jobs etc.

"This is obviously not an exhaustive list but it gives you an idea. Also, not all individuals will have all of these traits."

"So what do we *really* know about why these people do what they do?" Asked David.

"Well, that's a big question. Serial murderers tend to be special inasmuch as their crimes are not usually committed for greed, or jealousy, or profit. There usually isn't any revenge involved and the victims are usually unknown to the killer. Often there is a component of domination, manipulation, and control over the victims. Also you mustn't discount mental illness. Mentally ill people are not usually violent criminals but violent criminals are often mentally ill."

"Well that makes it really easy then!" Someone said.

"Of course it doesn't. Complex motives are what make serial murderers often so difficult to catch, but usually a profile emerges with continued offences. Also they tend to decompensate and become sloppy as time goes on. That's in our favour."

"So if we went back to our original idea that we're dealing with a soldier or ex soldier, what should we look for?" David asked.

"My guess is that you would find this is no ordinary foot soldier. For him to tolerate the structure and authority which underpins the psychology of the armed forces he would need lots of autonomy. A role away from scrutiny, outside the normal structure. Likely not a standard infantry type."

David nodded as he made notes. "That makes sense."

"Also if this person *is* a soldier it's unlikely that he's still serving in the military. It's not impossible but I would suggest that it's likely he has left the forces and whatever structure he operated under has been removed from his life."

"And another thing. If you have nowhere else to start, I'd be looking for a subset of those people who were discharged abnormally. Look for medical reasons, really anything at all that suggests they were discharged involuntarily."

CHAPTER 4

Sarah sits on the edge of the bed replaying the conversation in her mind. Thinking about his words and her responses, worrying about how she'd sounded. Maybe she'd been too eager, or maybe she'd sounded stuck up and cold. She didn't want him to think she was some sort of bimbo. Sarah is startled by the phone ringing and as she picks it up she knows who it will be.

"He phoned ye didn't he?" Maria asks, unable to conceal the excitement in her voice. "I've been callin' an' you were engaged for ages!"

"Yes he did…" Sarah pulls the phone away from her ear as Maria's scream of delight threatens to pierce her eardrum.

"Tell me, tell me, tell me!" Maria's tone that of a teenage girl.

"Well, he was very sweet. He apologised if I got a fright when he opened the door and he wants to take me out to dinner to make up."

"What did ye say?" Asked Maria breathlessly.

"I told him that he didn't have to do that."

"You what!" Maria shrieked.

"But that that I would be delighted anyway." Sarah added, laughing. "I may be slow but I'm not stupid."

"That's grand! Where's he taking ye?"

"He said he knows a little Italian place on Station Road, we're going there tomorrow night, he's picking me up in his car."

"Aye, all very nice. I reckon he might be the one, hen. You shoulda seen his face when he carried you in his arms, he couldna stop lookin' at you. If nothin' else, at least you'll get yersel' a little duvet action!"

"Maria!" Sarah exclaimed. "Give me a break, it's only dinner for God's sake."

"Aye, it starts wi' dinner but who knows where it ends. Anyway I want to know all about it."

After she hangs up on her old friend Sarah climbs into bed and closes her eyes. Sleep refuses to oblige. What if this *is* the one, she thought. Maybe this is how it begins. Certainly she'd never experienced such a profound reaction at meeting anyone else. She feels a tingle of excitement at the prospect of speaking with him face to face. And try not to faint this time, she tells herself.

* * *

Following the briefing with Natalie, David suggested a quick coffee in the canteen before she left. Ostensibly to thank her for her information, he was also more than a little curious about her.

"So you think it went okay? Natalie asks once they're seated.

"It was very good. If nothing else it stimulated people's thinking, got their minds looking at the case from different angles. I think that will be important given how little we have so far.

"I could tell that not everyone felt that way." She said. "Don't worry too much about that, they usually come around after a while."

"Oh, I'm sure they will. It sounds like you've done this before, I wouldn't have thought there was enough of these sort of cases to keep you busy."

"Thank God, no. I do get invited to work in various places, mostly in the UK but occasionally in Europe. Most of my time is spent lecturing and on my research. It's a thrill to get away sometimes even though it's inevitably a tragedy of some sort that gets me out of the university grounds."

"And do you find the reception pretty much like it was here?" David asked.

"Much the same, although it's getting better. There are times I get brought in just to make the force look good in the eyes of the press, I think. Even then I usually manage to convert a few at least."

"So, tell me about yourself," Natalie said, changing the subject. "You moved back to England from Australia."

"Yes, almost two years ago now."

"Why?" She said, as if this were the most natural question in the world.

"Well, my folks came back and then my dad had heart trouble and, well, I guess I don't want to be on the other side of the world if anything happens."

"That's very sweet."

David felt his cheeks burning. "Ah well, a blokes gotta do… etcetera etcetera."

"Do you like it here?" She asked.

"Not particularly, no." David said and they both laughed. David was struck by how her face lit up when she laughed. Not just pretty, she is gorgeous, he thinks.

"And you think you'll stay for a while?" Natalie asked.

"I think I'll need to knuckle down here in the medium term for my career's sake. I've got a very good position, actually better than I'd hoped for when I came over so I should consolidate that for a while I think."

"Good." Natalie said with a smile.

* * *

The compact four wheel drive pulls over on the side of the track, its tyres crunching through the loose stones, headlights off, moonlight alone guiding it to this spot. The man turns off the engine and winds down the window. Sitting in the dark he feels the crisp night air surge into the warm cabin. He savours the feeling of the cold air in his nostrils, rich with the smells of the country, wet grass and rotting wood, damp earth.

Above the wind he imagines he can hear the ocean and memories of his boyhood return with a startling clarity. Standing atop rugged hills, leaning into wind that threatened to knock him down, his young eyes scanning the rocks for treasures lost overboard from passing ships, glass floats inside rope nets, lobster pots, life-rings from failed rescue missions, wooden crates packed with provisions. Always searching, seldom finding.

He smiles as he remembers one special morning when he was convinced that he could see a body washed into a small crack in the rocks, the swell pushing and tugging at its clothes, a horribly smashed leg articulating in ways never intended by its maker. He can still taste the excitement as he scrambled down the cliff, his mind alive with the possibilities. A murder victim, perhaps a Mafia style execution with the bullet hole still visible in the centre of a shattered skull. A suicide leaper, her face smashed beyond recognition. A drug dealer, his body dumped from an exotic speedboat, skimming over the waves with running lights taped over. And then the crushing disappointment as he arrived with skinned knees and bleeding ankle to discover several broken pieces of wood bound to each other by ripped and faded plastic sheeting.

Zipping up his jacket, he steps out of the car, his boots crackling in the frosted grass. He listens, small ticking noises as the warm engine delivers up its heat to the night air. Satisfied that he is alone, the man walks around the vehicle and opens the rear hatch. Folded into the small space is a black rubber body bag containing the still limp body of a young woman he'd known only as Amanda. The man hadn't even bothered to disguise the bundle as he travelled through these isolated parts. He simply rationalised that if stopped by anyone, he had another bag hidden under his spare wheel.

Seemingly without effort he hoists the thick rubber sack onto his shoulder and starts walking toward a rocky point on the shoreline that the locals call Black Bull. He had meant to drive the body farther away from his base but he's tired and has lost interest in this one now a much more significant possibility has presented itself. The man is also confident that there is nothing to tie him to this dead woman.

After a ten-minute walk through steep and slippery country that worked some heat into his chilled muscles the man arrives at the ocean. He lays the body down carefully and flexes his back. Standing motionless for fifteen minutes he scans up and down the shoreline. He can see the lights from the power station many miles northwest of his position but he sees no tell-tale signs of human presence on the rocks. He learned patience in his former profession and can stand motionless for hours if necessary waiting for a betraying flash as a fisherman checks his watch or the characteristic tiny glow as someone draws on a cigarette.

As expected, he is alone on the rocks at this ungodly hour. He squats on his haunches and slowly unzips the body bag, the plastic and metal waterproof zip following the contours of the body inside. The woman's face is relaxed and peaceful in the moonlight. He picks her up and begins stepping cautiously over the rocks toward the water.

* * *

As the man retraces his steps to his vehicle Detective Inspector David Orbost is having a bad night and Cyril Morpeth's is turning into a nightmare.

Feeling like he was sixteen again, over their coffee in the canteen David had stumbled his way through an invitation for a drink sometime. To his very great surprise, Natalie had not only accepted but suggested dinner that very evening while she was in town. It was his first date in more than a year and his stomach was fluttering as he'd entered the pub in which they had arranged to meet. He saw her immediately, sitting at the bar speaking and laughing with the publican who was obviously lapping it up. She'd changed out of her severe business suit and looked comfortable and relaxed. It seemed to him that her laughter animated the room.

Following some initial nervousness (mostly on his part it seemed) they quickly relaxed and managed to chat comfortably all evening. His worries about finding enough to talk about had simply evaporated and afterward he was surprised to recall that not once had they spoken about the case that brought them together. That has to be a good sign, doesn't it? He asked himself. David had found her to be delightful company and, after walking her to her car, she had surprised him by giving him a kiss on the lips. In a bit of a fumble, he'd moved to kiss her cheek but she offered her lips instead. David hoped that he'd recovered fast enough to cover his blunder. She departed telling him that she'd enjoyed the night and that they should do it again. All in all, a pretty good result, he figured.

And now here he was lying wide awake at four o'clock in the morning, his head still spinning with recollections of the evening and his imagination sprinting ahead to where it might lead. He thought back to the way her shirt pulled tightly across her breasts when she sat up straight and wondered, not for the first time, whether women really had any idea of the effect they have on men. He figured that if they did, they probably underestimated it.

About ninety kilometres north of where David tossed restlessly in his bed, Cyril Morpeth spits over the side of his boat to get the taste of vomit out of his mouth. Cyril is a keen fisherman and enjoys sneaking out when the sea isn't too rough but he isn't keen on all of the "bloody regulations" that complicate his pastime these days. Cyril is known as a bit of a skinflint and prefers to fish quietly at night in a sheltered cove rather than fork out money for rod or boating licenses. Besides, he has to watch the pennies since taking early retirement from the power station where he'd worked as a welder for forty years.

As his stomach stops heaving, he turns to look back at the woman lying in the water. She is floating almost level with the surface and he'd nearly run her over as he motored toward the spot where he saw the man dump something into the sea. He had an awful feeling that it might be a dead body but actually seeing her up close was worse than he feared. It was the eyes that had frightened him. Wide open and staring, he thought for one awful minute she was some sort of apparition from the other side. Next thing he knew, he couldn't hold onto to his steak and kidney pudding.

At first Cyril couldn't believe that the man wouldn't see him sitting out there only a hundred yards offshore. Obviously the man was up to no good and he had his hand on the starter rope of the outboard motor in case he had to make a getaway. For what seemed like hours Cyril was forced to remain motionless as he watched the man checking the rocks, he dare not move a muscle lest he disturb something in the tin boat. Later he realised the angle of the moon left him and his boat in the long shadow cast by the rugged crag behind him. Still, he waited until he was absolutely certain the man was gone before motoring over.

He swears under his breath as he realises the situation he finds himself in. There is no way he can leave the woman out here. Not if it might mean the bastard who dumped her gets away with it. But he wasn't certain that he could pull her into his little boat without it overturning. He isn't sure if he wants to either. The thought of her blood (or worse) in his boat is more than he wants to contemplate. He's convinced himself that the boat would capsize and drown him should he attempt to drag her on board.

He smiles grimly as he imagines the gossip around the village if the pair of them got washed up dead together. Finally he decides to hold onto the woman's clothing with one hand and control the outboard with the other as he motors slowly toward the rocks. He tries to travel as slowly as possible but the woman's head is pushed completely under the water every time the boat moves forward and that just seems wrong to Cyril. He is also worried that she might slip into the motor's propeller as she moves around in the water. In the end he steels himself and puts his hand under her neck to support the head and in this ungainly fashion he tows her back to the shore from which she'd floated only twenty minutes before.

Her cold, wet hair sticks to his wrist as the water swirls around her face. Cyril chooses a tiny sheltered inlet, not much more than a large fissure in the rocks that holds a patch of sand onto which he can beach the boat. He drags the woman up above the high tide mark and lays her down on the coarse grass where he hopes she will be safe for the next hour or two. He then climbs back in the boat and heads for home, all the way thinking about how he can explain this to the wallopers without getting nicked for having no licences.

* * *

By the time the body is recovered and brought to the mortuary it was mid morning. Walter and David sat in the same interview room they had shared with Natalie Braithewaite and the rest of the team the day before. This time their companion is one very uncomfortable Cyril Morpeth, much closer to the law than he ever liked to come. Cyril twists his cap in large hands that, from decades of hard and dirty work, have come to resemble tree roots. As he clumsily tries to duck and weave his way through the story of how he found the body, he omits all mention of what he was actually *doing* in a little tin boat during the middle of the night. His efforts wouldn't have fooled a constable on his first day in the job. David decides to cut to the chase.

"Look, Mr Morpeth. My partner and I are not the least interested in whether or not you have the correct paperwork to be out and about in the middle of the night with a dingy full of fishing tackle. Or whether the fish are undersize or the right sort or too many or *whatever*. We really couldn't give a stuff."

"But you're both Polis."

"That's true, we are police but we're interested in the dead woman you found which frankly is much more important to us than your little fishing expeditions. Let me make a deal with you. You be absolutely honest with us about what happened, and I guarantee nobody will be digging into what you were doing out on the water that night. How's that?"

"That's right, is it?" Cyril's eyes narrow and he looks at them as if to say he hasn't come down in the last shower of rain.

"Absolutely, and my partner here can be a witness to our bargain."

Cyril looks across at Walter who dons his most serious expression and nods officiously.

"Is that one of them tape recording machines?" Cyril asks, nodding toward the black box mounted on a shelf above the table.

"Yes it is, and if you look closely you'll see that the tape is running, so you're covered if that's what's bothering you." David said.

"Well that sounds alright then." Cyril said, sitting up a little straighter in his chair, his face brightening.

"At the outset I want to ask you one very important question. Did you see the man's face?" David holds his breath waiting for the answer.

"No, it were too dark."

Cyril must have seen their disappointment for he quickly adds "But he was a big bastard, I reckon six four or six five by the look o' him. And strong too. The way he was carrying that poor lass, it was like she weighed nothin'. And she did, let me tell you. I struggled wi' her dead weight up the beach. That I did. But not him."

"Did you see what he was wearing?" Asks Walter.

"Clothes you mean?"

Walter nods patiently.

"Naw. Man, it was dark out there. He looked all black. I'll tell you one funny thing though. When he first arrived at the beach he laid the girl down on the ground and she was in some sort of a bag. Like a big sleeping bag wi' a zip all the way down. Like they used to have in the war. He took her out and floated her away. As gentle as you like. Didn't chuck her in, you know what I'm sayin? Sorta slipped her in the water, all gentle like, gave her a little push. Then he rolled the bag up and walked off. Toward the top of the hill. Didn't even look back once. I know, I was watchin' all't time."

After getting Cyril to point out on a map exactly where the man went, they made him repeat his story three times over, with a break for a late lunch between, asking questions along the way until they were satisfied that every scrap of information had been extracted from the old man. By the end, most of the day was gone. Walter stood.

"Thank you Mr Morpeth, you've been very helpful. We'll be in touch over the next week or so if we think of anything else."

"And, about the fishin'…" Cyril looked uncomfortable, seeking assurance but not wanting to meet Walter's gaze as though even the mention of it implicated him.

"Fishing Mr Morpeth?" Walter said with a smile. "I don't recall a discussion about anyone fishing."

"Aye, right you are then." Replied Cyril, heading for the door.

Walter closed the door and sat back down opposite David.

"What do you make of all that?" He asked.

Before David can respond, there is a knock at the door and a police constable pokes her head inside. "Excuse me Sir, but Mr Norwich from the mortuary is on the telephone, he says that you should be interrupted."

David and Walter exchange a brief glance and then both men leap from their chairs.

* * *

Sarah's Day in the shop passed with irritating slowness and the date she had that evening with Mathias was never far from her mind. She was both excited and apprehensive about meeting the man that had so spectacularly affected her at their first encounter. At closing time she had been the first through the door and on her way home. Now, freshly showered and standing naked in front of her full length mirror she appraised her body.

All things being considered she decided the image wasn't too bad. Maybe a little heavy in the hips but that was just being picky. Eric had once told her that if there was a best-breast competition she could easily be Miss Northumberland. Turning to see herself in a three-quarter view she was still pleased with what she figured were her finest physical attributes. No too big, not too small and perfectly shaped. The one part of her body that she wouldn't change at all even if she had a magic wand. Any man would be delighted to see these boobs she thought. Not that Mathias is going to see them tonight she cautioned herself, turning from the mirror and rummaging in the drawer for clean underwear.

Now dressed and standing in the front room her confidence was ebbing away. Being picked up at home from her parents place – he'll probably think I'm a real loser, she thought. Sarah wishes she'd planned ahead and met him somewhere else, perhaps arranged to meet up at the restaurant. Either that or she shouldn't have told her parents about it. She realised with annoyance that she was doing it this way because of her mother. To placate her mother who never stopped telling her how delinquent she was when it came to the production of grandchildren. As she had done many times previously, Sarah chided herself for trying to please her mother instead of living her own life, wished she could get a better grip on herself and start to care less about what others said. A bit more like Maria, she thought.

"You look lovely, you really do. You have nothing to worry about." Her father said.

"Anybody would think that you were fifteen years old the way you're fretting." Her mother added.

The doorbell rings and Sarah starts to get up. George holds up his hand.

"Let me get the door, I'd like to take a look at this chap."

George opens the door and is instantly taken aback as he looks up into the man's eyes. Against his olive skin, the light blue of his eyes is startling. Before he can speak, the big man offers his hand.

"You must be Sarah's father, nice to meet you, Mr Nelson. I'm Mathias."

"Please, call me George. No need for that Mr Nelson stuff here, my boy. Please, come inside, Sarah's waiting for you."

George leads the way into the sitting room, his hand tingling from Mathias's grip. Sarah and her mother wait, Dorothy affecting a casual pose that she apparently assumed made her look sophisticated while Sarah sat nervously with her hands in her lap. Before George can make the introduction, Mathias takes Dorothy's hand in his.

"You *must* be Mrs Nelson. You look so much like Sarah you could be sisters. I'm Mathias."

Sarah is amazed to see her mother actually blushing.

"It's lovely to meet you Mathias."

"It's so nice to see someone of Sarah's age still living at home, you must have a wonderful family environment here."

Sarah thought her mother gained an extra two inches of height following Mathias's comment.

"Well George and I do our best." She said, obviously delighted with the complement.

Mathias turns his gaze on Sarah. "You look wonderful." He says. "I've been looking forward to this evening all day."

Sarah isn't quite sure if her voice will work at this moment so she simply smiles, and feels a little silly.

"Shall we go?" Mathias says. "We have a booking for seven thirty and we don't want to lose our table."

"No, you get along." Dorothy said. "Have a wonderful time. And it's been lovely to meet you Mathias. I do hope we see you again."

Sarah shot her mother a warning look as Mathias escorted her outside and held the car door open.

"Let's hope she doesn't stuff this one up." Dorothy hissed through her smile as the couple drove away.

* * *

Mortuaries are pretty much the same the world over, thought David. Some are larger than others or more modern but they all had a clinical look about them that to David appeared to be a cross between an operating theatre and a butcher's shop. Lots of stainless steel and tiles. Not too much equipment and the equipment that was lying around looked as though it might have more in common with a bacon slicer than an infusion pump.

The little gutters that ran around and down the centre of the shiny table always left David feeling a little queasy, implying as they did, lots of runoff. He shuddered. He had yet to become accustomed to looking at the macabre invasion of someone's body. It wasn't simply that it was grisly although it definitely was that, it was more that it made him feel like a voyeur. Just the fact that the person was lying there naked for a start. The pathologists obviously had respect for the deceased and wouldn't tolerate anyone making jokes during the autopsy. They had a job to do, but *he* always felt as though he shouldn't really be there, seeing things that should be private. Normally, if he *had* to be here (which wasn't often) he would watch the autopsy through the glass window where he could speak to the pathologist via a microphone. It was surprising how much difference that sheet of glass made, it seemed to create a separation that went beyond the fact that the two rooms were divided by a window. On occasions such as this he was required to be inside the mortuary, standing next to the body laid out in the bright lights, sharing the same space, the same air. He would never admit this to his colleagues but it was way too close and personal for him on this side of the glass.

Standing next to Trevor, David and Walter gaze at the naked body of victim number four.

"Well I'll be buggered." David said, shaking his head.

"This is truly remarkable." Walter added. "It would appear that our brave girl has attempted to leave us a sign of some sort. Don't you think?"

"I guess that's for you chaps to figure out." Trevor said.

"But do you think she did this to herself, or did the killer do it for some other sick reason?" Asked David.

"Well, of course it's not possible to say with certainty but in my opinion she inflicted this wound herself."

"Based on?" David prompted.

"Based on several observations. We were very lucky with this woman inasmuch as she was in the water a relatively short time. We see bloodstain patterns on her jeans consistent with these marks as if she immediately covered the wounds after they were inflicted. Also, from the musculature I suspect she was right handed. In her right palm are several small puncture wounds possibly caused by the implement used."

"Any thoughts on what it might have been?" Said Walter.

"Hard to say. Thin but not sharp certainly; the skin isn't cut so much as torn. A piece of wire perhaps. Maybe a piece of tin or other scrap of metal. If I had to speculate I'd say a piece of wire based on the puncture marks in her hand. Right hand, left inner thigh, I'd say she did this herself."

"God, she must have had some guts." Said David. "Knowing we'd be staring at her like this." He looked away.

"I'm counting on you chaps to make her efforts worth it." Trevor said, his voice revealing an uncharacteristic amount of emotion.

"Another thing." He continued, businesslike again. "She has very obvious bruising to her right wrist." He held her hand up, palm out, to show them.

"Someone with a large and strong hand gripped her like this." He demonstrated the defensive grip with his own hands.

"Any chance of getting prints off those marks?" Asked David.

"It *can* be done and in fact the inside of the wrist is one of the more favourable places to experience success in removing fingerprints from human skin. But not after she's been handled and towed through freezing water I'm afraid."

"I feared as much." Said David.

"I thought you chaps might like this." Trevor said, handing over an eight by ten-inch glossy colour photograph of the marks on the inside of the dead woman's thigh. David noticed that the photograph had been angled to preserve her modesty and he was thankful for that small act of compassion.

CHAPTER 5

After the waiter has taken their order Mathias smiles and leans across the table toward Sarah, a mischievous light in his eyes.

"I'm glad to see that you're not still fainting at the sight of me."

Sarah reddened. "God I feel stupid about that, I don't know what came over me. One minute I'm lugging the shopping up four flights of stairs and the next thing I'm laying in a strange bed, flat on my back like some Victorian woman with the vapours. It's never happened to me before, you must have thought I was a complete idiot."

Mathias laughed. "Far from it. It's not every day that I have beautiful women swooning into my arms. I felt like I was carrying a princess."

Sarah searches his face, trying to detect any duplicity and is pleasantly surprised to see that he appeared to be sincere.

"Well anyway, it's nice of you to ask me out." She said.

"Nonsense, the pleasure is all mine, Sarah. And I don't think you are an idiot at all. I felt something between us in that first glance too. Something too powerful to ignore or trivialise."

"What do you mean?" Asked Sarah, toying with her wine glass.

"Well, do you believe that everyone has someone special waiting for them somewhere. A special person?"

"You mean like fate?" Sarah asked.

"Well, not so much fate as just a special connection. Someone who you've been looking for. I think that most people go through their whole lives without meeting that person and they end up settling for what they think is happiness without ever knowing what it could be like."

"I guess that could be true. Most of the couples I know just seem to knock along together. I don't know too many that are deliriously happy. I guess my parents are a couple like you mention. I'm sure they love each other but... Oh, I don't know."

Mathias puts his hand on top of Sarah's. His skin is smooth and warm.

"That connection we experienced when we first met, I'd like to explore what's behind that with you, Sarah. I think it might be too important for us to let go of."

Sarah is momentarily taken back by his openness and the intensity of his feelings. "That sounds good, I'd like to explore it too, but can we take it slowly?"

Mathias sits back and laughs. "I'm sorry, I know I can get a bit intense. Of course, we can take as slowly as you like. I was just gobsmacked when I met you and I don't want you to slip away from me."

Now it's Sarah's turn to smile. "I'm not intending to go anywhere soon."

"Excellent!" Replied Mathias, lifting his glass to propose a toast. "To special relationships and all the secrets they hold."

∗ ∗ ∗

As Sarah and Mathias enjoy their dinner and conversation together, thirty miles away in the tiny coastal village of Chidington, Janice Boulton turns out the lights and locks the door of her small souvenir shop. Business is slow at this time of year and the shop only opens for half the week. Friday is usually pretty quiet once the weather starts to turn and according to the sign on the door she should have stayed open until five thirty but at five o'clock there hadn't been a customer for over an hour so she decided to call it quits. It wouldn't be long now before they closed up completely for the winter. Really, she should have done it already but she kept postponing it, talking up the number of customers that she had during the day. While she wouldn't admit this to her husband, Janice actually enjoyed the solitude in the shop, looking out across the sea. It provided her some mental space and was one of the few places where she could get any reading done since her two children had arrived.

Peter, her husband, is a stay-at-home dad who manufactures various wooden "knick-knacks" as he calls them, in his garden workshop. Lighthouses, boats, placemats in the shape of ship's wheels, shells mounted on ornamental plinths and other trinkets having a nautical theme. To Janice's great pleasure, (and Peter's amazement) they are an unfailingly good seller during the summer. A man of immense patience, Peter never tires of the kids "helping" him in the workshop, even if that help consists of banging fifty nails into a single piece of wood. Janice treasures her time alone and so this arrangement suits her just fine. She gives the front door a rattle after removing the key from the lock, the small bell that Peter had installed offering a muffled note from inside the shop. Satisfied that the building is secure she starts walking home, her umbrella tucked under an arm just in case.

Janice has made this walk hundreds of times in the last few years and during the mild summer evenings she looks forward to strolling along the sea front before weaving through several laneways to her cottage situated about five hundred yards up the hill from the ocean. This night wasn't one for sightseeing however and she pulls her raincoat tightly around her shoulders as she zigzagged through the narrow cobbled streets. She bows her head against the wind as it sweeps through the alleyways pushing leaves and litter across her path.

The houses and businesses she passes are battened down for the evening and occasionally she catches the smell of a wood fire, a reminder of the warmth awaiting her. She knows that when she arrives at home Peter will tick her off for not phoning him to collect her from the shop. She smiles as she pictures his mock-stern countenance and his wagging finger. She also knows how lucky she is and what a production it can be getting the kids into the car just so she didn't have to walk for a mile and a half. Only on the foulest of winter days will she call Peter to pick her up.

Janice walks past Pinocchio's, her opposition in the souvenir business but this time she doesn't stop to have a look at the window display. She actually gets on very well with the elderly couple that run the shop and they often send customers to each other if they don't stock the exact item being sought. Tonight the shutters are down and the shop has closed early. Probably locked up ages ago she thinks to herself.

She turns the corner to the point where she always gains her first glimpse of the house that she and Peter have lived in for five years. As she lifts her head expecting to see it, a movement to her left startles her. She begins to turn, thinking it might be a dog but at that instant a hand clamps across her mouth with a grip so powerful that she feels one of her front teeth pierce her upper lip. Simultaneously an arm circles her chest and pins both arms at her side. She tries desperately to swivel her head but the hand over her mouth is too strong. The hand smells of stale tobacco and urine. Another more distinctive smell began to register in her brain. A hospital smell. She attempts to wrench an arm free but she doesn't have the strength. This man's grip is sucking the energy out of her body.

Something inside her mouth is burning her tongue but it doesn't seem to be important anymore, as though her brain is disconnecting from her body. She feels herself sinking down. As she is dragged back into the shadows, the lights from her house are slowly dimming and a great wave of sadness engulfs her as a mental picture of her family springs to her mind; her children playing in front of the fire, Peter, a glass of wine within reach, preparing their dinner...

* * *

This is becoming a huge operation, thinks David as he looks around the room at the twenty or thirty police, mostly men, that have assembled. The evidence boards have been moved to a larger space to accommodate the growing number of officers that are assigned to the case. Murder is not uncommon in the north of England with at least one case every month presenting itself somewhere in the large county. Serial killers however, are an entirely different matter. There had been some reluctance to accept the serial killer hypothesis in the early days but even the most sceptical among their number has no doubts now. The Chief Constable is coming under increasing pressure to make an arrest and it seemed that additional resources were being added on a daily basis.

A low rumble of conversation animates the room, the atmosphere charged with purpose and resolve. Chief Superintendent Richard Wallace, the area commander for Northumberland, makes his way to the front and raises his hands for quiet. Wallace is a large man with the confidence of a senior policeman who has seen most things at least once before. Respected for the man he is more than the position he holds, the room quickly comes to order.

"Good morning people. You all know Chief Inspector Jamison on my left who has, of course, overall responsibility for this investigation, and DI's Walter Pembroke and David Orbost who have been at the cutting edge of this since the beginning. I'll be handing over to these gentlemen in due course for an update." He pauses, his eyes sweeping over the officers seated before him.

"We've also had several offers of specialist assistance from the Met but so far we have indicated that their expertise, while unquestionably formidable, is not required at this time."

A murmur of discontent rippled around the room. The area commander nodded and raised his hand for silence before continuing.

"This is a bad business. Many of you are family men and so I don't need to tell you what concern this case is causing out there in the community. We have lots of people living in isolated and rural areas and they are frightened. Despite our public appeals, we don't have much to go on but this latest victim appears to have possibly given us something. What that something means, we don't know yet. One thing we simply cannot do is wait until the killer makes a mistake. The community will not allow it and neither will I. The reason that I'm increasing the resources on this case is that we simply have to dig in and find a way through. I want every stone overturned until we find out where this bastard is hiding. You've all seen the four sets of photographs behind me. Let's not allow another set to be pinned up because we didn't push hard enough. I'm counting on you all. Over to you, Chief Inspector."

The chief superintendent took a seat at the back as Jamison, who was small to Wallace's large, took control. As he started speaking, two administrative staff began handing out packs containing documents, notes and photographs.

* * *

It's Saturday evening and for the second time in as many days, Sarah is sitting in the passenger seat of Mathias's car as they head off together. Again she's impressed by how clean the car is. It even smells nice as though it's been sprayed with a subtle and yet delicious fragrance. The car is warm and Sarah is excited to be sitting next to Mathias as they glide through the empty streets. It crosses Sarah's mind that it would be nice to just keep on driving, not arrive anywhere, simply preserve the moment. The car is like a cocoon, a little world they inhabit together, protecting them both from the cold outside. Mathias is unlike anyone Sarah has been out with in the past. He appeared so confident and self assured but at the same time not arrogant or egotistical. Equally relaxed speaking with her parents as he seemed with her, he gave every impression of being comfortable in his own skin.

After bringing her home following their very pleasant dinner he had spent time talking to Dorothy and George, telling them about his plans to move up through the ranks in the security company where he worked. He took great interest in her father's job at the post office and asked lots of questions about the changes George had seen over the years and what he thought of the postal service these days. George positively glowed at the opportunity to talk about his modest career.

Mathias invested similar energy in her mother. Sarah marvelled at the way Mathias listened intently when someone was speaking to him, gave them all of his concentration as though what they were saying was of unique and particular importance to him. Sarah observed with wonder that when he spoke he had her parent's rapt attention for every word. His voice and his eyes were almost mesmerising. She was in no doubt that her mother figured him as a great catch for her. Certainly more than she had the right to expect had been her mother's insinuation after he left.

Sarah wondered whether her mother was aware of the subtle ways that she found of belittling her daughter or whether it was simply part of the venomous disposition that she was beginning to manifest as she got older. Either way, Sarah was determined not to let her mother undermine her confidence with Mathias.

"Almost there." Mathias said, jolting Sarah out of her daydreaming.

She looked around as Mathias parked the car and saw the same depressing council flats that she'd visited with Maria during the week. She thought she'd rather live at home forever with all of its aggravations than in one of these squalid and dismal little boxes.

Sarah felt a little nervous accompanying Mathias to this party. She wasn't terribly good with people she didn't know and Mathias had said that the conversations often became quite animated among this little group and if people got excited she was just to roll with the punches. Looking up at the grey concrete flats, she began to question her decision to come along.

"You'll be fine, really." Mathias said, once again sensing her mood. "Come on, let's go and meet everyone."

Mathias parked in an empty lot under a single street light that blinked on and off every few seconds, its weak orange light almost an afterthought. He locked the car and they began walking toward the block of flats. The wind had dropped but the night was cold and the sky black and moonless. As they turned into the narrow lane that squeezed between the rear of the flats and the back of a used car yard, two men step in front of them. Sarah freezes, panic rising in her chest. Unconsciously, she grips Mathias's arm, felt the rubbery spring of muscle and sinew. The men take several paces forward, the shorter of the two bouncing on the balls of his feet, his hand in his coat pocket, a shabby woollen hat rolled up to uncover his ears. The large man appeared to have something in his hand, an object he was trying to hide. The threat of violence charged the air like static electricity. The wire mesh fencing on either side of the laneway was at least seven feet high and was twisted into wicked spikes along the top. One way in and one way out. Mathias gently unlaces her fingers from his arm and leans close to whisper, his hand on the side of her face.

"Stay right here. I'm going to have a little chat with these boys and I'll be right back. Don't worry, everything will be fine."

Sarah wants to run, to put as much distance as she can between themselves and these thugs. She's frightened for Mathias, the men look hard, their faces set with grim determination. Something about Mathias's calm and unhurried voice makes her stay. He walks forward, his limbs loose like those of an athlete, until he's at arms length from the two men. His hands hang by his sides, his hands open. Relaxed.

"You're standing in my way." He says.

The short man smiles showing teeth yellowed by nicotine and neglect.

"That fuckin' so big man?" He said. He turns to his companion. "Mibee we ought tae…"

That was as far as he got. With frightening speed Mathias steps forward, his arm exploding straight out, his hand open and the heel of his palm striking the face of the larger man with monstrous force. There is a sickening crunch of bone as the man is lifted off his feet by the blow. He crashes backwards into the wire mesh fence surrounding the flats before spinning around and landing on his back as if he'd been smashed with a baseball bat. One leg twitched momentarily and then he was still. The only signs of life are the short bursts of steam and pink spittle that rise from his mouth in the freezing air. Mathias's hand falls back to his side before the big man even hits the ground. Woollen hat man takes a step back, his mouth open and his gaze darting between Mathias's calm face and his companion lying prostrate on the bitumen. The speed and ferocity of the blow have completely pummelled any spirit of bravado from his mind.

Standing several paces behind, Sarah didn't even see Mathias move. One second there were two men and the next only one was standing. She sees Mathias lean forward toward the smaller of the two men who recoils as though he's been slapped, backing off with his hands held up in surrender. Mathias turns his back on him and walks over to Sarah, taking her hand in his.

"What happened?" Sarah gasps. "What did you do?"

"Let's cut around this way." He said, leading her away from the man on the ground. Sarah looks up at him, her eyes wide.

"Just some lads out for a rumble. I suggested they look elsewhere for their fun and they agreed."

"But the man on the ground?"

"He'll be fine. His face might take a while to mend but I'm sure he's pretty tough."

Sarah's heart is still hammering in her chest and she shoots a glance behind her to see if they are being followed. She sees the small man bending over his broken companion, casting nervous glances in their direction, his eyes wide with fear. As they enter the grounds surrounding the flats Mathias stops, turns to face her and puts his arms around her shoulders, pulling her to him. She lays her head on his chest and listens to his relaxed steady heartbeat, feels the muscle under his skin, like hard rubber. He wraps his jacket around them both. The warmth of his body is comforting and her heart rate starts to slow. He kisses the top of her head.

"Let's not let those fools spoil our evening. We won't see them again."

Sarah presses her face into his sweater, breathes in his smell.

"You feel nice to me." She says. "What did you say to that short man with the hat?"

Mathias stares up at the flats with their patchwork of dark and orange-lit windows. "Nothing."

Sarah tilts her head back to see his face. "It didn't look like nothing."

"I just gave his heart a little squeeze." He said.

Sarah cocks her head to one side, her eyes seeking an explanation. In response Mathias takes her face in his hands and lifts her chin so she is looking directly into his eyes. Even in the semidarkness his eyes are electric. He kisses her lips tenderly.

"Let's go inside before we catch our death of cold."

She followed him down a dim corridor lined with linoleum that was worn right through to the concrete in places before stopping outside a blue painted door on the ground floor. Sarah could hear laughter and the sound of good-natured conversation from inside the flat. The volume swelled as Mathias pushed open the door. He put his strong arm around her shoulders and gave her a little squeeze before leading her inside. It felt good. Her first reaction as she entered was one of surprise that there were only five people in the room, somehow she had expected a larger group.

As her gaze swept across the individuals she was further surprised to realise that they were almost all women with only one man among them. Mathias led her by the hand and made the introductions. Looking around she was impressed by how pleasant the little flat was once you were inside. There were two welcoming sofas, woollen tapestries on the walls and colourful oriental rugs covered the polished floorboards. Not at all what she'd expected but very cosy. She started to relax and someone placed a glass of red wine into her hand. Perhaps the evening might actually turn out to be fun after all, she thought.

* * *

David felt sick. He and Walter sat in the kitchen opposite Peter Boulton as the man explained to them how his wife hadn't come home from work the night before, hadn't called, had simply disappeared. David watched as the man twisted and untwisted his handkerchief, his love and concern for Janice eating away at him. The children had been sent to stay with Peter's sister but signs of them were everywhere. Dread gripped David's heart as he thought about the devastation to this man and his young family if Janice turned out to be another victim. The small house spoke to him of a simple and loving family. Photographs of better times covered the walls and everywhere the warmth and smell of timber softened the space. While the house was clean, children's toys were dotted around in a manner that suggested a relaxed and unaffected atmosphere. It was plain to see that Peter's world revolved around his family and David desperately wanted this to be something other than what he and Walter feared.

"I have to ask you a difficult question." Walter said, looking Peter directly in the eyes. "In our experience, when a woman disappears from a circumstance like this," he waved his hand to encompass the domestic scene, "it's sometimes because she wanted to."

Peter stares at him, a puzzled expression on his face, his eyes red rimmed from tears, his skin grey. "You mean, maybe, she just ran away? Just up and left us?"

"I think it's a possibility that we have to discuss. My question, Peter, and I dislike intensely that it's necessary to ask, is, how were you and Janice getting along. Honestly, what state do you think your marriage was in?"

Peter stands abruptly almost tipping over the kitchen chair in his agitation. "Listen here, there was nothing wrong with our marriage!" He yells. "Janice and I were like peas in a pod. She never stopped telling me how happy she was! She loved her life. Her house. And the kids, she… she just…"

At this point he can't continue and slumps back into the chair, sobs shaking his wiry body as he covers his face with the damp handkerchief. Walter leans forward, his voice soothing.

"I'm sorry to have to bring that up, Peter. I have no reason to suspect anything other than that Janice was perfectly contented. It's a standard question we have to ask because we need to be sure. If she really has gone missing and, God forbid, has fallen victim to some sort of foul play, then we can't be wasting time checking with all the relatives to see if she's turned up in Shropshire with an overnight bag or something."

Peter nods. "I understand. But please, you have to believe me that she would never do a thing like this. Not to us, not deliberately. Never ever. I know this as sure as you're sitting opposite me."

Walter reaches across the table and places his hand on the grieving mans arm. Squeezed. "I do believe you Peter." He said.

David flipped back through his notebook and asked Peter to repeat the answers he'd given to some of their earlier questions. Where was her shop? How was the business doing? Did she work alone? When did she lock up? When did you speak last? How was she this morning? Why didn't you collect her? Which way did she walk home? What time did she normally arrive? The questions were never ending and David felt bad having to push the poor man but he knew that recollections, like photographs, faded with time.

Afterward the pair walk to their cars parked at the end of the narrow street. David flips up his collar and digs his hands deep into his pockets, the night air chilly after the warmth of the house they'd just left. As usual, Walter appeared entirely indifferent to the weather.

"A bad business methinks." Walter said.

"Christ, I hope we don't have to go back there and tell that poor sod that his wife's been found floating in the English Channel. It's bad enough when we're talking about young women but mothers with little kids. Shit, I felt bad for that fella."

"Well, she wouldn't be the first one to turn up in the embrace of another man. Under the current circumstances it would almost be good news." Walter replied.

"I dunno, I've got a bad feeling that we're going to find her in an entirely different embrace."

"Woman is the salvation or the destruction of the family, she carries its destiny in the folds of her mantle."

David didn't even bother to ask.

"Amiel, Henri Frederic." Walter added.

* * *

Sarah leaned back into the homely overstuffed sofa and rested her head on Mathias's shoulder. The room was warm and she felt mellow after several glasses of wine. The evening had been much more enjoyable than Sarah expected and she'd really hit it off with a woman named Rita, so much so that they had promised to meet for lunch in town. She'd also had a great laugh with Joyce, an older woman with a nervous tick in her eye who was in the throws of separation from her husband of twenty years. And Maggie, whose flat they were in, seemed to be such a sweet and gentle person. What she found really interesting was the dynamic of the group of friends. Mathias was clearly the leader and when he spoke, everyone listened and nobody interrupted.

What Sarah found odd was that this only happened when it was Mathias speaking. Anyone else was interrupted, talked over, and laughed at once the discussion became animated. Another strange thing was that they all appeared to be bonded in some slightly preternatural way. Mathias had surprised her by the depth of his spiritual understanding and the way he could hold forth on topics such as eastern religion, mysticism, reincarnation and so on. There was obviously a very complex side to his personality.

Sarah was pondering what all this might mean when Mathias leaned over with a hand rolled cigarette and offered it to her. Surprised, Sarah leaned away from him.

"I didn't know you smoked." She said. Somehow she hadn't pegged him for a smoker, he looked much too healthy.

"This isn't about smoking," he said, "it's about opening the mind. It's a little thing we do that helps us get in touch with ourselves."

Sarah thought that this sounded a bit like new age wank but she didn't want to embarrass him in front of her new friends.

"It looks like smoking to me." She said, trying to laugh it off. Mathias wouldn't be deterred.

"This is a very special herb. It's not tobacco and it's not marijuana in case you're concerned. It's a herb that's been used for thousands of years by holy men throughout Asia. Go on, take a puff."

Sarah looks around the room for support. Maggie spoke up.

"Try it Sarah, it's okay. I think you'll enjoy it. Have a puff and if you don't like it don't have any more. It's really quite wonderful."

Her inhibitions suppressed by the wine and the relaxed atmosphere, Sarah took the roll-up and pulled the heavily scented smoke into her lungs, held her breath for a few seconds and then breathed out. The others watched her carefully. At first nothing happened and she had to suppress the desire to cough. Then, a feeling of great calmness began to wash over her. It felt as though someone was pouring warm water over her head. A soothing wave of water that slowly enveloped her entire body. The sensation of relaxation was outstanding. She took another long draw. Her vision seemed to intensify, the tiniest details became visible to her, she could now see the pores on Rita's skin across the room and the stubble on the chin of Robert, Maggie's muscular boyfriend. It was amazing, like having telescopic vision.

Abruptly, the feeling heightened as though had it been thrust to a new level and Robert's skin began to disappear. Now she had x-ray vision and could see the bones of his face, the fillings in his teeth, his eyeballs like orbs of jelly resting in their sockets. The inside of his head appeared as his skull melted away and she saw a dark red patch with an inky black centre on one side of his brain. It didn't look right and suddenly Sarah was frightened. She dropped the roll-up on the carpet as she tried to push herself back, away from the awful vision before her. Robert was disappearing before her eyes, being peeled apart like an onion, layer by layer. She could now see into his chest, his heart pulsing, thick red blood vessels branching off into a maze of tiny tubes. His spine, the pieces of cartilage stacked on top of each other like anatomical Lego. And abruptly he disappeared.

Then the walls of the flat were gone and she could see outside. She screamed and tried to close her eyes but she couldn't stop the stream of images from entering her brain. It was as though she was in the cinema with her head in a clamp and her eyes taped open. Vaguely she felt hands on her body, voices in the distance calling to her. She couldn't hear what they were saying. A wave of bright light hit her eyes causing her to cry out and then a movie began to roll in front of her.

It was Joyce. She was walking across the road at the zebra crossing opposite the chemist in the High Street. The sun was shining and

Joyce had her coat open, her purse clutched under one arm. She was crossing the road toward the chemist and waving to someone on the other side. The breeze tugged at the edges of her parka. She was halfway across when a white car appeared from nowhere, accelerating toward her. A policeman ran around the corner shouting something. Sarah could see his mouth moving but couldn't hear any sound, this movie was silent. She wanted to scream at Joyce to get out of the way, to look to her right but she couldn't move. She could see what was going to happen.

The policeman blew his whistle and yelled. Joyce stopped on the crossing, in the middle of the road, her head began to turn. Then the white car smashed into her. Joyce's legs were knocked out from under her and she pitched onto the car's bonnet, her head smashing the windscreen and leaving a bloodstained dent as she bounced off. Joyce was flung into the air like a rag doll, her purse spinning wildly. The white car didn't even slow. Joyce's arms and legs cartwheeled out as she tumbled and then she hit the road like a bundle of rags and was still.

A second later her purse landed on the footpath and bounced twice before tumbling into the gutter. For a moment the entire street was motionless. Then people began to pour out of shops, cars pulled over and motorists ran toward Joyce's shattered body, the policeman yelling into a microphone clipped to his jacket. Sarah knew Joyce was dead, her legs bent at grotesque angles. As if floating above the scene with a perfect view of everything, she was surprised to see so little blood. The wave of white light hit her again sending fingers of pain into her eyes and the movie screen inside her head turned black.

Sarah's next sensation was of something wet and cold on her face. She was lying on the couch and Mathias was mopping her forehead, Robert fanning her with a magazine. She realised that she was drenched with sweat and her head throbbed mercilessly. She tried to speak but Mathias put his finger on her lips.

"Relax, don't try to talk. You've had a fainting spell again. Gave us all a fright, but you're okay now. She peered into the ring of concerned faces above her and she wanted to tell them that this wasn't just a fainting episode but she didn't have the energy. She looked up at Robert and remembered the dark patch she'd seen on the side of his brain and suddenly she was scared for him. Maggie brought some water and Sarah managed to push herself up on one elbow to take a drink, her throat scratchy. Sitting up made her a little dizzy and she lay down again, the room beginning to fade. The last thing she recalled was Mathias lifting her up and carrying her into another room.

* * *

Peter Boulton replaced the receiver and crossed off the last name on his list. The click of the telephone handset settling into its cradle sounded obscenely loud in the quiet of the empty house. Following Walter's line of questioning he'd decided to telephone everyone that Janice knew. Friends and relatives alike. It felt like a betrayal of trust but he had to do it. The calls had drained him and the effort of keeping his head upright seemed almost beyond his capability. He thought of the children and realised he had no idea how he would even survive this ordeal, let alone remain strong for them.

CHAPTER 6

Sarah opens her eyes to see an older man bending over her. His hair is white and his bushy eyebrows poke out above the rims of his black framed spectacles. He smiles.

"Hello Sarah, I'm Doctor Robertson. Your friend called me out to give you the once over. He tells me that you've had a couple of fainting spells recently. Are you on any medication? Changed any medication lately?"

Sarah thinks back to the new tablets that her own doctor prescribed and wonders whether there is a connection. As the doctor pokes and prods and listens she explains her medical history and tries to tell him about what had happened. When he's completed his examination the doctor recommends that she go back to her own GP and bring him up to date. Sarah promises to do exactly that but without any real determination in her voice. The doctor gives her a stern look, pronounces her as well as can be expected and suggests that she has a cup of tea before toddling off home to bed. A frown of disapproval creases his face as he adds that a little less alcohol might be in order for someone on permanent medication. He snaps his bag closed and shows himself out.

Feeling better, Sarah shuffles back into the front room and receives a cheer from the small group. Maggie stands up to make some tea. As Sarah goes to sit down she sees an ugly burn mark on the rug near the sofa.

"Oh God, I'm sorry, Maggie. I must have dropped the roll-up on the carpet. I'm such a klutz, I'll buy you a new one. I feel so bad about it."

Maggie waved her hand, dismissing it as trivial. "Nonsense, you couldn't help it, and we egged you on anyway. *You* should be mad at *us*!"

Heads nod around the room. Sarah sits back down on the sofa and rubs her eyes. Mathias perches on the edge of the coffee table opposite her, an expression of expectation on his face. Suddenly she realises that the air in the room is charged somehow, like a thunderstorm when there's lightening close by. She feels that sparks might jump out of her fingers if she touches him at that moment.

"What did you see, Sarah?" Mathias asks.

She can't be sure but it seems to Sarah that everyone in the room leaned toward her slightly. Even Maggie in the kitchen stops what she's doing to listen. Sarah is uncomfortable at being the centre of attention like this. She has the distinct impression that they have all waited, not to see how she was but to hear what she had to say.

"What do you mean?"

Sarah wanted to know how they knew she saw anything in the first place. She began to worry that she'd said something, maybe made a fool of herself. Maybe she'd described the whole thing as it unfolded? She didn't think so but she couldn't remember.

"We know you saw something, Sarah." Mathias insisted.

"Just some stupid hallucinations. It must have been a reaction to the smoke. It doesn't matter."

"It matters to us." Mathias said.

Sarah looks around the room at their faces and realises Mathias is serious. They really did want to know. She doesn't like the way that this situation is developing but she's also unsure how to handle it. Even though it's late they had obviously waited until she came out of the bedroom to give them an explanation of what she'd seen. And she had burned a hole in the rug after all. Having to recall the awful images so soon felt like a weight on her tired shoulders. She really didn't feel like talking about this now but she couldn't bring herself to say forget it, move on, next topic.

"Okay." She said rubbing her palms against the tops of her legs. She decided not say anything about Robert, the experience of looking inside his body and seeing that mark on his brain was simply too weird to talk about right now.

"It was like watching a silent movie. Like I was floating and could see everything."

"Like God." Mathias said, his eyes never leaving her face.

"I guess you could say that." Said Sarah. "I saw an accident and, well, it happened to one of the people here and I feel bad about relating it."

Mathias leaned forward and Sarah again had the feeling that to touch him would be dangerous. "You must tell us what you saw." He said.

"Look, I'm tired, okay?" Sarah said. "It was silly, it didn't mean anything."

Mathias didn't move. Nobody spoke.

"Well, it all happened very quickly." Sarah continued, trying to give herself a way out of explaining all of the minute detail that she could remember so clearly.

"Joyce was crossing the high street in town and was bowled over by a car. There it is. Told you it was silly."

Without warning, the oxygen appeared to drain from the room. There was a collective gasp and Joyce's hand flew to her mouth. Maggie dropped a cup and it exploded on the kitchen floor causing everyone to jump. Sarah was stunned by the reaction.

"It was only a dream." She said.

Joyce's eyes are wide, the pupils dilated. She looks at Mathias, her face a mask of terror.

"This is real, isn't it?" She said, her voice no more than a whisper.

Mathias doesn't answer but simply averts his eyes, unable to disagree with her. Sarah looks from one to the other, not understanding what's happening, unable to comprehend the reaction she has produced in them. Joyce leaps to her feet and runs from the room. Robert stands, not sure what to do.

"I better go and see if she's okay." He says.

Sarah turns to Mathias. "What's going on? Why is she reacting so strangely? What did she mean about it being real? I feel awful about this, I never should have said anything."

Mathias has a strange look in his eyes, one she hasn't seen before. Almost a look of veneration. Sarah is becoming frightened. As if reading her fear, Mathias takes a deep breath, kneels on the floor and put his arms around her, pulling her to his chest. To her surprise she doesn't get an electric shock when he touches her.

"I better get you home I think. Everyone's a little tired."

Sarah pulls away, she is being excluded from something and it was starting to irritate her. They had pressed her to reveal this for God's sake and now they didn't want to talk about it. When she looked at Mathias's face it had softened, the strange look had dissolved.

"But what about Joyce? What's the matter with her?"

Mathias took hold of Sarah's hands. "Joyce can be a bit highly strung. She has a phobia or two and I guess you touched a nerve. It's not your fault, you had no way of knowing."

Sarah was still confused. "What sort of phobias?" She insisted.

Mathias looks at her and she's startled to see tears welling up in his eyes.

"Joyce doesn't get out much on her own, sort of a bit frightened of her own shadow. In particular she's terrified of crossing the road, of being hit by a car." He said.

* * *

Detective Inspector David Orbost took one last pull from the beer bottle before dropping it into the flip-top bin in the corner of his small kitchen. It's midday and while he doesn't usually drink this early, he makes an exception on the Sunday mornings after he finishes cleaning the flat. A job that he loathes, he manages to find all manner of excuses to delay the inevitable until it simply can't be put off any longer and he's tired of living in morbid fear of a surprise visit by his mother. Looking around he feels satisfied with his work. The place smells clean, the shower is freshly scrubbed and all of the dust bunnies have been evicted from the corners.

Not for the first time he toys with the idea of getting a cleaning woman to come in. Trouble is, his policeman's instincts always rebel against giving a stranger the key to his place. It occurs to him that he should ask Walter if he knows anyone locally who could be recommended, someone who has a history of honesty and reliability. Maybe Walter even uses a cleaning person that he could contact. He has another thought. He could also ask Natalie where to find a good cleaning women. He thinks better of it. Might sound like a sexist comment. Complicated. Better get to know her a bit better first.

As his gaze wanders over the splendour of his sparkling flat, he's distracted by his briefcase that he can see in the hallway near the front door. His mind is dragged back to the case. He's been asked by Chief Inspector Jamison to give the briefing tomorrow morning. Standing up in front of a group of people doesn't actually terrorise him, particularly standing in front of police who are pretty much the same the world over, but he's uncomfortable at the thought nevertheless.

The problem really is that they're simply not making any headway, which leaves him without a whole lot to say. Despite extensive man hours invested in door-knocking and speaking with friends and family of the dead women, they haven't been able to draw much of a picture of the person they're looking for. He's reminded again of how difficult it can be to crack a case that appears to be motiveless. If the victims aren't known to the killer and the killer doesn't leave evidence for the police to find, it can be tough. Sometimes impossible even.

He reminds himself that there are serious crimes that have been on the books for decades, in some cases the perpetrator has probably died of old age by now. The reality is that most crooks are pretty stupid, most murders point to the murderer and those that don't usually provide some physical evidence that can be used to narrow things down at least. But not this time it would appear. With a sigh he walks over and picks up the briefcase, sets it down on the table and begins to read through the reports again.

* * *

"I tell you, Maria, I've had some crazy things going on in my head as you well know but that was the weirdest thing that's ever happened to me." Sarah said. "And the strangest part was that Joyce looked straight to Mathias to tell her whether she should take the whole idiotic episode seriously or not. I can understand someone having a phobia, Christ, me of all people can see how that can happen but what sort of normal adult person needs somebody else to tell them whether a dream is reality? I just don't get the whole thing."

Without responding, Maria pours the tea that she's made for them and hands a cup to Sarah before sitting down at the tiny kitchen table.

"And another strange thing, when Joyce looked to Mathias to tell her it wasn't real he didn't say anything! I would have thought he'd have laughed it off or at least told her not to worry about it. It was like there was some secret understanding in the group and I was the only one who didn't know about it."

Maria's face is serious; she is obviously trying to choose her words carefully.

"And ye don't know what the stuff was in the roll-up?"

"No. Some herbal thing, Mathias said. They all pushed me to have a toke. I'd had a few drinks, you know how these things can be."

"Well, hen. I guess ye don't need me tellin' ye that it was bloody stupid to be tryin' some unknown weed that gets passed around. Just daft is that. Specially wi' your history."

"I know, I know. But I was pretty relaxed and they weren't to know that I'd be spinning out like that."

"I have to say, pet, I'm no' happy about this whole thing. Are ye sure it's not some weird cult thing they're into?" The worry was written large on Maria's face.

"I don't know, I don't think so but it's hard to be sure. They seem like nice people and Mathias was very sweet about the whole thing."

Maria isn't her normal cheerful and irreverent self and Sarah is surprised to see her so serious. She is also startled to notice how old Maria looks when she isn't laughing and joking around, as she did most of the time.

"Mibee you need to give things a wee space." Maria said, not able to meet Sarah's eyes.

"What do you mean?"

"You know, just cool it for a while."

"Are you talking about Mathias?" Sarah said.

Without looking up, Maria fiddles with the jewellery on her fingers.

"Aye, mibee just be a wee bit more careful wi' him. Oh, I don't know. What the fuck do I know about these things? I'm just fretful that you don't get your bony arse into a mess wi' those people. I don't like all this weird shite."

Sarah can see the struggle that her friend is having to convey her concern without being a scaremonger. It's not like Maria to beat about the bush thinks Sarah. She leans across the table and takes Maria's hands in hers.

"Thank you. Thank you for being such a good friend. I don't know what I'd do without you."

"Aw, away wi' ye, yer daft bugger. Ye'll have me bawlin' in a minute. Just watch yer step wi' those fruitcakes."

* * *

When Sarah arrived home that evening her mother told her that Mathias had called three times. In her withering style she left Sarah in no doubt that being out of contact was a very bad move when dealing with a man like Mathias. Her implication was that whatever Sarah might do to give Mathias the slightest impression that she was anything but eager to see him, was simply stupid. Don't give him an excuse to look elsewhere, God knows, he has better options than you, seemed to be her message. Refusing to be drawn into an argument, Sarah filled a glass with milk and took it into her bedroom where she could return Mathias's calls out of her mother's hearing.

"Sarah, I'm so glad you called, I've been out of my mind worrying about you. It was so stupid of me to press that smoke on you last night, I can't imagine what you must think of me." Mathias said as soon as he realised it was Sarah on the phone.

"That's okay, I'm fine now." Sarah said cautiously.

"Our little group of friends must seem weird to you." Mathias said, apparently doing his mind reading act again.

Sarah sighed. "Look, it's probably just me but… I don't know, Joyce's reaction, well actually everyone's reaction. It's just, sort of, strange. I guess I'm not making myself clear."

"No, no, it's perfectly clear and I can understand why it all seems odd to you. Why don't you let me take you out to dinner to make amends?" Mathias said.

Sarah was torn. What to say? She decided to stick to her resolution and give herself time to get her mind straight.

"That sounds lovely but I was thinking maybe things are going a bit quickly, perhaps we need to slow it down. You know, not rush things."

There was a silence on the other end of the phone and Sarah's breath caught in her throat as she wondered whether he was about to tell her to go jump.

"Okay. Okay." Mathias said. Sarah could detect the caution in his voice. "Are you saying that you don't want to see me again?"

Sarah began to panic; she didn't want to swing the pendulum too far in the opposite direction.

"No, of course that's not what I'm saying. I *do* want to see you again. It's just that, I guess my head's a bit mixed up right now and I'm not sure what I want."

"I understand that you were frightened last night," Mathias said, brightening, "I should have explained a few things to you. Listen, what about this for an idea. I'll take you to dinner and I'll try to help you to understand what it is that holds our little group together and then maybe it will make more sense. If you still feel the same way after that we can take it at any pace you like. How does that sound?"

"Well, that sounds fair I guess." Sarah said, unsure of whether she was doing the right thing but still hoping there might be a rational explanation at the bottom of it all.

* * *

The man's shovel slips easily into the wet sand. The night sky is relatively clear and the quarter moon provides all the light he needs to complete his task. Looking up he can see high clouds scudding across the sky, giving the moon an ethereal glow. Like a halo, the man thinks. Probably some shitful weather on the way. Bending to his task he continues to dig. The sand is damp and piles up nicely making the job much quicker than trying to dig a grave in dry sand where the loose grains insist on pouring back into the hole. The man congratulates himself on having the foresight to have predicted this. He has chosen this spot because he knows that it's off the beaten track and also just high enough above the tide line that it shouldn't be disturbed by the waves. The bottom of the hole begins to fill with water and it's obvious that it can't be dug much deeper. It's not quite the depth that the man had in mind but he tells himself that it will have to do. A line has been crossed and there is no turning back now.

He stands up straight and stabs the shovel into the large pile of sand to his left. As he wipes a sheen of sweat from his forehead his eyes scan left and right to ensure that no one lurks nearby. The man knows it would be unlikely for anyone to come to this spot at night but he's nervous nonetheless and is anxious to get the job done so he can be on his way. Inspecting the hole again, he decides that it will be adequate for the purpose. He takes hold of the woman's feet and positions her at the side of the hole. Using his boot he shoves her body over the edge. With a soft splash she lands on her back in the centre of the trench but her left arm is sticking up out of the hole at almost ninety degrees. The woman has been lying on her side and rigour mortis has left her arm poking out from her body. He's reminded of a Nazi salute.

"Stupid bloody woman." He whispers under his breath as he attempts to push the arm down. It's more difficult than he expected. Using his boot to hold the dead woman's arm down he shovels the heavy wet sand on top of her. Filling the hole is much quicker than making it in the first place and in a few minutes the job is done. Scattering the excess sand around him, the man stands back and inspects his work in the weakening moonlight. Satisfied, he walks to edge of the water and hurls the shovel as far as he can. It disappears into the night before making a reassuring splash some distance away. Rubbing his hands on his trousers to remove the sand that clings to his skin, the man turns his back on the water and trudges away.

CHAPTER 7

Business was slow for a Friday evening and the trio had no trouble getting a quiet table near the window where they could speak without being overheard. The pub is a favourite haunt of the local force and it would be a rare night that there wasn't at least one table of boisterous police. In no way was the establishment remarkable but to the practical minds of the local coppers, what it lacked in ambience was more than made up for by its proximity. David and Walter had taken to having a drink after work on a Friday evening and just lately David was starting to pine for that first beer by mid afternoon. A little voice at the back of his mind nagged at him that this was how alcoholics got their start. Another more agreeable voice countered that it was simply the unique and temporary pressure of this case.

Walter raises his glass. "I drink when I have occasion for it, and sometimes when I have not."

"Cervantes. Don Quixote." Natalie replies.

"Splendid!" Cried Walter. "How heart warming to be in the company of someone with taste as well as style. Thank you my dear for joining us at our humble pre-prandial tipple."

He leans forward conspiratorially. "David is a fine chap, but I have to say, something of a Philistine where the finer things of life are concerned."

David simply shakes is head, feigning hurt. "That's right, just talk about me like I'm not even here. I'll just be off outside to eat dirt."

Smiling, Natalie puts a hand on his arm to prevent him from rising. "Don't you take any notice. Just being a fine chap will get you a long way."

Not for the first time David wonders whether she is teasing him with a double entendre or if her words are simply innocent. Sometimes the complexity of male-female relationships leaves him bewildered.

The three sipped their drinks in response to Walter's toast. A shadow passed over Natalie's face and she placed her glass of wine carefully in the centre of the paper mat.

"You know, there's one thing that I think doesn't get enough airing at our briefings." She said.

"Go on." Walter replied.

"Because this case is so difficult in terms of motive and forensic evidence, I think we're putting too much effort into trying to analyse the minutiae of what we *do* have to the exclusion of the broader issues."

"For example?" Said David.

"Well, for instance, we've debated endlessly the question of how he gets these women to wherever he imprisons them. Does he have a car, does he drug them, does he trick them etcetera."

"And these are important questions." Adds Walter.

"Of course they are but they aren't the only ones we should be thrashing out."

Walter nods. "It's certainly true that our progress has been underwhelming this week. What questions would you like added to the agenda?"

"For one, what does he *want* from these women?"

David picks up his glass and leans back in his chair.

"How can we know? The man's a serial killer, surely it's just about domination and power over his victims. That sort of thing?"

"Yes but look at the way he treats them. It's almost reverential in some respects."

Walter's head snaps up, a surprised look on his face. "Reverential! Now there's an interesting word choice. If you don't mind my saying so, he most certainly chooses an unusual way of showing it!"

"Sure." Natalie replied. "But then people who think like you and me don't usually become serial killers either."

"Tell us what you mean, Natalie." David said, his drink momentarily forgotten.

"Remember what Cyril Morpeth said? How the killer carefully floated Amanda's body into the water?"

Walter flicks through his notebook. "As gently as you like."

"That's right. He didn't toss her in the ocean or roll her off a cliff. He floated her gently out to sea. And have any of the victims shown any signs of physical mistreatment, beating or torture? Other than being restrained? And haven't they all had food in their stomachs? He even kills them quickly for Christ's sake."

Natalie sits back, a smile plays at the corner of her mouth as she watches the wheels turning in the minds of the two detectives.

"So…" David begins, his brain trying to reorganise the pieces of the puzzle, trying to find if there was a new arrangement that yields a different picture, "what *does* he want from them?"

"Well that's obviously my point, David. We're not giving that question enough attention. Perhaps he's looking for something from these women and when he's disappointed, he reluctantly kills them. My speculation is that it takes him some time to make up his mind and that's why he keeps them alive. I'm not sure that the abduction is about the killing at all. There's something else going on here."

A look passes between David and Walter. David slumps back in his chair and runs his fingers through his hair.

"Bugger. She could have a point, Walter. Jesus."

"And while you're worrying about that, here's another thing. Perhaps you should give some thought to what might happen if he *does* find what he's looking for. If I'm correct, you'll either catch him quickly or never hear from him again."

* * *

It's after midnight but Joyce Matthews is wide-awake. As she fidgets restlessly in her double bed she simply can't banish Sarah's words from her mind. Mathias had said since the start that when the right person came along they would know it. And now it had happened. How else could Sarah have known about her fear? Only Joyce's closest friends knew and even then they didn't really understand the absolute gut wrenching terror that Joyce experienced whenever she neared the curb. In fact crossing the road wasn't the worst of it. She had reached the stage where she could no longer even walk along the footpath if there was traffic on the road.

She would go out early in the morning to do her grocery shopping and if a car approached as she walked down the street she would scurry into a shop entranceway or an alley. It was if it were beyond her control not to scan the road for cars and potential hiding spots when she stepped outside. While she knew she was getting worse, Joyce simply invented new ways of trying to survive that didn't involve going near the roadway.

When she first met Mathias she was in a bad way. Her mind wandered back to that day when she was attempting to cross a quiet street at the zebra crossing. In the distance, some kid with a hot car had screeched away and she had been paralysed with a fear so overwhelming that she could go neither forward or backward. Mathias had seen her and somehow he read her fear. He put his strong arm around her shoulders and led her away from the road. She thought her legs would give way but he steered her inside a café and insisted on buying her a hot drink. He asked no questions but she found herself pouring her heart out to him, maybe because he was a stranger. He didn't make her feel silly and he didn't try to help, he just listened.

Never in her life had Joyce felt such a profound sense of unburdening. It was then that Mathias told her about Rachael Telford. He revealed something to her that had changed her life. How Rachael was born in 1594 in London but sailed for Massachusetts in America when she was thirty six. How she fought in the religious struggle for Puritanism before establishing a women-only Bible study group. How she realised the extent to which women had been pushed out of traditional religious beliefs and generally dominated by men and how she had been called by God to begin rectifying that situation.

Joyce was entranced by Mathias's stories of this strong minded woman and listened in amazement as he explained what had come to be her controversial but little-known religious teachings. For the first time, Joyce began to feel a sense of self worth, a realisation that maybe she could be complete and whole on her own, just as she was, despite her fears. That maybe she could even be powerful, in control.

Over the next few weeks she met Mathias for lunch at the café many times and each time he revealed another story to her, another aspect of Rachael's personality and beliefs. She was speechless on the day that Mathias told her about Rachael's prophecy regarding the coming of a woman, The Redeemer, who would have powers beyond anything seen on earth since Jesus Christ. In her mind's eye, Joyce could still see the fire in Mathias's eyes as he explained how this woman would reveal herself in the new millennium and prove her identity by seeing into the future. While she might not acknowledge it at first, when she gained control of her power she would strike a great blow for women worldwide.

She gasped when it was explained to her that all of the signs had now been fulfilled and the women could appear anytime. And that when she did arrive, she would trigger a struggle between good and evil, which had the potential to destroy the world.

And now the woman was here. In Maggie's flat no less. And the dreadful, dreadful words she had spoken about Joyce. Spearing into her very soul. After everything she'd learned about and hoped for and craved from this woman, when she finally arrived her first vision represented a death sentence of the most unimaginable cruelty. Joyce's heart ached with despondency and fear.

Without switching on her bedside lamp, Joyce reaches into the drawer and takes out the bottle of sleeping pills prescribed by Doctor Baxter. The only thought in her mind is to bury the fears that haunt her. Without looking she shakes out a small handful of the pills, puts them in her mouth and swills them down with a gulp of water. That ought to do it, she thinks. And if by some miracle I don't wake up again, all the better.

* * *

As Joyce slipped in to the kind of merciful unconsciousness that only prescription drugs can offer, Peter Boulton was dealing with his own demons. There was still no news about Janice and he was starting to lose hope. In the last couple of days he found himself thinking of life without Janice. He hated himself for it because if felt like betrayal. A week had gone by and there was no trace. A serial killer was targeting women in the area. Those dots were too obvious to remain unjoined.

The thought of Janice dead was somehow more bearable than the alternative of her kept prisoner in some God-forsaken hole. Peter knew that in the absence of anything concrete, *a body*, he forced himself to articulate, the time would come when he'd need to face the fact that she wasn't coming home. He didn't even want to think about how he'd tell the children. For what seemed like the thousandth time since Janice had disappeared, his eyes strayed to the phone fastened to the kitchen wall, willing it to ring. It didn't and he slumped in his chair, his tired body aching with grief.

* * *

An explosive burst of tea shoots from Maria's nose and she almost chokes following Sarah's revelation.

"What the fuck!" She splutters.

"That's what he said." Sarah replied.

Maria struggles to bring herself under control as she mops a trickle of tea from her dirigible-sized bosom.

"Let me get this straight. He's sayin' ye are some sort of fuckin' virgin Mary?"

"Well, not exactly, but you get the idea."

Maria's mouth opens and closes without a sound.

"What did ye tell the daft bugger?" She said.

"I asked him if he knew how weird the whole thing sounded."

"And did he?"

"I don't think he really did." Sarah said. "He takes this very seriously, I think he truly believes it. He banged on about how this Rachael Telford had said that The Redeemer wouldn't know that she was special at first. A bit like Jesus. Did you know that Jesus had no idea that he was the Christ until he was thirty? Before that he was just a carpenter with his dad."

Maria shakes her head in frustration, her accent thickening as her anger rises.

"Give me a break girl, don't be tryin' to analyse this shite! The man's heed's full ae mince!"

"Come on Maria, you have to admit it's rather flattering being the chosen one." Sarah says, smiling.

Maria's eyes drop to the floor for a few seconds. Sarah can see she's struggling to find the right words.

"I really don't like this, hen." Maria said. "I know you think it's a bit of a laugh…"

"I just can't take it seriously." Sarah interrupts.

"Aye. I know that. But I'm telling you that you should!"

"Look." Said Sarah. "It's bollocks, we all know that. I'm not going to play along with it and I told Mathias that it was probably best we didn't see each other and that it was all too weird for me."

"And what did he say?"

Sarah can't meet her friend's eyes. "He said that I didn't really have a choice."

"Fuck that for a game o' soldiers!" Maria snapped.

"Not about going out with him. He said that was up to me. What he meant was that if I am the one it was because I've been chosen. If you're chosen you're chosen. You don't get a say."

Maria shook her head. "Promise me ye'll no' have anything to do wi' these nutters. Promise."

"Of course not." Replied Sarah, leaning over and giving Maria's plump hand a squeeze. "It's over. And here I was wishing for a more exciting life!"

"Exciting my arse! I'll give that big bastard some excitement when I see him next, and no mistake."

CHAPTER 8

At first Joyce isn't sure where she is. Her head pounds and her throat is parched. She pushes herself up onto one elbow and is immediately overcome by nausea. Settling her head back onto the pillow she notices with a jolt that the sun is shining outside, must be mid morning. Little by little she eases herself up until she can drink the rest of the water in the glass by her bed. After a minute she sits up and places her feet on the cold wooden floor of her bedroom. Without daring to look down she feels around for her slippers and manages to hook them with her toes.

Using the bedside table for support she pushes herself upright. Objects in the room bounce up and down as pain throbs inside her head. She plods to the bathroom and fumbles through the cabinet looking for painkillers. She shakes a small pile into her hand and stares at them for a few moments before swallowing them all. She knows that she shouldn't take so many but somehow it doesn't seem to matter anymore, the part of her mind that relates actions to consequences seems to have been disconnected.

Joyce feels like she's floating as she picks her way downstairs toward the refrigerator and the cold drink that she craves. Suddenly the fridge is before her but she can't quite remember how to open it. Laying her head against the cold metal, she knocks on the door. No answer, must be empty, she thinks. Time passes as she rests her head against door, enjoying the feeling of the cold steel pressed to her skin. The sensation of floating is deepening. She feels separated from her environment in a strange way. Not in any way frightening but tranquil and calm. It's wonderful not to worry anymore. She's so tired of worrying. Joyce knocks again at the refrigerator door before remembering that there are no drinks at home. She decides to go to the corner shop for some lemonade.

Without understanding how it's happening she seems to float outside and on to the footpath. The wind tugs at the bottom of her nightie and feels deliciously cool against her damp face. She hadn't been aware of putting on her coat but she can see it flapping as the breeze plays with it. She looks down at her skinny white legs and thinks to herself that the sun will do them good. Across the road she sees a person who looks like a policewoman and she decides to ask her if she has anything to drink. The woman is waving as though she understands what Joyce wants.

With no concern for the traffic whatsoever, Joyce simply floated into the path of a vehicle driven by a vending machine repairman who at that exact moment was keying in a text message to his girlfriend on his mobile phone. As he raised his eyes to the road he heard a bang and his windscreen shattered. He skidded to a stop imagining someone had thrown a rock at his van. Tossing the phone onto the passenger seat, he was about to leap out in an attempt to grab the cretin responsible when he saw the blood and the hair trapped between the shattered pieces of glass in his windscreen.

$$* * *$$

Sometimes Ken McLeish wondered who was more crazy, himself or the dog. Ever since he'd been a boy Ken loved to walk for miles on the beach. Since his retirement and especially after his wife passed away, no matter what the weather he'd walk every afternoon. Even when the rain hammered and the sea was grey with wind-blown foam streaking across its surface, Ken would walk the dog along the sand. The pair didn't get too far these days but it was just about the only time he felt really alive, the wind punching into his chest and the sand mounding up against his boots when he paused to catch his breath.

Amazingly the dog seemed to love it too and whenever Ken pulled the animal's little waterproof coat out of the cupboard he'd bound up with his tail thumping the wall like a drum. The two had become inseparable and Ken couldn't bear the thought of the house without his old mate. Ken's stomach gave a rumble and he checked his watch. He suspected they should probably head back soon and get the dinner on. He had a shepherd's pie in the fridge that his daughter brought when she last visited and his mouth began to water as he contemplated cutting into it.

"One more throw, Bobby and then we turn round." He said to the dog as it dropped the soggy tennis ball at his feet and looked at him expectantly. He watched as the ball arced gracefully over the wet sand, bounced twice and then began to roll toward the waves. Never tiring of this simple pleasure, the dog charged down the beach after its toy. Ken was surprised to see it skid to a halt ten yards short of the ball and lift its nose to sniff the air. As he began to walk toward it he saw the hackles on the back of its neck rise. The forgotten ball began to bob at the water's edge.

"Come on lad, grab the ball before you lose it!" He called.
Ignoring him the dog began sniffing along the sand toward a clump of low vegetation above the high water mark. As he approached, the animal took several paces back and began to howl in a way that sent a shiver through Ken's body. He shuffled over to the dog who was so agitated he didn't even acknowledge the presence of his master. At first he couldn't make out what was upsetting the dog to such an extent and then he couldn't make sense of what he was seeing. Something sticking out of the sand. Something gold there too. A wedding ring. On a finger. A woman's hand. Ken fell to his knees, grabbing Bobby by the collar to hold him back. In an instant he was transported back seventy years to a time when he was a frightened teenager on another beach in a foreign country.

* * *

The mood in the little flat flips between sorrow and excitement. Joyce's death has rocked everyone including Mathias. There is absolutely no doubt in any of their minds now. They heard Sarah's vision with their own ears. Its fulfilment so soon has them gasping at the enormity of what they've become a part of.

"But I don't get it." Said Robert, shaking his head as if to clear his vision. "You say she doesn't want to see us again? After what she's shown us? Hell, who she's shown herself to be?"

Mathias raised his hands and the small group fell silent.

"Look. We know from the writings that when The Redeemer arrives she might not realise who she is..." He said

"Yes but..." interrupted Robert.

"Let me finish. Sarah has been through the wringer in the last couple of days. The vision itself obviously took a lot out of her. Who knows, she may even have had more visions and become frightened and confused. God only knows how she'll react when she finds out that her first vision has already been fulfilled. Rachael also said that The Redeemer might even try to fight her calling at first, push away the responsibility. Sarah is doing exactly that and proving by doing so how accurate Rachael's prophecy was! It's amazing!"

Robert jumped to his feet, his large frame causing the glasses on the coffee table to rattle as he towered over them. "But we have to make her see." He said.

"Sit down, Robert." Mathias said, waving his arm. "What we have to do is to give her some time."

Maggie blew her nose and dabbed at the tears in her eyes. "But Mathias, why Joyce? She wouldn't hurt a fly."

"Of course she wouldn't and I know that it's not easy to see the whole picture yet but look at it this way. Obviously what's happened has been given as a sign for the people in our group. Nobody else is aware of the vision; nobody else in the entire world knows that Sarah is The Redeemer. Not the Pope, not the Archbishop, nobody. Except us. What an incredible thing that is. What an awesome responsibility we have been given. We can't begin by questioning the rightness or wrongness of what we've witnessed."

"I guess you're right, I'm sorry. I'm being weak." Replied Maggie.

Mathias reached over and gave Maggie's knee a reassuring squeeze. As he sat back the smile dissolved from his face, like a cloud passing in front of the sun.

"There's something else. Something you all need to remember."

The silence in the room was absolute as they waited for Mathias to continue.

"Do you remember what Rachael said about the dark powers and what they might attempt to do when The Redeemer arrived?" He scanned their faces for an answer.

"She said they would try to silence The Redeemer." Rita whispered.

"That's right. And when would she be most vulnerable to that attack?" Mathias asked.

"Before she realised who she was." Maggie answered, nodding her head.

Robert shook his head again. "My God, we have to do something."

"We do Robert." Mathias said, his voice soothing. "But we have to be careful. This phase is very delicate. The Redeemer needs our protection and guidance but doesn't know it. In fact I think I see the dark forces already moving to intercept her."

"What?" Maggie cried. "Where?"

"From my last conversation with Sarah I know her good friend Maria is already trying to turn her against us. This woman probably means well but she doesn't realise that she's being used as a pawn in the great struggle."

"She has to be stopped." Robert said. "We can't let this happen."

"I agree with you, but how? That's the question."

"Well we can't bugger around with this, Mathias, we need to act!"

"Calm down Robert. Let's think about it. Rita, do you still have an arrangement to meet Sarah for lunch next week?"

"Well she hasn't cancelled it." Rita replied.

Robert looked as though he might explode. "Next week might be too late!" He cried.

Once again Mathias raised his hands for silence. The group dropped their eyes to the floor.

"We need action but it must be considered action. The direct approach may be too confronting at this time. Rachael said that a protector would be raised up at the right time. It's obvious to me that we have been selected to occupy that role. I don't think we would be permitted to stray too far from our responsibility."

Robert nods his head, not trusting his voice to speak. Outwardly he appears to be in agreement but the muscles in his shoulders are bunched and a vein pulses in his neck as he struggles to keep himself under control. He and Mathias go back a long way, even signing up for the army on the same day, but he can't shake the feeling that something's not right with Mathias's cautious approach.

* * *

Sarah was in two minds. She sat in her bedroom staring at the cordless phone that she'd just replaced in its little cradle. On the handset, the red light was winking, indicating that its batteries were being charged. It crossed Sarah's mind that maybe the red light was a warning for her. Put on the spot, she'd agreed to keep her lunch date with Rita and now she didn't know if she'd done the right thing. She *had* made a promise to Maria but it wasn't as though she was going out with Mathias and Rita seemed to be so normal when they had chatted at the party.

She rationalised it away by telling herself she would say nothing to Maria and when she had lunch with Rita she'd only talk about stuff other than religion and prophecies. Secretly she was also curious to find out how Mathias had taken her decision that they shouldn't see each other again. She was a little surprised that he hadn't called her since their last conversation and she found herself missing him and the way, for a while, she'd felt really special. An expression popped into her head 'All the good men are either married or gay.' Yes, and you can add 'or are religious nutters' to that list she thought.

Her eyes began to fill with tears and she shook her head in annoyance. Snatching up the phone she decided to call Maria and suggest they get pissed together to commemorate the demise of yet another potential relationship.

* * *

The three settle down in their usual place near the window. After toasting their health, David takes a long pull from his glass and sets it down on the small table.

"My God, what a week." He said. "I don't know if I'll ever get used to delivering shitty news. I just feel so bad for Peter Boulton. The man's aged twenty years in the last week or so."

"It's awful," Natalie said, "But in a way it's better for him now that he knows. At least he can begin to work through the grief and start putting his life back together. It can be much worse for people who never find out what happened to their loved one. Sometimes they get stuck in limbo for decades and don't seem to be able to move on. Still, I guess it's easy for me to say, it wasn't my spouse who turned up buried under the sand on a remote beach."

"The torment of suspense is very great; and as soon as the wavering, perplexed mind begins to determine, be the determination which way soever, it will find itself at ease."

"That's lovely, Walter." Natalie said.

"Robert South. Another great English divine. Educated at Christ Church in Oxford, he was said to be the favourite preacher of Charles the second. A man of great wit also."

"How do you know all this stuff, Walter?" David asks, shaking his head.

Walter pulls himself upright in the chair. "Ah, the superiority of a British education."

David makes a face and rolls his eyes at Natalie who flashes him a conspiratorial smile.

"And speaking of superiority," Walter continues, turning to Natalie, "I thought you acquitted yourself rather well at the briefing today, my dear."

"Yes, you were pretty insistent that Janice wasn't killed by our man." Added David.

"Well, really, what can I say? Janice was bashed, sedated with and probably even killed by a massive dose of chloroform, sexually assaulted and buried inexpertly on the beach! My guess is the miserable cretin thought he could jump on the bandwagon and the local plods would blame the serial killer. Stupid sod."

David nodded his agreement. "I think you're right about the stupid part. I spoke with Greg just before and one of his fellas found a shovel with a set of initials carved into the handle about twenty feet into the water at low tide. He reckons they'll have the bastard by tonight. We should have it so easy."

"The irony is that the dullard may not even have intended to kill her in the first place." Walter said with a sigh of resignation. "The current thinking seems to be that the chloroform was meant to somehow anaesthetise her so he could perform the rape and then make his escape leaving her to come round at some later point. He wouldn't be the first felon to conceive of the scenario."

"And so what went wrong?" Asked Natalie.

"Well, this chloroform substance isn't to be trifled with. Apparently it doesn't work the way it does at the cinema unless it's in the hands of an expert, which our killer obviously was not. Too much of the chemical or exposure for too long and one's heart and lungs stop working. Inevitably, death follows. We may find out in due course but it wouldn't be at all surprising if Janice's death comes down to that all-too-common but lethal mix of rage and ignorance."

"Tragic." Said Natalie, shaking her head. "To change the subject, has there been any progress in figuring out what those marks mean? The ones scratched into the thigh of the latest victim?"

"Nothing yet." Replied David. "We thought at first it might be a map but if it is we can't figure out what it refers to. A few people seem to think it's a drawing of a building or a sign on a building but it doesn't look like one to me. Wallace has had people driving past every old building they can think of looking for something that the marks resemble. My own guess is it's some sort of distinguishing mark or scar on the killer that might not make sense unless we suspected him and saw it for ourselves."

As David is speaking, Walter draws on his beer mat the basic shape that is burned into the memory of everyone involved with the case. They stare at it again without any new inspiration.

"Another round?" The barman collecting their empties snaps them out of their private world.

"God, you made me jump! I didn't hear you come up." Natalie said, laughing.

On a whim, David scoops up Walter's sketch and hands it to the barman.

"You see anything that looks like that 'round here?" He asks.

The barman waggles his head from side to side. "Looks a bit like a tree."

He's in the process of handing it back to David when he stopped.

"Ah but, come to think about it, you know what it does look like?" He asked.

"Give us your best guess, old man." Walter said.

"It's not a tree that's in my head, mind."

"Just call it as you see it, you can't do any worse than us." David prompted.

"Well it looks like the insignia of the British SAS. You know, the flying dagger."

For a second nobody spoke and then they jumped to their feet.

"Was that the right answer?" The barman asked, a surprised look on his face.

Natalie put a hand on his shoulder and gave him a noisy kiss on the cheek. "It might just be the best answer you've ever given." She said as they headed for the door.

CHAPTER 9

Burt Harrison, still dressed in his filthy boilersuit, sat on the metal seat, his shoulders slumped. A thin trail of smoke rose from the cigarette hanging off his bottom lip, a dozen crumpled butts lay in the aluminium-foil pie dish on the steel bench before him. The welt on the side of his head from the "accidental" elbow he'd received when the coppers kicked in his door throbbed like a bugger and added to the hangover he was nursing from the night before.

What a shitful way for a man to end up, he thought. Harrison knew he was in serious trouble. As soon as that stupid shopkeeper had stopped breathing on him he knew it. Not that this was his first brush with trouble, that miserable cow that he'd been married to had made sure the law knew where he lived. What sort of a world is it when a man can't even give his own wife a clip 'round the ear when she deserves it? What goes on in a man's house is nobody else's business. He gave the table leg a vicious kick, scattering the cigarette butts across the floor.

Harrison looked up as he heard the door to the interview room open. Squinting against the spiralling cigarette smoke he watched the two men cross the room and pull up chairs opposite. The uniformed policeman that unlocked the door took up his position in the corner of the room behind Harrison.

"More bloody Polis." He growled, picking a strand of tobacco from his tongue and flicking it into the centre of the table where it lodged, poking up like a tiny stick. "I've already told them other wankers all you need to know."

"Excellent." Replied David. "Then you can tell us as well."

"Fuck off."

David looks at his watch and turns to face Walter. "Actually look at the time, it's nearly midnight. This fella obviously doesn't want to talk to us so we may as well head off. What say we come back after breakfast in the morning, say nine o'clock? See if he feels any different then?"

"That's a capital idea old chum." Replies Walter. "I myself would be delighted to repair to my bed."

"Come on, Sergeant, lock the door behind us and we'll see you back here in the morning." David said as they rose to leave.

"Hang on a minute! You can't leave me in here all night! I haven't even had me bloody dinner."

"Well we're not going to hang around listening to your whinging. Do you want to talk or not? Come on dickhead it's getting late and I'm out of patience." David snapped.

"Can I have somethin' to eat?"

That's more like it, you miserable shit, David thinks as he pulls his chair out and sits down again.

"I could probably get someone to fetch some fish and chips I suppose."

"Aye, that'd be grand." Said Harrison, giving them a smile that showed off his few remaining teeth.

David takes his time as he flicks through the interview notes. Harrison uses the dying ember on the end of his cigarette to light another.

"Okay. You've admitted to the killing of Janice Boulton but you claim it was accidental."

"That's right."

"So you really just wanted to rape this women, is that all?" David asked, not attempting to hide his contempt.

"Aye. Nothin' she hadn't 'ad before."

David closes his eyes momentarily as he fights the urge to splatter Harrison's nose all over his face.

"Why did you choose this particular woman?" He asks.

Harrison shrugged. "No reason. I seen her walking home that way before. Who gives a toss."

"You wouldn't tell the other detectives why you chose her. I'd like to know."

"It's my business."

"Private business."

"Aye."

David tosses his notes on the table and pushes his chair back on two legs. "Oh I see. You were having trouble at home, is that it? Couldn't get it up for the missus so you went looking for a bit of excitement. Some poor little woman you could bully. You chose her because she was tiny. The wife kicks you out of bed I suppose so you go creeping around like some miserable little pervert..."

Harrison smashes his fist onto the table and is halfway out of the chair before the uniformed officer clamps a meaty paw on his shoulder and pushes him back down.

"What do you fuckin' know!" He yells, spittle flying from his lips. "There were nothing wrong wi' my missus until she got mixed up wi' them fundamentalists! Nothin' that a good clout wouldn't set straight. Fillin' her head wi' daft stuff about women's power and fuckin' independence bollocks. And now she's run off and left me to cook me own bloody dinners. Made me look like a right fool. Fuckin' women, they're all the bloody same. Every one of 'em."

Harrison slumps back in his chair, folding his arms across his chest like a petulant child.

"Well, now we're getting somewhere." David said.

"So, your wife finds religion and you get stuck with the housework. You then decide a little vengeance on the fairer sex is the order of the day. Doesn't matter which woman you choose because, as you say, they're all the same. Right?"

"Aye. Close enough. And any road, that shopkeeper should have been at 'ome lookin' after the 'ouse instead of takin' a man's job."

"My God! A working woman! She was obviously asking for it then."

"Fuck off."

"But you overdid the chloroform and she didn't wake up. And now it's murder."

"It weren't murder, it were an accident." Harrison shot back.

"When someone dies in the course of a deliberate and premeditated act of violence committed against them, it's murder. Whether you set out to kill her or not makes no difference. She's still dead and two little kids have no mother."

"Aye, it's a fuckin' tough world."

"If it was an accident why didn't you at least call an ambulance? You could have buggered off and left them to it."

"Like I told them others. Me 'ead wasn't straight. I'd been drinkin' most of the day as it was."

"So give me a name. What's this religion she's mixed up in?" David asked.

"I don't bloody know." Harrison growls. "She kept gabbin' on about some fella called Mathias. Should've killed the bastard. He's probably bangin' her silly right now. Good riddance I say. He's the one you should be lockin' up, not me. He caused all this, puttin' his stupid bloody notions in 'er head."

"Oh I don't know." David replied. "We'll have to talk to her but it sounds to me like Mrs Harrison's the only winner in this miserable situation. She's got you off her back for good to start with."

"Fuck off."

David signalled to Walter and they stood up to leave. "Take this delightful fellow back to his cell Sergeant, if you would be so kind." Walter said.

"Ere! What about me bloody chips then?"

With an expression of raw fury on his face, David steps toward

Harrison who pulls back in alarm. In an almost inaudible whisper he says, "If I thought I could get away with it I would gladly smash your miserable face to a pulp against that fucking brick wall and all you'd get is a trip to the morgue, you pathetic shit. I suggest you go back to your cell and quietly hang yourself tonight. Save everyone's time and money putting you away."

David turns on his heel and walks out leaving Harrison with his mouth agape.

* * *

Sarah, mobile phone in hand, paces up and down outside the cafe where she's arranged to meet Rita. Come on Maria, where the hell are you? She thinks back but can't remember a time when her old friend has been out of contact like this. It's not like she's gone away, Maria hates holidays for God's sake. Neither her home phone or mobile has been answered since yesterday morning and Sarah is becoming worried. Already she's been to Maria's flat and banged on the door without success. She even called Maria's mother in Glasgow and only managed to upset the poor woman as well with her concern.

There's been times, it's true, when Maria has gone on benders of such epic duration that she didn't resurface for a day or so but on most of those occasions, Sarah was by her side anyway. It would be very out of character for her to simply up and leave without telling Sarah she was going. Particularly with all the stuff that's happening right now. Sarah looks at her watch and snaps the mobile shut in frustration. Have to deal with this later, she thinks as she stuffs the phone into her coat pocket.

Her worry about Maria is bringing on a migraine and she contemplates taking some tablets. She decides against it, empty stomach, probably a bad idea. Picking her way through the lunchtime crowd she catches sight of Rita sitting alone at a table for two by the wall. Their eyes meet and after a small wave of acknowledgement Sarah makes her way toward her new friend.

* * *

"What's this?" David asked, looking up from his desk.

"It's only the list of all British Special Forces personnel discharged for medical reasons during the last twenty years." Replied Walter, wearing a cat-that-got-the-cream expression.

"You managed to get it!"

"Yes, and not without difficulty I might add. These Special Forces Wallahs do value their anonymity."

"I know, how did you pull it off?"

"I became tired of beating my head against a brick wall and so decided to get Wallace involved. Our identifying the marks as potentially the flying dagger of the SAS tipped the scales. Wallace threatened to call the minister, and low and behold here it is."

"Jesus, there's quite a few names here." David said, flicking through the computer printout. "I hope they have a good recruitment program to replace all these poor sods."

"I'm reminded of a German proverb the provenance of which I don't recall." Walter said. "A great war leaves the country with three armies - an army of cripples, an army of mourners, and an army of thieves. I guess this represents a section of the army of cripples."

"My God, in more ways than one obviously."

"Quite. Methinks the life of a professional killing machine must be a difficult one."

"Any ideas about how we whittle this list down?" Asked David.

"Well I guess we could begin by striking off those men who got their leave ticket by being physically injured in some way as opposed to suffering mental damage. Stepping on a mine or whatever."

David took a deep breath and bulldozed the rest of the paperwork on his desk into a drawer. Roping in a couple of Detective Constables that had been assigned to the case, he quickly briefed them on the objective.

"Let's get to it then."

* * *

The memorial service for Janice Boulton was held in St Mary's Church by the Sea. The Church is more than six hundred years old and, although he considers himself to be practically an atheist, David couldn't help but be affected by the antiquity and beauty of the building. Ironically, the day of the funeral dawned bright and while the winter sun held no warmth it was a welcome relief from the leaden skies.

Along the side of the church facing the ocean, stained glass windows depict scenes from the Bible. The flood of Noah's day, Daniel in the den of lions, Jonah inside the belly of the whale, Sodom and Gomorrah, the plagues of Egypt, the loaves and the fishes, Jesus on the cross, the judgement day. All in full colour and vivid detail. David found himself fascinated by the power of the images and, not for the first time, wished he knew more about these stories that held such theatre and spectacle.

He isn't quite sure what he's doing here and had rationalised it as an opportunity to see a building and a location that he hadn't been to before. Part of it he knew was that he felt in some way indebted to the family. Despite being charged with the welfare of these people the system had failed them and this obscene tragedy had occurred. He knew it wasn't quite rational but sometimes these things just got to you. Anyway, if nothing else it made him feel better to show his respect.

His daydreaming was interrupted by the congregation standing noisily on the bare wooden floor. He hadn't yet mastered the standing and kneeling business so he just kept an eye on everyone else. When the moderately large crowd filed out he scanned the faces for anyone that he might know. As Peter Boulton, flanked by his family, shuffled toward the door and the beginning of his new life David nodded and offered his condolences. In a daze Peter shook his hand and thanked him for coming. David was sure that there wasn't even the vaguest flicker of recognition in Peter's bloodshot eyes.

One of the last people to clear the church was a woman. She had obviously been waiting for the crowd to disperse and she wore a heavy black veil that almost completely hid her identity. Working on a hunch, David timed his exit so the two passed through the door together.

"Lovely service." He offered.

"Yes. So sad." She replied, not looking up.

"You knew her well?" David asked, trying to keep his tone conversational. He though he detected a stiffening in her neck and shoulders.

"Not terribly well, no."

"Mrs Harrison?" He asked.

She stopped mid-stride. Standing this close David could see the fear in her eyes through the veil.

"Who are you?" She asked in a small voice.

"I'm a policeman. I've spoken with your husband."

As her hand flew to her mouth David hurriedly continued.

"Don't worry, you've done nothing wrong. I'm not surprised that you came. I think it was very brave of you. Would like to come and sit down with me for a moment?"

Without waiting for a response David led her toward a park bench under a massive oak tree. He waited for her sobs to subside and she was the first one to speak.

"I was so scared coming to the church. I'm sure the family wouldn't have wanted me here but I'm just trying to make sense of it all. She sounded like a lovely lady and when I saw those little children with their..." She couldn't continue. David waited until she got herself under control again.

"I know that my husband is not a good man. I used to think it was just me, that I wasn't a good enough wife. But I know it wasn't true. In the end I just couldn't take it anymore. Do you think it was my fault? Did I push him over the edge by leaving? Tell me honestly please."

"I *know* it wasn't your fault." David said. "I've been a policeman all my working life and I've seen men like your husband before. He has a grudge against the world and it could just as easily been you in that coffin today. What happened is absolutely no fault of yours."

She lifted the veil and threw it back over her head. David was startled to see how attractive she was, despite her eyes puffy from crying. After spending time with the husband he had expected her to be a dowdy little oppressed housewife.

"You're very kind to say that. Thank you." She said.

"Your husband tells me that you've found something special in your life. A faith that's obviously affected you greatly."

"Yes, that's right." She said, her face brightening. "I feel like a different woman now."

"Would you like to tell me about it?" David asked.

CHAPTER 10

"It's so lovely to see you again, Sarah!" Rita came around the table and gave Sarah a hug and an affectionate kiss on the cheek. "Sit down, you're looking really well." She said.

Sarah wasn't sure if the woman was being genuine or over compensating for the incident that she'd witnessed when they were together in Maggie's flat. Probably a bit of both she guessed. Sarah decided to give her the benefit of the doubt.

"Thank you, it's good to see you too." Sarah said, looking around. "I don't think I've been in here before."

"It's new, they've only just finished renovating it but everyone says that it's a great place so here's hoping."

"How bad can it be? As long as I can get a nice glass of red I'll be happy." Said Sarah, her eyes scanning the specials board. "That and a huge chunk of the lasagne ought to do me. God I'm starving!"

"You don't waste any time choosing do you!" Rita replied with a smile.

"No point dicking around. I'm a cut to the chase sort of girl, at least where food is concerned." Said Sarah.

The pair passed the next half an hour or so companionably, Sarah talking about her job and relating a couple of amusing anecdotes at her own expense about living at home beyond age thirty. Rita laughed at Sarah's self-deprecating style and told a few stories of her own.

Sarah was amazed to hear that Rita, despite being no older than herself, had been married twice already and had only recently split from her second husband who she said tried to suppress her as a woman. After the coffees had been served, Rita toyed with the thin sugar packets on her saucer.

"Sarah, can I ask you a personal question?" Rita said.

Here we go, thought Sarah, her back stiffening a little.

"Sure, as long as you don't get offended if I decide not to answer." She said, trying to keep her voice light as she delivered the line she'd rehearsed previously when thinking about what to do if the conversation became difficult.

"Of course not, I don't want to put you on the spot. It's just that something very unique happened that time at Maggie's place and I've wondered how much thought you've given to what it means."

Sarah sighed. "Well, the thing is, Rita, I'm not sure it means anything really. I don't want to go into it but I've had a bit of a history with funny turns. Not so much any more but when I was younger particularly. I've been a bit slack lately, you know, drinking a bit much, careless with my tablets, that sort of stuff. I just put what happened down to a bad combination of medication, alcohol and whatever was in the wacky-backy."

"Mathias doesn't think that's what it was." Rita replied in a small voice.

"I know he doesn't and I guess we won't agree on that but at the end of the day it doesn't really matter."

Rita sat back in her chair as though she'd been punched in the chest. "Doesn't matter! How can you say that, Sarah! It matters more than anything!"

This was what Sarah had been afraid of. She'd almost decided that perhaps she could be friends with Rita despite her connection with Mathias but now that seemed impossible. Suddenly the whole thing was just too much like hard work.

"Look, Rita, I like you. I've enjoyed your company today as I did last time we met. But this stuff is just too weird for me. I respect that you might sincerely believe it and I'm happy for you if it's helped in your life. But, and here's my point, I *don't* believe it and it *doesn't* matter to me. End of story. I'm sorry to have to lay it out like that but there it is."

A tear coursed down Rita's cheek leaving a dark track.

"I just don't understand it, I really don't. Especially since Joyce..." Rita's voice trailed off as she remembered that Sarah probably didn't know about Joyce's accident. Instinctively she covered her mouth with her hand, a look of panic on her face, terrified of what she'd said.

Sarah cocked her head to one side. "What about Joyce?" She asked, irritation creeping into her voice.

"Nothing. I shouldn't have said..." Tears were now flowing freely down Rita's cheeks.

"Come on Rita." Sarah snapped, becoming aware that the headache behind her eyes was building. "Finish what you've started."

"Joyce is dead!" Rita wailed, causing several other groups nearby to look up. "Killed by a car, just like you said! What you saw!"

Sarah sat back in her seat, her mouth opening and closing soundlessly. Nausea swept over her and for a second she thought she would vomit. She tried to speak but couldn't form words. Her head began to pound and her vision seemed to compress to a tiny square that was completely filled by Rita's mascara-streaked face. She was struck by the blinding light she'd experienced in Maggie's flat and as her head began to fill with grotesque images she pushed back violently against the table scattering cups, plates and cutlery onto the floor.

As Sarah's chair tipped back and she tumbled to the floor she let out a scream that froze every person in the restaurant. Her eyes rolled back in her head and her limbs were twitching. People nearby looked on, uncertain what to do. In a voice that chilled the hearts of the diners close enough to hear she whispered "Oh no, Rita, so much blood."

A second later, in a dead faint, Rita joined her on the cold tiled floor of the restaurant.

* * *

Under the timeless stare of stone gargoyles the man unloads his burden onto the top of an ancient sarcophagus, which is unceremoniously doubling as a temporary bench. The exertion has cost him and he sits heavily while catching his breath. The weather outside is cold and the wind biting but despite this his shirt sticks to his back, slick with sweat.

The portable generator with the bright red fuel tank that he brought on his first trip from the car sits on the stone floor looking oddly time-displaced in the archaic chamber. One more trip to get the balance of the fuel for the generator and then I'm done, he tells himself. It's taken most of the morning to transport the food and equipment but as he looks around at the boxes stacked neatly he's pleased. Mentally he ticks off his provisions; Food, water, toiletry needs, rope, cables, portable lights, medical kit. Could last a month with this lot. A month, maybe more. Easy. He doesn't think he'll need that long but he knows the value of being prepared.

He has a new spring in his step because he knows the mission is almost over. This is the real thing. After wiping his damp hands on his jacket he stands and turns his attention to the generator encased in its tubular steel cradle. A smile plays at his lips as he catches sight of the yellow warning sticker and its cautionary two-man transport instructions. Bending his knees he lifts the seventy-five kilogram generator chest high before heading down the vaulted passage and into the darkness.

* * *

David tosses his pencil onto the desktop and places both hands behind his head before straightening out his cramped spine. He and Walter have been slogging through the short list compiled by the two constables and spending hours on the telephone without turning up anything of interest.

"I can't believe how little use this whole exercise has been." He says in frustration. "They're either overseas, still in hospital, dead and buried, or getting on with life."

"As you say, a relatively tiny pool of geographical possibilities, all of whom appear to be furnished with unassailable alibis. Most inconvenient of them really." Replied Walter.

"Perhaps we're barking up the wrong tree with this idea of a medical discharge. Perhaps there's some other thing, you know, some crisis or life changing event that's caused his switch to flip."

Walter nodded. "Perhaps you're right. I still wouldn't discount the possibility of some sort of nascent mental illness though. Maybe not severe enough for him to be drummed out of the service but perhaps enough to predispose him to his new vocation."

"Maybe he found God? He wouldn't be the first to decide that he had to go on a religion-fuelled killing spree." David said, shaking his head.

"Methinks you have religion on the brain since your conversation with the Harrison woman. You've raised the topic several times since."

"Well it's sort of fascinating. You have what appears for all intents and purposes to be a normal rational woman. Attractive, by all accounts intelligent, and yet she's able to hold the most bizarre set of beliefs in her head. What's really weird is that those beliefs act as a sort of filter to the world. Everything she takes in is filtered through this new religious knowledge as a way of testing its veracity. If it doesn't agree it's discounted. You know, work of the devil, stupid earth-bound knowledge or whatever. But if it supports the religious hypothesis she holds, even obliquely, then it's seen as some sort of sign. It's almost like she has a virus in her mind."

"That idea is guaranteed to win friends an influence people. Religion is the virus of the masses, as it were." Walter replied.

"Remember that woman who was run down the other day in the High Street?" David said.

"The substance abuser that simply walked into the road?"

"That's the one. Anyway it turns out according to the Harrison woman that this woman belonged to the same religious group as she did. And apparently some modern day prophetess had a vision or something that she would be bowled over by a car."

"Who, the Harrison woman?" Asked Walter, struggling to follow the thread.

"No, the stoner who was actually run down."

"Ah, I see. The prophet spoke..."

"Prophetess." Interrupted David.

"Quite so. The prophetess spoke and the poor addled woman was compelled to meet her destiny."

"Yes. I told her the dead woman had a cocktail of drugs in her system so strong that it was amazing she could even walk, but that part of the story was suppressed by the filter in her mind."

"Your religious mind-virus at work."

"Absolutely."

"But don't we all carry a similar thing in our heads? As a result of our upbringing and our experiences in life? Some sort of a metaphor for how the world works which, at least to an extent, is peculiar to us?" Walter asked, adopting the devil's-advocate position.

"Yes, that's true." David countered. "But the thing is, most of the people who really believe this stuff accepted it as adults not as kids. They become infected, as it were, by some well-meaning but contagious person. They willingly embrace it as thinking adults even though the consequences can be disastrous for them. Joyce Matthews for example."

Walter nodded.

"There are stories about the Australian aborigines and other very old cultures where some medicine man puts a curse on a person and the person so fundamentally believes that he's going to croak that he simply lays down and dies! The virus in his mind is so strong that he just gives in. He no longer *believes* that he can go on living."

"Interesting." Walter said.

"Come on, Walter, you've got to admit that my mind-virus idea's got legs."

"Legs indeed." Replied Walter. "I believe that the Templeton prize is worth a million pounds this year. Perhaps you should enter. I'm sure your theory qualifies."

"You may laugh, Walter. Let's see you come up with a better theory."

"My theory of the fundamental gullibility of people has served me well so far."

David's mind is obviously far away and Walter taps his pen on the side of his cup.

"Earth to David, come in David, I think we've lost you." He said with a smile.

"Sorry Walter, I just had a thought. You know I'm not a big fan of coincidences. It just crossed my mind that we have two dead women..."

"Two?" Interrupted Walter.

"Yes, I mean Janice Boulton and the stoner that stepped in front of the car. Two dead women with one thing in common. A set of crazy religious ideas."

"You sure that you're not stretching a long bow here old chap? There's no suggestion that the "stoner" as you so uncharitably call her was pushed in front of the oncoming motor and Janice Boulton was at least one step away from this group with nothing to connect her to Burt Harrison except time and unforeseen circumstance."

"I'd agree if we were talking about the Church of England or the Roman Catholic Church but this group is tiny. Mrs Harrison said there were only a few pockets of them around the world and they keep in touch via email. I think we have the only group in England right here in our backyard." David said. "Less than a dozen of the mad buggers."

Walter adopted his gravest countenance. "One could say, old bean, that we have a surfeit of work presently with our current endeavours. I'm not sure what is served by our getting involved in this. The murder of Janice Boulton is closed bar the paperwork, and the Matthews woman was a walking pharmacy whose self-motivated and terminal perambulation was witnessed by a policewoman, for goodness sake. I must say, we have bigger fish to fry, as the aphorist would have it."

"I guess you're right. I might still have a chat with the leader of this little mob when I'm out that way next. Just to satisfy my curiosity."

"As you wish my friend. But, do you know what Henry Wayland would say?"

"No but I have this feeling you're going to tell me." David said.

"Curiosity is looking over other people's affairs, and overlooking our own."

"All I can say is your mate Wayland obviously wasn't a copper."

* * *

For a few seconds the lunchtime crowd in the restaurant appears to be paralysed. Sarah's scream had echoed from the four walls and accompanied by the sound of crockery smashing and chairs tipping it wasn't clear to everyone what was actually happening. Someone yelled out to call an ambulance and the spell was broken. A man in a business suit began to take charge and tables were moved out of the way to provide some room. Sarah appeared to be having some sort of fit and so she immediately became the focus of attention. The businessman rolled Sarah onto her side and ensured that nothing was in range of her flailing arms and legs. As best he could he tried to hold her so that she wouldn't compound her injuries.

A waitress appeared with a broom and mop and began herding the crockery fragments into a dustpan. Two women in jeans attended to Rita who was breathing but had a nasty bump on the side of her face. A hand appeared from the crowd and one of the women took a moistened napkin and began dabbing at Rita's face. Some people started to back away as they realised that they couldn't offer any assistance and were just looking on like guilty voyeurs.

As Sarah's seizure began to ease, the sound of an ambulance

approaching could be heard. A couple of men ran out onto the street to give directions and a woman who had been sitting at a nearby table ensured that any personal items were gathered up. There was a collective sigh of relief when the paramedics with their equipment cases entered the restaurant and knelt by the injured women. The mood in the restaurant lightened immediately the professionals arrived as the weight of responsibility was handed over and the feelings of helplessness began to subside.

As if the drama hadn't been sufficient for one day, as Rita was being lifted onto the stretcher to join Sarah in the ambulance she began to gain consciousness and almost immediately became hysterical. Screaming at the top of her lungs, it took both of the paramedics as well as one of the restaurant's staff to restrain her. As the ambulance roared down the street the diners were left to wonder and hypothesise about the strange behaviour they had witnessed. Those individuals who had played an active part in the crisis stood in a small group and replayed the events that had thrown them together. Whichever way they looked at it, there were more questions than answers.

* * *

Peter Boulton slumped in his chair, a half empty bottle of scotch on the table. Never in his entire life had he felt so desperately miserable. Since Janice's funeral he just hadn't been able to pull himself together. He knew he had to. Had to find away out of the blackness and back into his life again. He knew that Janice wasn't coming back, that miserable sick bastard had made sure of it. The problem was he wasn't sure if he wanted to go on without her. He still couldn't imagine what sort of life it would be. When he tried to think about it, it didn't seem to *be* a life, it felt more like torture. Everywhere he looked he saw reminders of Janice. Any moment he expected her to come bustling into the house like she always did, never failing to give him a hug before doing anything else. But of course she wasn't going to bustle into the house. There would never again be a hug waiting for him.

He had seen the children only once when his sister brought them over and it had been a disaster. After telling himself that he had to be strong for their sake he just broke down and became inconsolable. The children were distraught and his sister had to take them away again. As soon as she left he drank himself into unconsciousness.

The problem was he didn't know *how* to live anymore. He knew how to live his old life. He knew how to make Janice happy, he knew how to be a parent with Janice, knew how to cook a meal for the four of them. But he didn't know how to do it on his own. It was as though he'd been transported to a foreign world where everything worked differently, where even the basics had to be relearned, and he wasn't sure that he could do it. Or worse, that he even wanted to.

And on top of all this he couldn't stop thinking about the man that had wrecked everything for them. Harrison's picture from the newspaper floated in his mind, never far from his thoughts. It made Peter almost insane with rage to imagine this man sitting only a few miles away. Being fed and looked after while Peter himself couldn't even eat because of grief. He knew the police were still talking to him as they worked through a complex murder case. The man had been charged with Janice's death but the paper said he was helping them with other inquiries. Sick bastard's probably killed other women. It seemed worse somehow to imagine that Janice was just another victim. It didn't make any sense but in his depressed state it served to further diminish her specialness.

His life was over. He wasn't dead yet but that was just a function of time. He didn't believe that he had what it takes to pull himself out of this one. He was no use to his kids, Jesus, they were better off without him. He didn't even recognise the man that he once was. He walked over to the small cupboard in the hall, the one that contained the shotgun his father had given him many years before when he sold the farm and they all moved up here to the coast. Janice hated him keeping it in the house but he couldn't bring himself to get rid of it.

He even had a box of cartridges hidden on a high shelf in the cupboard. Not that he'd fired it since he was a boy, but what good's a gun with no ammunition? Fumbling with his key in the tiny lock he pulled the door open and took out the gun. He liked the smell of it and the feel of the finely engraved stock, liked the weight and unambiguous purposefulness of the weapon. Holding the gun in his hands always reminded him of his dad and he started to cry. His father wouldn't be proud of the way his son was thinking.

Peter Boulton wiped his eyes and put the gun back into the cupboard. For now.

CHAPTER 11

David hadn't been entirely truthful with Walter when he said he'd visit Mathias next time he was in the area. The more he thought about it the more he was troubled by the two women and the religious cult in the background. While he recognised that Walter was correct about the coincidence being weak, something kept nagging at the back of his mind. During the night when sleep was again elusive he made the decision to pay Mathias a visit the very next morning.

He suspected that Mrs Harrison had been in bed when he called to ask for the number but he also thought he detected a certain pleasure in her voice at speaking to him again so soon. He'd tracked Mathias down at the building were he worked and arranged to meet at a local cafe of Mathias's choosing. If he was disturbed by a policeman calling him at work, Mathias certainly hid it well, David thought as he strolled toward their meeting place.

As he approaches the cafe a tall well-built man turns from where he'd been leaning casually against the wall and smiled.

"You must be Inspector Orbost." He said.

David was astounded at the intensity of the man's eyes. "Yes, how did you know?" He said. Curious.

The big man held out his hand. "I'm Mathias. Just a lucky guess I suppose. Nice to meet you Inspector."

The two men selected a table near the window and David noticed that Mathias smoothly manoeuvred things so he could take a seat that ensured his back was against the wall providing clear sight lines within the restaurant. David felt a tiny pang of disquiet at this behaviour. As the waiter left with their order Mathias was the first to speak.

"So Inspector, are you going to tell me what this is all about?" Not concerned, not worried, mild curiosity is all that his tone conveyed. David decided to go for the direct approach.

"I've been speaking with Mrs Harrison. At the funeral of Janice Boulton actually."

"Really? She has been through hell and back that poor woman. As much as I grieve for the Boulton family, it's probably the best thing that's ever happened to Fi."

"Fi?" David asked.

"Oh sorry, Fiona. Fiona Harrison?"

"Yes of course. You were saying?"

"Just that Fiona's husband is an absolute bastard and if they lock him up for life we'll all be the better off for it I think." Mathias said.

"I agree. The funny thing is, I was also talking to my partner about another woman. Someone who was killed in a car accident recently. Just stepped out into the road."

David thought he saw a troubled expression pass across Mathias's face but it was fleeting and was almost instantly replaced by the relaxed smile.

"Joyce." Mathias said.

"That's right."

Their conversation was interrupted by the waiter who set down two pots of tea and cups. He placed the bill face down on the edge of the table and David slid it to his side indicating that he intended to pay.

"Thank you." Mathias said, not missing the gesture.

As David stirred his tea, Mathias pulled off his jacket and draped it over the back of the chair. Just for a second, David caught a glimpse of something that caused the breath to freeze in his throat.

His heart began to hammer in his chest and he took a moment to compose himself before speaking. He placed the spoon in his saucer with just the slightest rattle betraying the elevated level of adrenalin coursing through his veins.

"I noticed a mark on the inside of your wrist. Would you mind showing it to me?"

Mathias gave him a strange look but pulled up his sleeve and offered his arm for David's inspection. "This?" He asked.

There was no question in David's mind. No doubt whatsoever. He realised that he'd stopped breathing and forced himself to take a couple of slow breaths as he made a show of examining the marks. Almost identical in outline to the self inflicted wounds on the thigh of the last victim.

"Can I ask you what these scars are from?" David said, hoping his voice sounded normal, hoping his internal turmoil wasn't visible. Mathias casually rolled down his sleeve.

"We seem to be hopping all over the place here Inspector, I hope you'll explain what all this means in due course. Since you ask, it's a scar. I had a tattoo done years ago when I was younger. More recently I tried to have it removed. Obviously the fellow I chose to take it off was not as skilled as the man that originally applied it. The whole thing became infected and what you see is the ugly result."

One more thing. One more thing. David thought. "Can I ask what the original tattoo was of?"

"You mean what was it?" Mathias asked.

"Yes what was it."

Mathias sighed. "I was in the forces. It was our insignia. Quite a few of the lads did it afterwards."

"Special Forces." David added, his hands clenched under the table to stop them shaking.

"Yes. Special Forces. When I found my religious calling I decided that I didn't really want to advertise the Special Forces connection for the rest of my life. Obviously I failed to achieve that objective as you so astutely observed."

"What had you done that you weren't proud of?" David asked, his mind racing.

"Do you realise how tactless you're being Inspector? I hope this isn't your normal bedside manner. Anyway, You asked so here's my answer. Her Majesty's government isn't keen on people like me saying too much about which specific bit of dirty work we did for them but the long and the short of it is that during my military career I killed several men who had been deemed to be bad by our superiors. Isn't that what you expected me to say? Killed them with my hands, if you must know. Up close and personal. Felt their life ebb away. Looked into their eyes as they died, that sort of thing. Satisfied? It was my job, Inspector, what I was trained for. And you know what's one of the great things about being Special Forces?" Mathias's voice was heavy with irony.

"You don't even need a war to kill someone. So when you're back home and lying in your bed thinking about the women that now have no husbands thanks to you and the kids with no dads, you can't even comfort yourself with the old war-is-war bullshit."

Mathias dropped his eyes to the tablecloth and was silent for a few seconds as he gathered his thoughts. As their eyes met again, a memory flashed into David's mind from his childhood. As a small boy his father had taken him to the London Zoo. A male tiger stalked up to him with only the glass window of the enclosure separating them. David was terrified, unable to move. The tiger's head was level with his own and for a moment their eyes locked. In a part of his brain that civilisation had managed to dull but not to eradicate, David was completely certain that the creature would kill him in an instant if not for the thin veneer of glass that separated their worlds.

It would kill him without hatred or temper or remorse. Simply because a tiger has to eat and so something dies. As a detective he'd stared into the eyes of killers and experienced that same certainty. Only in those cases the veneer separating their worlds had been his badge or some other social context in which he had even less confidence than he'd had in the armoured glass of the zoo when he was a boy.

Mathias's tone was flat and businesslike. "Look Inspector, I no longer choose to advertise what I was and that's something for me to deal with in my own way but I don't care much for you dragging all this up with no good reason. I think you better come clean as to why you're here or you should leave. You capice?"

The tumblers were falling in David's mind. The mark, the Special Forces soldier, the religion, the reverential treatment of the female victims that Natalie spoke about. His mind was spinning. Rather than taking on extra work, as Walter had feared, it looked like the death of Janice and Joyce were *connected* to the serial killings in some way and this man was the link. He needed backup. Suddenly he felt isolated and vulnerable being here on his own. How could Mathias not suspect anything with all of his clumsy questioning? He was in no doubt that he couldn't physically prevent Mathias from leaving if he decided to. He was also pretty sure that Mathias could kill him quickly and silently if he felt it necessary. Shit. What to do.

David took a deep breath and flashed his best smile. "Yes, I capice. I'm sorry for interrogating you; sometimes I just get a little carried away. Anyway, I'm just going to duck out to the toilet and when I get back I'll explain everything. Okay?"

Mathias gave him that strange look again. David felt the hair on the nape of his neck bristle.

"Sure, you do that. I'll be interested to hear what you have to say when you return."

David stepped out the back and immediately grabbed his mobile phone. Armed Response Unit, low key approach, no sirens, front and back doors, make it fast. He waited as long as he dared and then casually walked back into the restaurant where Mathias waited patiently.

"Feel better now?" Mathias asked, a slight edge to his voice.

"Yes, I can't think under pressure." David replied with a weak attempt at humour, taking his seat. It suddenly occurred to him that he had no idea what to say next. How to keep Mathias from walking. "More tea for you?" He asked, instantly realising how lame it sounded.

Mathias leaned forward with his elbows on the table, a look of resignation on his face. "Listen Inspector. Why don't you stop fucking with me and get to the point. I have no idea what's on your mind but I'm guessing you've just called the cavalry and now you're trying to keep me here by making small talk until they arrive. Am I right?"

"Why would you..." David began.

Mathias's voice was ice cold, his electric blue eyes never wavering. "I asked you to stop fucking with me. If you had wanted me down at the station you just had to ask. You're making a serious mistake. You don't know it but I do because I *know* that I haven't broken any laws lately, not unless putting yourself in harm's way to serve your country has suddenly become a crime. However this unfolds, will you remember one thing for me?"

David simply nodded.

"When your special operations people, or whoever you've called arrive, I'll go quietly. No need for a fuss. But remember this. Whatever you think I've done, and I'm guessing it must be serious, if I really *was* guilty and wanted to escape you wouldn't be able to stop me. You obviously know my background so you must realise that it would be stupid of you to try and prevent me from leaving if I so desired. Do you believe that?"

"Yes I do." Answered David.

"Good, and yet here I am still sitting opposite you anyway. I'd like you to remember that later, when you realise what an arse you've made of yourself and think about what that tells you. And when this is over I'll expect an explanation and an apology from you personally. Now, why don't we wait outside in the street, no point in alarming the customers in here. Perhaps you could make a call to your squaddies as well. We don't want anyone getting hurt because some nervous copper is jumpy."

Mathias rose to leave and David followed.

"Aren't you forgetting something?" Mathias asked. David looked at him blankly. Never in his life had he felt so totally impotent.

"The bill, Inspector. I believe you offered to pay."

* * *

The ceiling is beige. And something about it is odd. As Maria's vision begins to clear she sees that the ceiling paint is lumpy, like a bowl of porridge. A sort of stippled effect. And the light fitting is different, it has little brass arms with three tiny glass shades. It's switched on, the light making her headache worse. It isn't her ceiling. She closes her eyes and tries to remember where she is. The feeling isn't entirely unfamiliar, Maria has woken up in strange houses after a big night before. But this feels different somehow, the headache for one thing, she doesn't get headaches from drinking. She tries to concentrate, to think above the pounding in her temples. She remembers a man, a big bloke, tall with shoulders like a weightlifter. He bought her a drink. That's all she can dredge up.

Maria opens her eyes and eases her head to the side. She is alarmed to see that she's lying on top of the bed wearing only her underwear. Oh God, she thinks, what the hell did I do? Slowly she pushes herself up onto one elbow. The room is pleasant enough, small but neat, prints on the walls, curtains closed. She sees a small refrigerator and with alarm realises she's in a hotel. She has absolutely no recollection of going to a hotel with a stranger. It isn't her style anyway, not that she got many offers.

She rubs at her eyes, frustrated and confused. The bed groans as she wrestles herself into a sitting position, the room slowly revolving, making her stomach lurch. She swings her legs over the side of the bed. Her throat is dry, feels like sandpaper. She struggles to her feet and shuffles over to the mini-bar. It's full of small cans of soft drink and half bottles of white wine and champagne.

Maria pops the top of a can of lemonade and takes a long drink. She steps carefully back to the bed, looking for her bag and the headache tablets she keeps there, not for herself but for Sarah. The bag isn't by the bed so she pads into the tiny bathroom, her fingers tracing the wall for balance. It looks unused, the band of paper still around the toilet seat, the end of the toilet roll folded into a neat point. Two little inconvenient gestures to remind you that you're paying good money to be here she thinks. She crosses to the wardrobe and opens it. Two white bathrobes hang inside and a midget sized ironing board leans against the back of the narrow cupboard, otherwise it's empty. Now she has looked everywhere. Not only is her bag missing but so are all of her clothes.

Maria sits back on the bed, her mind struggling to make sense of her predicament. No clothes, no bag therefore no money, car keys, house keys, credit cards.

"Fuck." She says.

Maria crosses to the hotel door and pulls it open far enough to peek outside. She is greeted by a long and empty hallway with doors identical to her own set out on each side. A table with a vase of flowers stands in a small alcove opposite her door. A mirror hangs on the wall above giving Maria a glimpse of her own worried face. On the floor outside the door is a copy of The Guardian newspaper. Obviously standard fare for British tourists. Maria carefully bends to pick it up, closes the door and takes the paper back to the bed where she sits again. Her eye is drawn to the date and she's alarmed to see that a whole day has passed. A day of which she has no recollection whatsoever. This is just getting worse.

She finishes the can of soft drink and stepping over to the curtains, pulls them aside just enough to peek outside. It's night and the hotel faces onto a road. Cars cruise past, white, orange and red reflections in the wet street. Nothing she recognises. She flops into the chair at the small desk by the window and opens the drawer looking for clues. She discovers a glossy brochure with a photograph of the hotel on the front, full sunshine, blue sky. She is momentarily confused as she attempts to read the name and address. It takes her tortured drug-impaired brain a few seconds to determine that the writing on the brochure is in French.

* * *

As the light stabs into Sarah's eyes she knows no power on earth will prevent her from throwing up. She rolls onto her side and her lunch is ejected violently from her mouth and nose. Spasms grip her stomach and she retches again and again until there is nothing left, she's simply trying to vomit up air. For a moment longer she lays there with her head hanging over the side of the bed, a long string of drool connecting her to the floor. Her chest feels as though she's caused permanent damage, ruptured something vital. As she rolls onto her back her head throbs so forcefully that it's almost more than she can bear. Turning her head toward a sound she sees a nurse framed by the doorway, hands on hips.

"So, you're back with us I see." She says, looking down at the pool of vomit by the bed. "Hang on and I'll get a mop and clean this lot up."

Sarah closes her eyes and keeps as still as she can, trying to will the pain in her head to subside. She hears the nurse push the clattering steel bucket into the room. It sounds like a car crash inside her head.

"Sorry." Is all Sarah can manage.

"Ah well, look on the bright side. You're not the one who has to clean it up." The nurse says with a lopsided grin. "The doctor will be along presently. I'll put a pan on the side of the bed, do your best to use it instead of the floor next time, pet."

Sarah closes her eyes against the glare of the ceiling lights. Why do these places have to be so damn bright? Don't they know how sick people feel? She thinks back to the nightmare she had in the restaurant and suddenly she remembers Rita telling her about Joyce. The shock causes her heart to speed up and that sends the jackhammers in her head into warp speed. She forces herself to breath deeply, to relax, calm down. As her heart rate slows she turns the news around in her mind, looking at it from all angles. Can't be a coincidence she decides but the alternative that Mathias was right and she is some sort of prophetess is simply too absurd to allow. It occurs to her that maybe Joyce committed suicide by jumping under a car. After all, she was pretty upset at what Sarah said. That's probably what happened.

At that moment she decides she will tell Rita nothing about what she saw in the latest episode. In fact she isn't entirely sure of what she'd seen herself but she knew it was ugly. Sarah also knew she had been pretty slack in not telling her doctor about the turn she'd taken in Maggie's flat. Now it had happened again she had to get serious and do something about it. Fear slipped its icy hand down her back as her mind raced ahead and the possibility of confinement presented itself. The ghost of Sarah's future. She shuddered. Sarah fought the idea back down again. No way, not these days. That's not going to happen again. Just have to get the drugs right and take better care of myself is all.

Sarah's train of thought is interrupted by a rattling noise at the foot of her bed. Opening her eyes, she is surprised to see the doctor examining her chart. She hadn't heard him enter the room. He is Indian and has skin the colour of dark chocolate, about fortyish she guesses.

"So, how are you feeling Sarah?" He asks, taking her hand, his finger locating her pulse. His skin is smooth and cool to the touch.

"Sick, and my head's absolutely killing me."

The doctor unrolled the wide black band and strapped it around her upper arm, gave a few pumps on a rubber bulb. Sarah felt her arm squeezed in its grip.

"Sounds like you took quite a turn, I am thinking you need some rest. Do you think you could keep a tablet down?" He asks.

"I'm not sure I could."

"Okay, a needle then." He said, crossing the room and opening a small cabinet on the wall with a key from around his neck.

"The good news about needles is that they are working very fast."

The doctor turns to face her, the hypodermic needle skilfully concealed in his hand.

"Arm or bottom?"

"I prefer bottom." Sarah said, carefully rolling on to her side.

"Yes, I also am somewhat of a bottom man." He replies with a smile. "Wiggling toes for me please."

Despite the pain in her head Sarah manages a chuckle. As the drug begins to take effect Sarah feels the most wonderful sensation of warmth and comfort slide over her. Her problems seem to melt away and she becomes relaxed and sleepy. Without warning, a negative thought shouldered its way into her gently slowing mind. She remembers that she hasn't been able to get hold of Maria for a while. She briefly turns this fact over in her mind, feeling its weight and then decides that in all likelihood a perfectly good reason will emerge in due course. She can hear Maria chiding her for worrying so much. The last thing she remembers is deciding to close her eyes, just for a few seconds.

* * *

As Sarah sank into drug induced oblivion, Rita, on the floor below, was anything but relaxed. She'd been strapped into her bed and now she was being wheeled down the corridor to have her head CT scanned. One eye was black and almost closed and the side of her face throbbed. It had been patiently explained to her as if she was a child that the scan had to be done before they would give her any medication. She'd yelled and cursed at the doctor when he declined to remove her restraints and then she'd burst into tears. Eventually through pain and exhaustion she had calmed down. Now she wanted to get the scan over and done with so she could have some drugs and sleep.

After she is wheeled into the radiology department a nurse starts to unbuckle her from the bed. With the nurse's hand in the middle of her back, Rita sits up and attempts to swing her legs over the side of the gurney. The room spins and the nurse has to grab her to keep her from falling.

"You're a little concussed, Rita." She says. "You need to move slowly and you'll be okay. Just rest for a moment and then we'll try again."

As Rita's breathing returns to normal the room slows and finally stops rotating altogether. Just as well I *was* strapped in, Rita thinks. I'd have more than one black eye otherwise. She closes her eyes and is abruptly gripped by a feeling of absolute hopelessness and despair as she remembers her lunch date with Sarah. As if a door has suddenly slammed shut on her future. As certainly as night follows day she knows her fate is to join Joyce in some ghastly accident. Sarah's whispered words have etched themselves indelibly into her memory and she hears them again, every nuance clear as a bell, the sadness and despair unmistakable as she had peered into Rita's future;

Oh no, Rita, so much blood

CHAPTER 12

The man whistles to himself as he hammers a high-tensile steel nail into the centuries-old masonry. Around the walls of the chamber at a height of about six feet, a stone ledge held groups of exquisitely carved creatures. Above the ledge the ornate ceiling was shrouded in darkness. His current endeavours were watched intently by a trio of gargoyles. All had wings, one had the face of a bulldog and a heavy chain ran from its neck to a ring set into the stone wall. The second sported a powerful body protected by armoured plates and topped with the head of an eagle while the third was half monkey and half dragon, small horns jutting up from a monstrous primate's head. The man smiled and winked at the grotesques, continuing to string the electrical wire that would lead back the generator and allow electric light inside the tomb for the first time in its history.

With a deft flick of his wrist he looped the end of the cable around the neck of what appeared to be a bizarre vomiting lion before standing back to admire his work. Patting the distressed creature affectionately he sprinted up the stone staircase taking them several at a time, eager to complete his preparations.

* * *

David pushes his chair back and settles his feet on the desk.

"So what do you think, Walter? Tell me honestly." He said. The pair has just returned from a two hour session with Mathias in an adjoining interview room.

"I think we have nothing upon which to hold him. In fact his cooperation has been remarkable. Patient, polite, cool as a cucumber, as it were." Walter replied.

"Too bloody cool for my liking. Shit. There's something going on here Walter. It all fits together way too tightly for my liking."

"I agree that the coincidence, allowing that's what it is, seems remarkable. Certainly this man represents a link between the two cases but he has a cast iron alibi for at least one of the murders. He wasn't even in the country according to his passport, that's pretty solid, old chap."

"But Walter, really. What's the probability that this bloke is guilty? He's Special Forces, has the marks in a place on his wrist that the last victim could have seen, has the same physical profile as the man seen by Cyril Morpeth, seems to be in charge of a religion that elevates women above all else and can't account for his whereabouts at the time of two of the murders."

"I'm not denying the facts. It's just so circumstantial at present. We just don't have any hard evidence to actually *join* those dots. He also appears to be a genuinely nice fellow who is sincere in his beliefs, strange though they may seem. And, as you well know, innocent men don't need alibis so his inability to recall what he was doing on the two dates in question doesn't mean he's guilty."

"You forgot to mention that he's as sharp as a tack." David added bitterly. "Could you believe it when we threatened to get a search warrant to toss his flat he said it wouldn't be necessary?"

"Just put things back where you find them and show respect for my property was what he said, I believe. Doesn't sound like a man with something to hide, now does it?"

"Either that or he's way too smart by half and knows we'll find nothing."

Walter slid a page from the fax machine across the desk toward David and then cocked his head for an answer. David glanced at the page but didn't pick it up.

"Just because the man is a decorated hero doesn't mean he's innocent. Christ, the bloody medals have probably got a string of bodies behind them anyway!" David said. Frustrated.

"That's not really the point old chum. All I'm saying is that the record reveals a consistently careful and controlled soldier with bravery and resourcefulness. His commander said he was a natural leader and was sorry to see him leave. Could have had quite a career in the forces had he wished it. Doesn't sound like Natalie's profile of the flawed soldier to me."

"Walter, I agree with you, it doesn't. But, you know, some coppers are analytical thinking machines and some are like me, instinct driven. I admit the analysis doesn't hold any water yet but I tell you, my instinct is pinging like a bugger."

Walter sighed. "Let it go, David. You know as well as I do that we can't hold him. I don't think he'll run, he's had ample opportunity to do that already. We'll keep chipping away and if he's our man we'll find a chink in his armour at some point."

David shrugged, dragging his feet off the table. "Okay, Walter you win. But my gut tells me there's something going on and I've learned to listen to those instincts. Shit! I guess I better go and apologise to the big bastard and get it over with."

"And make it sound sincere dear chap. Methinks you don't want to get any deeper into this fellow's bad books than you already are."

* * *

The edges of the towelling bathrobe didn't quite meet when Maria had attempted to cover herself. She improvised by putting her arms through one robe and tying the belt behind her as if it were a straightjacket and then putting the second robe over the top in the normal manner. She felt stupid but at least she was spared the ignominy of speaking with the police with her belly poking out. She took another look at the street. Dawn was beginning to break. After no little confusion, the staff of the Hotel De Lausanne had been wonderful. When it became clear this was a police matter, the night clerk had been summoned and, in broken English, Maria was able to deduce that she had arrived in the early evening and was fast asleep in her wheelchair from the long journey. The reservation, previously secured with a credit card, was in order and so her husband had wheeled her straight to the room so that she could retire for the night. Nobody saw him leave. The clerk was shamefaced when forced to admit that he hadn't checked Maria's passport. The man was big and tired and grumpy from the train trip and his passport looked fine. He didn't want to risk aggravating the guest. How was he to know that an invalid in a wheelchair could be a problem?

Nothing could be done until the police arrived. The kitchen prepared a huge cooked breakfast and brought it to Maria on a foldout table with silver cutlery and a small vase of flowers. The manager, dragged from his bed, was most anxious to demonstrate that this was a very unfamiliar circumstance and that in no way could it be suggested that the hotel was implicated in such a heinous crime as kidnapping. Despite her headache, Maria was able to wolf down the whole breakfast and drink the entire pot of coffee. Only then did she begin to feel human again.

* * *

Rita opens the door to her council flat and lets herself in. Bolting the door behind her she uses the toe of her shoe to slide the small pile of letters sitting behind the door into the corner. Bloody bills, she mumbles under her breath. The concentration required for this normally simple action causes the room to begin moving. Rita holds on to the doorknob until the feeling passes. She catches sight of herself in the hall mirror and tears well in her eyes. One side of her face is blue-green and her left eye is still almost closed from the swelling. She has a lump like a duck's egg on her elbow and a bruise as large as a saucer on her hip.

None of these injuries really occupy her mind however. As the doctor in the hospital said, there's nothing here that won't get better given time. No permanent damage. He wasn't too keen on her discharging herself this morning but one night in that place was enough for her. She hadn't had a minute's sleep and her heart was weighed down with dread. Black, crushing, inconsolable, all-consuming dread.

She couldn't flush Sarah's words from her mind. A voice that she just couldn't squash kept on telling her it was only a matter of time. Just like Joyce, she now had an appointment with a premature and ugly death. But unlike Joyce, she didn't know where it would come from, she had no way to protect herself, she was helpless in the face of it. As sure as the sun rises in the east she knew in her heart that she was powerless to avoid her fate. But that didn't mean she understood it. Mathias had said that when The Redeemer arrived they would know it.

But why would she use such horrible signs to reveal herself? Why not turning water into wine or sticks into serpents? Or even better, why not raise the dead or cure the sick? Why should people who had believed in her, and wanted her to come, and hoped they'd live to see her, have to die? It made no sense to Rita but she knew that didn't matter. After Joyce was killed she was certain something momentous was happening and that she was just dust on the scales by comparison. She'd even felt guilty at being excited by the prospect of more visions and signs, but never in her wildest imaginings did she expect this.

Rita's face ached and every time she closed her eyes she felt the waves of nausea from the concussion grip her stomach. The painkillers she'd taken only served to dull the pain, its sharp edge was just under the surface ready to strike like a rattlesnake if she moved too quickly and in the meantime her head felt like it was stuffed with cotton wool. She shuffles into the bathroom and eases herself down onto the toilet seat. When the room stabilises she opens her small bathroom cabinet with its chipped and peeling mirror. Her tongue feels as though someone had laid carpet over it while she was asleep and she wants desperately to clean her teeth.

Her eye is drawn to the shaver propped up in the bottom corner of the cabinet, used by her long-gone husband. She picks it up and wonders how she came to have it and why she hadn't thrown it out before. It is one of the older types of razor that employs the double sided blades. Rita fiddles with the handle and works out that if she turns the bottom half inch of the handle the top of the razor opens like a clamshell. She can see the blade nestled in its holder. No fuss, industrial, clinical. She becomes aware of a powerful emotion, a commanding voice spurring her to act, to take control while she still can. She carefully removes the blade and holds it up to the light, marvels at its thinness, the invisible lethality of its edge. Rita leans back on the toilet seat and tilts the blade so it reflects the light from the single bulb in the ceiling.

Yes, she thinks. There is one thing I *can* do to end this. One thing I can do to avoid whatever awful fate I'm supposed to encounter. She imagines Joyce with her splintered bones and ruptured organs and her body shudders.

Without conscious thought Rita presses the flat of the razor blade to the inside of her left wrist. She sees the faint blue veins beneath her skin, understands the delicacy of that membrane. She turns the blade so its cutting edge is about four inches above her wrist. Pressing down hard she draws the blade swiftly toward her hand, slicing trough skin, fat muscle, and artery.

The flesh of her wrist opens like a flower. Immediately arterial blood begins to pump over her fingers. She clenches her fist and the blood paints an arc across the bathroom wall. Suddenly Rita is frightened. Her mind snaps into the present and she realises what she's done. The blood continues pumping, so much blood. Not just trickling but spurting out, hot and sticky. She looks at the blade in her hand and immediately lets go of it. There is so much blood on her hand that the blade stays there, stuck to her index finger. She screams and flicks her wrist as though she has some disgusting insect crawling on her. The blade winks through the air before lodging in a pool of blood on the tiled floor.

She tries to cover her mutilated wrist but the blood pulses out around her fingers. Terrified now, she stands up and tries to make it to the door. Call an ambulance, call an ambulance *now*. The bathroom tiles are slick with blood and Rita's sudden movement, conspiring with her concussion, leaves her unstable. She feels her bare feet slipping in the blood and then the edge of the bathtub is accelerating toward her. Her last thought is that she's going to strike her face again in exactly the same spot that only yesterday took the brunt of her fall to the restaurant floor. The doctor will be mad with me, she thinks. Fireworks explode inside her skull and then darkness.

* * *

Twenty four hours after being admitted to the hospital, Sarah is discharged. She felt conspicuous and silly being pushed to the hospital's main entrance in a wheelchair but apparently it was hospital policy. She is not looking forward to seeing her mother. Her parents have promised to collect her this morning and she knows what she's in for. Another haranguing session as her failures are enumerated by her mother while her father drives the car in silence. Why was she so useless, wasting her life? Couldn't even be trusted to take her medication. Drank too much. Partied too hard and didn't get enough sleep. Socialised with losers.

She had ignored the doctor's advice, and so it would go on. Sarah apologising and promising to do better but inside knowing she probably wouldn't. She sighed. It was just too much like hard work. As the doors to the main entrance slid open the climate controlled atmosphere of the hospital was replaced by the biting cold of the outdoors. Sarah hooked her bag over the armrest of the wheelchair and pulled her coat tightly around herself. She had become used to the antiseptic smell of the hospital and the stench of exhaust fumes out here under the covered driveway is assaulting.

Distractedly, she watches a small four wheel drive roll by and pull up just beyond where she sat. It was one of those popular "lifestyle" cars that promised picnics in the fields with beautiful people and access to exotic beaches with white sand and palm trees. If only it was so simple she thinks. The car stopped and a tall well-built man stepped out and began walking directly toward her. Surprised, she realises that it's Robert. She remembered him from that night at Maggie's flat and how attentive he'd seemed. Robert walks directly toward her as though he knew she'd be here.

"Hello Sarah." he said.

"Hi, what brings you here?" She asks, looking up at him.

"Actually I'm here to collect you." He replied.

"My folks are coming to get me." Sarah said, puzzled.

"I know that was the plan but their car's broken down and they phoned Mathias to help. He's tied up so he asked me to collect you. Hop in and I'll take you home."

Sarah was confused. Her parents phoning Mathias? Maybe her mother had saved his number. Maybe from a message he'd left for her. But her mother knew they weren't seeing each other anymore so why phone him? For a moment she toyed with the idea that this was one of her mother's stupid schemes. A daft idea to get them back together again. But it didn't sound likely, even for her mother. And anyway, even though Sarah didn't own a car, her parents had *two* cars, a small one that her mother drove and which was almost new and a larger car they used when setting out on longer trips. They can't both be broken down, surely. She opens her mouth to ask a question but Robert has turned away from her.

Sarah looks up at the nurse holding the handles of her wheelchair. The nurse has been tasked with seeing to it that Sarah leaves the grounds safely but she has lots more to do before her shift is over. Her head was turned and her mind is obviously elsewhere.

"Well, these things happen, dear." She says distractedly. "The main thing is that you have a ride home. We can't have you sitting here in the cold all day."

Out of the corner of her eye Sarah spots a parking inspector walking toward them, pulling a pad from his back pocket. Robert sees him too.

"Come on, Sarah, I can't leave my car here, this spot's only for collecting patients. Jump in before they give me a ticket."

The situation makes little sense but Sarah doesn't want to get Robert into trouble, particularly as he is doing her a favour by taking her home. She grabs her bag, untangles herself from the wheelchair and heads around to the passenger door. Robert holds it open for her and closes it when she settles into the seat, careful not to trap her clothes in the door. He jumps into the driver's seat and pulls away smoothly.

As they leave through the main gate, and unseen by Sarah, her parent's car turns into the hospital grounds, her mother unmistakable in the front seat, her stabbing finger pointing out the route to her long-suffering husband.

CHAPTER 13

The district nurse checks her notes and scans the numbers in the narrow street. Satisfied she's in the right place she turns the engine off and gets out of her car. She remembers her sports bag on the rear seat and decides to put it in the boot. One look at the neighbourhood tells her that if she wants to have a racquet to play squash with tonight she'd better put it out of sight. Straightening up she spots a group of early teenagers watching her from the steps of a block of flats across the road.

"Hello boys. Be good lads and keep an eye on my car would you."

Better to show no fear and to remind them that they've been seen. She also knew that her uniform conveyed a slight edge in the adult / youth power dynamic. Not much, but every bit counted. She locked the car with the remote and walked straight-backed toward Rita's flat. She was used to these areas, many of her patients barricaded themselves inside council owned flats just like these. Sometimes it was all she could do to get them to open the door.

The unmistakable smell of stale urine floated toward her as she approached the building. Stepping around an overturned rubbish bin, its contents kicked down the steps, she made her way to Rita's door. Paint hung from the door in long strips like burned skin and the doorbell had been smashed leaving only slender wires poking out from the doorframe. There was a suspicious stain on the concrete to the side of the door and she made a mental note not to step in it on her way out.

She still had the keys in her hand and she selects the chunky square key with the built-in remote opener. What is it about car keys these days, she thinks, they don't even resemble keys at all. Just some weird stick of metal. She uses the end of the key to tap firmly on the door and is rewarded with a solid resonance. The flat is silent. She tries again, tapping harder this time. Her efforts cause a small flake of paint to dislodge from the door. It falls to the floor and breaks into several pieces. With her shoe she gives the door a push. It moves a quarter of an inch and stops solid. Bolted from the inside, she guesses. Behind her she hears the creak of a door opening and turns to see a pair of rheumy eyes peeking through a crack secured by a solid chain.

"Hello." She said in her brightest voice. "I'm the district nurse. I'm looking for Rita. Have you seen her today?"

For a moment she thought the old lady wasn't going to answer.

"Seen her yesterday. Come 'ome in the mornin.' Probably still inside. I aint seen her go out again. Mibee in the back yard."

She thanks the old lady for her trouble and walks back outside. Down the side of the building is an alleyway, stone cobbles, wide enough for a single car, bordered on one side by the solid brick wall of the neighbouring building and on the other by high wooden fences enclosing the gardens of the lucky ground floor tenants. She counts the flats until she comes to Rita's gate. Finding it unlocked she lets herself in to a space roughly ten feet wide and fifteen feet deep. Old bricks have been laid over the earth to provide a path to the door and a tiny garden shed stands in one corner.

An ancient deck chair hangs from a hook on the side of the shed, its once colourful canvas faded to a dirty grey. Obviously fond of plants, Rita has about fifty pots of various sizes scattered around the tiny space. Moss grows everywhere and she guesses the little garden doesn't see much of the sun, surrounded as it is by tall buildings.

She tries the back door but it too is locked. Cupping her hands around her eyes she peers through the kitchen window. Rita's bag and keys sit on the small table; her coat is slung over the back of a chair. Concern builds in her mind as she considers the possibilities. Standing on the back step she pulls her file from the black case she carries and checks Rita's history again. The concussion and early discharge worry her. People often underestimate the effects of a head injury. Rita could be lying injured inside the flat after a fall in the shower or something. She deliberates for a few moments and decides that she had to know. They will need to open the door. Pulling her mobile from a coat pocket she dials one of the emergency numbers she has programmed in the phone. Almost every time she has to use one of these numbers, her day goes all to hell.

* * *

The police were not quite as generous as the hotel staff. Maria gained the distinct impression that they didn't believe her story. Why would someone drug a woman, bring her to the centre of Paris, book her into a decent hotel, steal her clothes and then leave? What is to be gained by all this? The Gendarme had asked.

Maria fought to contain her temper when the officer had suggested that perhaps the only crime was that she was here in Paris, unable to pay her hotel bill and completely lacking in passport or identification. The hotel manager, sensing that things were turning nasty and not wanting the hotel's name connected with the unfortunate incident any more than necessary, quickly stepped in. The manager indicated in no uncertain terms that the hotel would not be charging the unfortunate mademoiselle for her stay and so the officer should not concern himself with such details.

The passport was another matter and it took Maria two more days before she finally sorted out the mess and was allowed to return to Britain. Graciously, the hotel allowed her to call her mother and using her mother's credit card details Maria was able to obtain a cash advance from the hotel to buy some clothes. Maria insisted on paying the hotel for her stay, as they had been exemplary in their kindness towards her. The manager responded by arranging a tour of the city for her while she was waiting for the British Embassy to arrange a temporary passport.

When she finally departed, the staff assembled to waive her off and the manager kissed her hand and presented her with a bunch of flowers and his best wishes for her future. As the taxi pulled out to take her to the station, Maria couldn't stop the tears from welling in her eyes.

* * *

After Robert merges with the traffic on the main road, he reaches into the centre console and hands Sarah a warm drink.

"I picked up a latte for you, I know you like them." He said.

Sarah took it carefully out of his hand, not wanting to spill it. Through the cardboard cup the heat from the warm liquid was welcome against her cold hands.

"That's very sweet of you, Robert. You didn't have to do that."

"It's nothing." He replied. "I figured the stuff they serve in there is probably undrinkable, thought you might be ready for a real coffee." He turned and smiled at her.

"That's thoughtful of you and yes, I am ready for one." Sarah said.

Sarah eased the thin plastic top from the paper cup. Even sick she wouldn't stoop to drinking through the silly little beak that poked up from the lid. Looks for all the world like a baby's cup she thought. Another Americanism inflicted on us. She sipped the hot liquid. Despite a vague and slightly metallic taste it was pretty good. She settled back in the comfortable seat, pleased that Robert didn't seem to feel the need for small talk. She was angry with her mother for calling Mathias. It was completely inappropriate for her to call him. She could have caught a cab for Christ's sake. Her mother *knew* she had broken up with Mathias.

After her experience with Rita she'd decided that she definitely would have nothing to do with any of them ever again. And yet here she was sitting in Robert's car, a ride that Mathias had arranged and now she was in some way indebted to both of them. Inexcusable. She's gone too far this time. She had to have this out with her mother when she got home. No question about it.

Sarah's mind jumps back to her immediate situation as she sees the street sign at the end of her road go by. Of course, she reminds herself, he's never been to my house before.

"Sorry, Robert." She said, gulping the last of the coffee and replacing the infantile plastic lid. "I was daydreaming. We've just passed my street. Never mind, you can take a left up ahead and go around the block."

"No problems." Said Robert, smiling. But he drove right by the next street.

"Oops, that was the one." Sarah said. "Sorry, but you pretty much have to do a U turn now to get back."

Robert turned and smiled at her and continued driving. Sarah felt relaxed and warm in the car. These seats are so comfortable, I could fall asleep she thought. She waited for Robert to find a good place to turn around but he just kept on driving.

"There's a park coming up on the left. You could turn around in there." She said.

"No problem, thanks."

Robert passed the park without slowing, now heading directly away from Sarah's house.

"Robert," she said, "you're going the wrong way. We've gone miles past my house."

Robert turned and smiled at her. "You think so?" He said.

Sarah was confused. Her mind wasn't working the way it should. Had she really passed her street or just imagined it? Maybe the episode with Rita was still impairing her thinking in some way. As the sports stadium went by on her side she knew she was right. They *had* passed her street and every minute they continued driving they were putting more miles between where they were supposed to be going. She looks over at Robert, notices the bulge of muscle under his shirtsleeve and sees how casually he grips the steering wheel with his large right hand, his other hand resting in his lap.

What is she supposed to say? Again she had that odd feeling that reality was sliding out of her grasp, causing her to question what she'd seen only a moment ago. And she was tired. Really tired. The kind of tired that comes from sedatives. Hospital drugs. Suddenly she is frightened. The coffee. She remembers the metallic taste in her mouth. She knows that taste.

Sarah struggles to keep herself calm. Can't let him see that I suspect anything. Whatever happens she decided she would jump out of the car next time they stopped at a traffic light. She checks to ensure she knows where the door handle is and an icy fist closes around her chest. The handle has been removed. Where it should have been there's a hole. She can see inside the door, can see the impression in the plastic trim where the handle had been. The car looks new, how could the handle be missing? Trying to appear casual despite the pounding in her ears, she slips her hand down to the seat belt buckle and presses it. Nothing. The buckle doesn't unlock. The car has been tampered with to stop her getting out. What else could it be?

Her vision is starting to shut down. The world is sliding into monochrome like an old black and white television. In desperation she tugs on the seat belt, hoping to pull out enough slack to allow her to slip out of it. The belt gave a couple of inches and then locked solid. She pulled it with all her might but it didn't budge. Her vision was dimming to the point that only a small circle of light appeared at the centre, like looking through a dirty porthole. She slumped back, unable to fight it any longer. Her head slipped to the side. Gently, Robert moved her head so it rested against the top of the seat belt. Anyone passing in the opposite direction would see an altogether common sight. Man drives while woman snoozes.

* * *

The hospital called the police immediately. After listening to Sarah's increasingly hysterical mother and interviewing the nurse who had witnessed Sarah's departure, the conclusion is quickly reached that abduction was a real possibility. The climate of fear surrounding the finding of the dead girls provided such an obvious context that Dorothy had to be sedated to calm her down. She was admitted to the hospital for observation. George paced the floor wringing his hands, unable to bear the thought of his girl in danger but unable to think of anything else. The nurse involved was distraught at her own failure to remember the details. She hadn't taken any notice of either the vehicle involved or the man. She was preoccupied with the fact that she was running late and falling behind in her tasks. So many cars come and go outside the hospital picking up and dropping off patients. She was fairly sure the car was white and had a boxy sort of shape, maybe a van of some sort. Her recollection of the man was even more vague, all she knew was that he was big and she only remembered hearing one name. Mathias.

* * *

Robert arrived at his destination with Sarah sleeping soundly in the passenger seat. He'd only needed to pull over twice to clear his head. He would have preferred to do this at night but he had to seize the opportunity when it presented itself. He knows from experience that success in an endeavour can come two ways. From planning and meticulous attention to detail or from decisive action when presented with an opportunity that can be turned to your advantage. In this case he suspected that both could required. It was obvious to Robert that Sarah was in great danger and needed his protection. He'd come to realise in the last week or so that Mathias wasn't who he'd pretended to be.

There was obviously a strange side to the man that he'd never seen before and he cursed himself for his stupidity in not realising it sooner. After all they had been through together. Weird how you never really know someone. Ever since the wasps had started coming, Robert was seeing situations and people with a new clarity. Things were simplified, black and white. His doubts no longer troubled him. Sarah needed protection and Mathias was sitting on his hands, not doing anything. Well, she will be safe now, he thinks.

He winds the window down and listens carefully. Nothing. He takes a brisk stroll up the hill and scans the countryside with high powered binoculars as the wind tugs and pushes at his clothes. Every few minutes he shakes his head in frustration, trying clear the wasps that he can hear inside his head. Lately there seemed to be more of them and they visited him with increasing frequency.

He reminded himself that it was simply the stress of the situation he'd been thrust into. Satisfied that he is truly alone, he returns to the car. Pulling a small screwdriver from his pocket he crouches down and pops open Sarah's seat belt. He notices the plastic hospital band is still on her wrist. It strikes him as particularly inconsiderate of the hospital not to have removed it for her when she was discharged. In one fluid motion he reaches into his pocket and pulls out a four inch folding knife, opening the blade with his thumb without even being conscious of the action. The blade simply materialises in his hand. He slices through the plastic band and the knife folds and disappears again with as much thought as one might give to blinking. He is very fond of his knife.

Robert looks down at the severed band in his left hand and at that moment the wasps return. Lots of wasps. He hears them an instant before they swarm behind his eyes, momentarily blocking his vision. He stands and shakes his head vigorously, the hospital band slipping from his fingers. Seconds later his vision clears and he hears the wasps retreating, their evil hum growing softer. A sheen of sweat covers his face and he wipes it away with his sleeve. He's irritated to think the wasps are getting the better of him. He needs a drink.

Momentarily disoriented, he looks down at Sarah sitting in the passenger seat and remembers where he is. He lifts her out of the car like she's a sleeping child. She's light in his arms, her head resting on his shoulder. He closes the door with his knee. Something bothers him, he can't put his finger on it. He shrugs.

"You'll be fine now, your protector is here." He whispers as he begins the long walk that will take Sarah to safety.

* * *

The police were not surprised to discover that Mathias had called in sick today. They were also correct in their assumption that he wouldn't be at home in his flat. Using strategically parked cars, officers on foot, as well as rooftop surveillance they threw a security cordon around his home as well as the building where he worked. They didn't have to wait long. Mathias strolled down the street, a newspaper tucked under his arm. He saw the surveillance teams as soon as he turned the corner. At first he didn't associate this operation with his time spent at the local nick. A few more paces and it became obvious that his building was the focus of all the attention and the penny dropped in his mind. He experienced a momentary flash of anger at what he considered to be nothing less than harassment by Inspector Orbost. It wasn't like he hadn't cooperated. Christ, he'd given up almost an entire day to their stupid suspicions last time. Credit where credit's due, Orbost did apologise to him for the misunderstanding. Mathias knew his heart wasn't in it though. And anyway, despite the apology here they are again, even more cavalry this time making even bigger fools of themselves.

The whole thing was becoming a bloody nuisance. When would they learn that all they had to do is knock on the door and ask for a polite chat? Without breaking his relaxed stride, he began to wonder whether it might be time to get a solicitor involved. Perhaps someone at work might be able to suggest a good one.

He spotted David and Walter sitting inside a dark coloured sedan on the opposite side of the road. As he crossed over he could see several men on nearby rooftops and he caught a flash from the lenses of a pair of binoculars. Sloppy, he thought. He approached the car and the driver's window slid down with a soft hum.

"What can I do for you gentlemen?" He said. In his peripheral vision he spotted the other officers closing in. Mathias didn't wait for an answer.

"Don't make a scene. Surely you know me by now. What's it about this time? Or do you want me back at the nick again?"

"That's what we want, yes." David replied, conscious of the security perimeter tightening around them.

Mathias shook his head. "This is getting fucking tedious, Inspector. I'm really in no mood for it. I woke up with a rotten cold this morning and these stupid theatrics will probably cost me my day off."

Mathias is aware of the men closing in on him. "Tell your goons to keep their hands to themselves if they don't want them broken. Come on, let's get this over with."

"I'm arresting you on suspicion of the murder of..."

"What the fuck?..." Mathias exclaimed.

"You do not have to say anything but anything you do say..." Continued David, speaking under Mathias's outburst.

"Come on!" Mathias shouted. "Get real guys, what the hell is wrong with you?"

The car is now surrounded by several armed police standing back far enough to allow them time to react if rushed.

"Sarah Nelson." David said. "Where is she?"

Mathias looks at him blankly. "Sarah? What's wrong with Sarah? Tell me."

"We have reason to believe that you abducted her from hospital this morning." Walter replied.

"What! You think I abducted Sarah? Hospital? Listen, if Sarah is in danger, you have to tell me right now." Mathias said.

"We'll tell you at the station." David said. "But we have to cuff you first."

"Shit. You stupid bloody fools." Mathias holds his wrists out in front of him. "Get on with it and let's go. Fuck, if anything happens to her while you're wasting time with me I'll make sure you lot burn for this."

"Go easy lads." David said as a large officer wearing black fatigues and body armour grips Mathias's wrist and pulls it behind his back. Mathias's eyes flash at him and the officer eases his grip slightly. As Walter steps behind Mathias and snaps on the handcuffs a police van pulls up and Mathias is placed in the rear.

A radio call is made and at Mathias's innocuous looking office building across town, armed police wearing bulky vests stand down and begin packing up their kit leaving curious locals trying to guess who the guilty party might be..

CHAPTER 14

Sarah Nelson floats toward consciousness as the powerful sedative slowly loses its grip on her mind. She becomes aware of a low hum, like an air-conditioner running in another room. She opens her eyes to subdued light but can't immediately figure out where she might be. The events of the last forty eight hours begin to replay in her mind at an accelerating pace. Lunch with Rita, the frightening episode, hospital, Robert, the car! Her pulse races as she battles to access the details of that frightening memory. She recalls the seat belt, the missing door handle and the not-quite-right coffee taste.

Her memory surges back so forcefully and vividly that she has to screw her eyes shut and concentrate on her breathing in an attempt to bring her mind and body under control. When the feelings of panic began to subside she reopens her eyes. Lying on her back, it's odd but she can't see a ceiling above her. She turns her head and a grinning skull returns her gaze. Sarah screams and attempts to curl into a ball before she realises that the skull isn't real. It's surrounded by a garland of carved leaves and rests on a stone pillow. On either side it is flanked by marble busts of men long dead.

Sarah pushes herself up onto one elbow and is immediately aware of something on her leg. She is covered with a blanket, like a travel rug with a red Stuart tartan and she drags it off and tosses it on top of her thin pillow. Looking down she's astonished to see that her ankle is enclosed in some sort of leg iron. A steel cable sheathed in plastic joins the leg iron to a fastener in the stone wall. She lifts her leg and sees a couple of coils of wire on the floor. Maybe twenty feet of cable all up. She struggles into a sitting position on the simple camp bed on which she's been lying. Swinging her legs over the side she examines the leg iron. It appears to be made of a light metal, perhaps aluminium. Two nuts and bolts on each side to keep it closed. She knows there will be no point but she tries to unscrew the nuts anyway. The inner surface is covered in a sort of thick carpet material, obviously to protect her leg from being scratched by the metal. This seemed odd. She'd been secured with a comfort version of something out of the middle ages. This was just too weird

She attempts to stand and the room spins. When the feeling passes she again moves cautiously and this time she is fine. It's cold and she zips up her coat as far as it will go. Careful to ensure the cable attached to her ankle didn't become tangled she explores her surroundings, testing out the limits of her movement in all directions.

A single globe casts an anaemic light that is insufficient to penetrate into the corners of the chamber. She can reach what she guesses to be a stone sarcophagus on which had been placed a metal plate and knife with some bread, a jar of peanut butter, some dry biscuits, a packet of muesli bars and several bottles of water. Chained up and fed bread and water she thought grimly. She can also reach a portable toilet with its own holding tank and instructions on the side for flushing. Lying nearby is a plastic shopping bag containing several rolls of toilet paper and an unopened box of tampons.

She shivers and instinctively folds her arms across her chest. Somebody wants me here for a long time. Her gaze falls on what looks like a large ornate birdbath but which she suspects had been designed for a more ceremonial purpose. A full bucket of water stands next to it together with a washcloth and a towel still in its plastic wrapper.

In the opposite direction she can climb up eight of the stone steps which lead out of the chamber before the wire becomes taught. On one side of the steps, ornate figures and shapes have been cut into the rock. Small mythical creatures made up in a Frankenstein like fashion from bits of wildly different animals stand at silent attention next to every step. She picks her way down again, flicking the wire ahead of her to ensure she doesn't trip. Her eyes wander over the walls with their intricate carvings and Latin inscriptions. In one corner of the chamber, out of her reach, a folding chair has been placed. A light globe hangs from a wire above the chair and although the globe isn't lit she can just make out the shape of a thick writing pad and a packet of pens. Sarah thinks it almost looks as though the chair has been placed to allow someone to observe her and then make notes in the pad as though she was a kind of specimen. Too weird.

Sarah shuffles back to the bed and sits down. She finds her handbag on the floor next to the bed and snatches it up, rummaging through its contents. As she expects, her phone is missing but she's relieved to see her emergency medication hiding behind a crumple of tissues. Tossing the bag aside, she asks herself whether Robert has done this to her or whether he'd simply delivered her up to someone else.

She takes small comfort from the fact that whoever is keeping her here obviously has made an attempt to provide for her needs. Keeping her alive. For what? She thinks about the tampons again, imagines being carried into this place unconscious. A stranger's hands on her body as they bolt the manacle closed. She fought the urge to cry. She stands again and walks to the wall where the cable terminates, examined the fitting, gave it a tug. The cable has been formed into a loop and a heavy steel band crimped the end solidly. Sarah figures the cable would be strong enough to tow a car.

A pang of alarm hits her as she suddenly remembers she only has one day of medication in her bag. This setup looks as though it's designed to keep her here for a while. While she isn't as diligent as she ought to be about never missing a day, the thought of not having her medication available for an extended period frightens her. It's all too much. Without warning her head feels heavy. Her investigations have left her feeling weak, the residual effects of the drug she has been fed. She flops onto the bed. She doesn't even have the energy to think anymore. Pulling the rough blanket over herself, she is asleep within a minute.

* * *

Mathias folded his arms across his chest, his cold adding fuel to his already blazing mood of frustration and anger. Walter and David sat opposite, the metal table separating them, defining two sides. Us and them. Two police wearing side arms stood like sentinels in the corners behind Mathias. One more in front of the locked door and another outside. They knew his capabilities and were taking what they estimated to be appropriate precautions. So far and almost instinctively, Mathias reacted to this heightened security by giving them no reason to assume he would be violent. It took a significant effort of will to maintain this veneer in the face of increasingly hostile questioning.

"So, let me summarise." David said, using his fingers to count off the points as he made them. "You don't have anyone that can confirm your movements at the time Sarah disappeared. You have admitted to beginning a relationship with her, a relationship which she broke off and which by your own admission you were upset to lose. We now have two women, well known to you who have apparently killed themselves in the last few days. Sarah's fingerprints are in your car. Your physical profile fits the description of the killer of the dead woman found in the water. You have identifying marks approximating those recorded by the last victim. Your name is mentioned at Sarah's abduction. You have the skills required, and you seem to be at the centre of this whole tawdry mess. Do you see my problem?"

Mathias sighed. "Your problem Inspector is that you're talking out of your arse. Everything you say is true. You've managed to name a whole lot of the cities on the map but then you've just gone and invented a new road that connects them all so you can drive wherever you please! And by the way, for the record, Rita was my friend. She was a troubled person but it's enormously sad that she took her own life. And also by the way, as I've said repeatedly, had I known that I needed an alibi, I would have been more careful to ensure I had one. If I'd only gone to work this morning instead of calling in sick, your entire case against me wouldn't exist. You'd be out there now doing what you're supposed to instead of wasting all of our time barking up the wrong tree. Again."

"But you didn't go to work this morning, did you." Walter said.

"Obviously I didn't. I'm so stupid that I go and abduct someone I know in broad daylight, allow my name to be heard and my face to be seen by a witness, knowing that you already have me in the frame for some other crime, then I waltz down to the paper shop, have lunch and then stroll back into the blindingly obvious open arms of you lot. Why would I do it?"

"I don't know why you would do it." David replied. "Perhaps you're playing silly buggers. Maybe you think you're smarter than we are. Probably it has something to do with your weird-shit religious cult. That's my guess."

"Have I at any stage tried to convince you of my religious views? Have I even raised it as a topic for discussion? No Inspector, you're the one who keeps banging on about it. I could tell you that your resistance and objections were foretold long ago but I suspect..."

Mathias's voice trailed off and he fell silent. His mind raced, grappling with a realisation that battered him like a blow to the head. He closed his eyes for a moment, almost dizzy with the understanding. The entire picture unfolded in his mind, like an organised landscape spread out before him. All the facts fell into place. The gasp as the final twist of the Rubiks cube solved the puzzle. Robert had taken Sarah. The stupid bloody interfering git.

Orbost was very close. He knew now why he'd been suspected. He also knew he had to gain his freedom, the most important mission of his life lay in front of him and he had to accomplish it quickly. The words of Rachael Telford, the words he lived by, sprang into his mind: *'And in those days two will be raised up, one to protect and one to destroy.'* Mathias opened his eyes to find David studying him intently. Before the shutters fell Mathias knew David had seen into him.

"What is it?" David asked. "You've just realised something, haven't you? I know, I saw it. Tell me."

Mathias's face retuned to its impassive state. Disconnected, controlled. Inside, Mathias cursed himself for allowing the slip.

"You must be mistaken, Inspector. As I've told you, and as you can no doubt hear in my voice, I have a cold. It was the reason I didn't go to work today. If you wish to continue I would be grateful for a glass of water and some aspirin."

* * *

When Sarah opened her eyes and looked at her watch she was astonished to realise she'd slept for ten hours. Her gaze quickly swept the chamber but everything appeared as before. She sat up, the camp bed creaking with her movement. After stretching her legs and back she splashes some water onto her face from the bucket. Tearing off the plastic she dries her face and hands with the new towel before hanging it over the edge of the bird bath or whatever it was. As Sarah looks around she realises that she's starving. She tries to calculate when she'd last had a meal but she couldn't recall whether she'd eaten breakfast at the hospital or not.

Either way, it was a while back she tells herself. Flipping the steel cable around the edge of the bed she walks over to the portable toilet. Sarah squats down and reads the instructions. It looked pretty easy and it appeared to work just fine. Afterward she rummages in the plastic bag containing the toilet rolls and tampons and finds a bar of soap still wrapped in its brightly coloured paper. She washes her hands and sets about preparing some food.

The bread isn't exactly fresh but with a liberal application of the peanut butter it tastes pretty good. She freezes, a chunk of bread halfway to her mouth. A stainless steel thermos sits next to the muesli bars. She is certain that it wasn't there before. She puts the bread down and quickly looks around the chamber, suspecting that someone might be hiding in the corner. Everything is as before with the exception of the thermos. Goose bumps ripple down her arms at the thought of someone watching her while she slept.

She turns her attention back to the thermos, picks it up, heavy, full. She unscrews the top that does double duty as a cup and then the stopper underneath. A wisp of steam rises into the chilled air and the aroma of coffee fills her nose. She attempts to identify the smell of the drug that had knocked her out previously but she can't detect it. She pores a little into the cup and the heat radiates into her fingers. There wouldn't be much point in drugging me now, its not like I can go anywhere, she rationalises. She takes a sip, it tastes wonderful, not even the slightest metallic aftertaste. Bugger it, she thinks and fills the cup, carefully replacing the stopper to keep the rest warm.

As she clutches the cup for warmth and chews on the bread and peanut butter she starts to feel human again. The sedative is working its way out of her system and, with the effects of the food and hot coffee, she feels fresh and alert.

She allows herself a second cup before using some of the toilet paper to wipe her mouth and fingers.

* * *

In the police cell, Mathias sat on the steel-framed bed with his back against the brick wall. His eyes were closed but his mind was working feverishly, considering and weighing options, angles and tactics. He chided himself for not seeing it sooner, for being so stupid. Must be getting rusty in my old age. He considered again taking Inspector Orbost into his confidence and came up with the same answer; too risky. He couldn't allow anything to interfere with what he had to accomplish and the only person he really trusted was himself.

He thought of Sarah and the other dead girls, how the police were hell bent on nailing him. Put the case to rest, lock him away for good. Even blame him for Rita's suicide and mad old Joyce's accident. Well, that wasn't going to happen. Mathias knew that unless they could charge him, they would be compelled to release him at some point. His confidence that they *wouldn't* actually charge him given their flimsy circumstantial evidence was beginning to wane in the face of Orbost's single-minded determination. He also guessed they could get a court order to hold him for longer if they were desperate. He couldn't allow either of those contingencies to occur. He needed to get out before he was moved to a more secure facility. If that happened he would be useless.

Shouting from outside interrupts his thoughts. Someone is yelling, he snaps back to the here and now and moves toward the bars at the front of his cell. A gun goes off, the report terrifyingly loud inside the building and a man screams in pain. Shotgun, Matthias thinks. Suddenly the shouting man is inside the cell block, smoke still lingering at the end of the double-barrel shotgun, blood trickling from a wound above his eye.

"Harrison!" He yells. "Where are you, you fucker?"

The man walks unsteadily down the row of cells, checking each one, looking for Harrison, swinging the shotgun left and right. Mathias glances around and realises that he is totally exposed. If the man chose to fire at him he could hardly miss in the tiny cell. Behind the gunman a form appears in the doorway, shouting at him to put the weapon down. The gunman spins around, staggering a little as he does so and a police officer jumps from inside an empty cell and tackles him to the ground.

As the pair crash to the floor, the shotgun discharges, blowing chunks of plaster from the ceiling and sending clouds of white dust into the air. Suddenly officers come from everywhere. The gun is kicked away and the madman handcuffed and dragged back through the door. Outside the cellblock he continues yelling and struggling with the police.

From beneath the night-desk at the end of the cellblock, a young officer raises his head, his face drained of all colour. He glances around to see if any of his colleagues saw him hiding under the desk. Outside the yelling continues and he hears a crash like a chair being smashed. His focus totally centred on the commotion beyond the cellblock, the fresh-faced policeman hurries to find out what's going on. Mathias sees the keys clipped to his belt, judges that he will pass carelessly within arms length of the bars of his cell and decides to seize the opportunity.

As the officer hurries by, Mathias shoots out his hand and seizes the man's left arm above the elbow. The man's own momentum causes him to turn in towards Mathias who then grabs the front of his jacket and pulls him with frightening strength toward the bars of his cell. Before he has a chance to raise his hands to protect himself, the officer's face smashes into the heavy steel bars with a sickening crack, his legs giving way under him. Mathias holds him upright as he fishes the keychain from his belt, offering silent thanks that when the building was renovated the old cell block had been left as it was with its key lock doors.

Working quickly he opens the door and drags the officer inside.

Ripping the thin blanket from the bed, Mathias tosses the officer on top of the mattress and covers him with the blanket. No more than ten seconds have elapsed. Outside the sound of yelling is growing fainter, the shooter had obviously been subdued. Mathias scans the cellblock and sees a door leading to the toilets used by the officer on duty during the night. Pushing the door open and stepping inside, he finds what he was hoping for. A small window above one of the stalls. It had been fitted with two vertical bars screwed to the timber frame.

Mathias climbs onto the toilet bowl, grips the right hand bar, braces himself, and tears it clean off the wall, the screws old and rusted in the damp atmosphere of the washroom. He uses the bar as a lever on the other side and in moments the second bar surrenders in a shower of splinters. The window itself consists simply of frosted glass louvers, which he quickly removes.

Cautiously he peers out of the window. A car park. Perfect. Officer's private cars are parked here while they're on duty. In the distance he can hear the sound of an ambulance siren approaching. Another excellent diversion, he thinks as he eases himself through the small opening and drops like a cat onto the ground. He elects not to steal one of the cars on offer given the fact that many of the police will be out at the front of the building and could be expected to notice someone driving away. Instead he works his way to the back of the lot, which is surrounded by a wire mesh fence. He pauses for a moment and then flips over into the waste ground on the other side before sprinting to the cover of nearby trees.

He spares a thought for the young officer that he knows is hurt quite seriously, but desperate times call for desperate measures he tells himself. From the trees it's a short jog to a shopping centre car park and freedom.

CHAPTER 15

Unfortunately for both Mathias and his victim he was a little heavy handed when stealing the keys to his cell. In the young officer's collision with the cell bars he sustained a depressed fracture of the skull, which resulted in an acute subdural haematoma. A seriously bleeding brain. Inside the police station, it took some time to subdue and attend to the injuries of Peter Boulton.

An officer who was caught by a few pellets from the first shot had to be treated at the scene and then in hospital for puncture wounds to his neck and shoulder. For a while the station and the cellblock became a crime scene where photographs were taken, diagrams compiled and evidence collected. Having already been charged with murder, Burt Harrison had been moved out of the cellblock several days before. In what would later be characterised as a tragic breakdown of police procedure, it was almost three hours before the young constable was identified as missing and eventually found under the blanket in Mathias's cell. By that time young Justin McKenzie was dead.

* * *

Sarah becomes aware of a new sound. She has grown accustomed to the muted drone of the generator and the occasional report of surf breaking over rocks somewhere far away. She quickly realises that someone is approaching, heading down the stone steps toward her. She sits upright on the bed, bundling the blanket up in front of her chest and her anxiety increases as the footsteps grow louder. Robert steps into the chamber, his eyes take in everything at a glance. She has the feeling that he instantly knows all of the objects she has touched since arriving. He walks over to the folding chair, picks up the pad and pens from the seat and sits down, his eyes never leaving her.

"I see you found my thermos." He said.

"I did." Sarah replied. "You must have brought it while I was asleep."

"Yes." He said. "I'm sorry I had to lie to you and drug you, Sarah. I wanted to bring you here without a fuss so that we could talk. I didn't think you'd come otherwise."

He shrugged, a sheepish expression on his face. Sarah pauses, waiting for him to continue. When he doesn't, she asks the obvious question.

"Why have you brought me here?"

Robert paused before answering. "For your own safety, Sarah."

"What do you mean? What danger was I in?"

"You are The Redeemer, Sarah. Sooner or later you'll have to acknowledge that fact. You have proven it twice now, soon you'll possess The Mastery and until then you are in great danger. Here you won't have enemies trying to stop you. Here you can speak openly, Sarah and I, as your protector, will record your words."

Sarah's head is so full of questions she almost doesn't know where to begin. She hates the way he keeps saying her name. It's creepy.

"What enemies? I don't think I have any enemies!"

'Her own enemies will prove to be those at whose table she sups and upon whose bosom she reclines' Robert quoted Rachael Telford.

"What?" Sarah exclaims.

"The point is, Sarah, sometimes friends can turn out to be enemies. Particularly if they try to turn you away from that to which you are destined."

"What the hell are you on about Robert?" Sarah said. "For a start I don't have many..."

Sarah stopped. A feeling of absolute dread gripped her heart. Please God, no.

"Maria?" She said, her voice not much more than a whisper.

"For example." Robert replied, his voice level, calm.

Sarah's shoulder's droop. Tears well in her eyes. She tries valiantly to prevent her voice breaking. Suddenly her legs begin to shake uncontrollably, she's glad to be sitting down.

"Please Robert, tell me that you haven't hurt Maria. Please tell me that."

Robert was having difficulty speaking. His left arm waved crazily at something invisible, his eyes began to roll back and he let out a grunt of frustration. A few seconds later he struggled to pull himself together.

"What was the question?" He asked.

"Maria!" Sarah screams. "Tell me about Maria!"

"She was a just another problem that I had to deal with is all." Robert replied calmly.

Sarah felt the world collapsing in on her, crushing the breath from her lungs, her vision turning grey. Her scream echoed around the chamber. She buried her head in the blanket from the camp bed.

"No, no, no."

"Sarah you have to learn to trust me. I am your protector, I know what's best for us."

"You sick, miserable bastard!" Sarah screamed. "How could you..." She collapses back into the bed, giant sobs gripping her entire body, absolute despair tearing at the very centre of her being.

Robert appeared to be confused at her reaction. In the face of her overwhelming distress he wasn't sure what to say. How could she be so aggressive to him after all he had done for her? What had tipped her over the edge like this? Then the wasps returned, even stronger and more determined this time. He cried out as they threatened to suffocate him, flying into his eyes and ears and nose. When eventually they gave up their torment, he wiped the sweat from his face, turned and made his way up the stone steps. Sarah sobbed until she thought her chest would split. Thoroughly exhausted from grief she fell into a deeply troubled sleep.

* * *

Natalie glanced across at David, noticed how he seemed to have aged over the last couple of weeks. His skin was pale and black smudges had appeared under his eyes. It was obvious that he wasn't getting enough rest. They knew so much more about the murders now. The religious connection vindicated what Natalie had said about the girls being treated reverentially. The fact that they had made so much progress only served to magnify the disaster of Mathias's escape. Everyone involved with the case was bitterly angry that somehow they had managed to snatch defeat from the jaws of victory. No one wanted to acknowledge Natalie's other prediction; that if the murderer found who he was looking for the police might never hear from him again. By all accounts he had found her.

The killing of the young constable had sent a surge of energy through everyone involved with the investigation. Thousands of police were now on high alert for Mathias's face. It was personal now. Strong enough before, by but killing their young colleague Mathias had driven their determination to a new level. Individually, officers all over the north of England and Scotland were hoping they'd find the bastard and that he would resist arrest. Not many wanted to see this one locked away.

"You know, it's interesting." Natalie said. Walter looked up but David continued gazing into the depths of his beer. It was late and he was exhausted.

"With all of the other girls," she continued, "we haven't found a single witness to their disappearance. Not one solitary person has come forth to say they saw any one of them carted off."

"So what are you saying, my dear?" Walter asked.

"Just that it's unusual. Sarah Nelson was taken in broad daylight with people everywhere. Very different."

"Or maybe not." Walter replied. "Perhaps just as many people saw the others climb into cars or whatever. It's nothing unusual so nobody notices. As William Wirt observed; The great herd of mankind pass their lives in listless inattention and indifference as to what is going on around them etc."

"He's probably right, Walter."

"Or maybe because he thinks his search is over, there was no further need for concealment." Walter added.

"Makes no difference now." David observed, looking up from his drink. "The bastard killed a young copper. He has to go down."

Despite attaining a sort of a celebrity among his colleagues for forging the links that led them to Mathias, David hadn't quite recovered from the ignominious body blow that they all felt at allowing him to slip through their fingers.

Natalie leaned over and put her arm around David's shoulders, gave him a squeeze. "And you're going to be an old copper before your time if you don't get some sleep. Come on boys, let's call it a day."

* * *

Mathias knew he was a wanted man. Although unaware of the young officer's death, he realised that his actions would be interpreted as an admission of guilt and in the minds of the police he was a serial killer on the run. He suspected also that the police would be watching the homes of the other group members. He had to be careful. For the last thirty minutes he had been monitoring the factory where Maggie worked. He was now quite confident that the police did not have it under surveillance. Checking his watch he began to walk back to his car in the underground car park. The wintry weather suited his purpose, enabling him to rug up so that only part of his face was visible. His timing was perfect and he spotted Maggie walking to the bus stop, the collar of her coat turned up against the biting wind. He pulled alongside, leaned across and opened the passenger door.

"Hi Maggie, hop in." He said.

As their eyes met he knew that the police had already contacted her. She hugged her coat around herself as if to protect herself from evil.

"Mathias, they told me..." She stammered

"Maggie, this is really important. I can't sit here with the door open. It's about Robert. Please, get in."

Maggie was torn between the person she knew and trusted, and the awful story the police had given her. The mention of Robert's name was enough to sway her judgement. She glanced up and down the street as if expecting she might be under observation and then climbed into the car. As the passenger door closed Mathias was pulling out into the traffic and melding with the afternoon rush.

* * *

Sarah opens her eyes and is immediately assaulted by a cruel headache. Above her left eye a steel lance of pain bores into her head with every heartbeat. She sits up slowly, not daring to move her head too quickly, guessing that all of the crying has triggered a migraine. She fishes around with her foot to locate her bag and then pulls out the packet of Paracetamol capsules that travel everywhere with her. Squeezing out three of the blue tablets, she washes them down with a cup of the now lukewarm coffee from the thermos before lying back down and closing her eyes.

Her stomach empty, the medication soon takes effect and the pounding starts to ease. She thinks about Maria, hopes that she hadn't been made to suffer. Strangely there are no tears this time, just a cold place in the pit of her stomach where a rage is building. Gathering up the steel cable she crosses to the wall and examines the fastening again, this time more carefully. She sees that the steel hoop to which it is attached has been screwed into the stone wall. Some sort of a plug has been inserted into a hole in the wall. She picks at it with her fingernail, it feels like hard plastic. A small pile of stone dust rose like a tiny pyramid on the floor directly under the hoop, Sarah kicks at it causing it to fan out across the floor. She grips the hoop, the shiny steel cold against her skin, and tries to rock it. She detects no movement whatsoever. Clearly she isn't going to remove this end of the cable.

Sitting back on the bed she turns her attention to the ring around her ankle. It looks home made. Sarah supposes it would have to be, it isn't something you could buy from Marks & Spencers. It's constructed from two pieces of aluminium strip about two inches wide and a quarter of an inch thick that have been bent over a cylindrical object to achieve the correct shape. Flanges were formed at each end of the strips to allow them to be bolted together. Two holes had been drilled into one half and the steel cable was inserted in one hole and then out of the other. It was crimped in the same fashion as the end attached to the wall. Sarah pulls off her shoe and sock and attempts to slip it over her foot but it won't go past her heel.

She turns it around, examining it from all sides. It looked large enough to slide off but it won't. Why not, why won't it come off? Sarah thought, puzzled. Suddenly she has an idea. She imagines it without the thick carpet that lines the inside. *That's* why it won't come off, she realises. The carpet is making the inside diameter too small. She almost doesn't dare to believe she is right but for the first time she senses a glimmer of hope.

Jumping up she snatches the knife from the stone table, licks off the remaining peanut butter and bounces back down on the bed, pulling her manacled foot into her lap. She'd already examined this knife which was all steel, looking as though it belonged to a dining setting and she'd dismissed it as a weapon. It had no sharp edges and while it was suited to spreading peanut butter it was useless for cutting, even less so for stabbing. However, it seemed to Sarah that it might be just the thing for prising the carpet away from the inside metal surface of the manacle.

Excited, she attempts to slip the knife between the metal and the carpet. It's attached with an extremely strong adhesive. She starts worrying the edge of the carpet and slowly manages to raise up a tiny corner. It's going to take time but Sarah is beginning to believe she can do it and the prospect infuses new energy into her weary body.

* * *

Mathias drove to a large multi-storey car park, circling up to one of the higher levels before sliding into a vacant spot and turning off the engine. The car was silent, Maggie was frightened.

"They said you killed a man." She said. "Breaking out of the police cell."

That's torn it, Mathias thought. "It was an accident, Maggie. I didn't mean to kill anyone but I had to get out of there. I have to find Robert."

"Why? Where is he? Is he in some kind of trouble?" She asked

"I think he's kidnapped Sarah." Mathias replied.

"What! Kidnapped Sarah? What are you saying? You know Robert, he's just a big softie. That can't be right."

"No Maggie, it *is* right, but my problem is that the police think it was me. And it gets worse. Haven't you noticed Robert behaving strangely just lately?"

Mathias saw fear rise up in Maggie's eyes.

"I have. He's got this sort of nervous thing he does, he kind of blacks out for a few seconds then he can't remember what he was saying. I think it's stress. We've all been under so much pressure since Sarah came. He's had to take time off from the hospital and I've begged him to go to the doctor but he won't go. He just won't. What can I do?"

Maggie starts to cry. Mathias leans over and takes her in his arms, allowing her to sob on his shoulder for a couple of minutes. When he pulls away she wipes her eyes and looks at him expectantly.

"This is not going to be easy for you, Maggie but I think Robert is responsible for the deaths of the girls that have disappeared over the last few months."

Maggie is dumbstruck. "Robert?" She gasps.

"Yes, the police found some sort of message from the last girl. It points to Robert in a specific way. And they've seen his car too."

"But this is all crazy! You know Robert; he's not into killing people, he always wants to save people! That's why in the Army he became a medic instead of…" She falters.

"Instead of someone like me." Mathias finishes her thought.

Maggie can't meet his eyes. "And Sarah? Why would Robert kidnap Sarah? I just don't understand."

"That's the reason I had to run, the police think it was me. We're about the same size and they have a witness for one of the killings that didn't see a face but said it was a big guy. Like Robert. And now Sarah has gone missing and they say a big guy picked her up. My name was spoken between them so they think it was me. But I *know* it wasn't me. I have to find him, Maggie. Before he hurts Sarah."

Maggie's eyes are wide with fear. "Just lately he goes out and he won't tell me where he's going." She sobbed. "I thought he was having an affair with someone but this is worse. Are you sure about this? I mean really sure?"

Mathias looked into her bloodshot eyes. "I'm sorry, Maggie, but I'm certain."

"What can I do?" She wailed.

"We need to work together. You have to be strong. This is not about Robert, he's not in control anymore, he's being used by the forces of darkness, exactly as Rachael foretold. Exactly as we expected. We just didn't anticipate that the destroyer would be one of us. But think about it, who is better placed than one of us to harm The Redeemer? Who was it that betrayed Jesus? That's right, one of his own disciples, his closest companions, and here we go again. No, this is not about Robert, this is about Sarah. If we fail her, Maggie, she will die. Nothing can be more important than this. *That's* why I had to get out of the police cell at any cost"

Maggie gasped, the full weight of the responsibility settling over her.

"Tell me what I have to do." She said.

* * *

Sarah had worked on the manacle for over an hour and had loosened half the carpet on one side. Her wrist was beginning to cramp and she had a blister on the palm of her hand from the handle of the knife. She allowed her foot to flop onto the bed and rubbed her thigh to get the blood circulating again. She needed a break. She carefully positioned the carpet so it wasn't obvious that she'd been tampering with it. Then she looked at the blade of the knife. It was badly scratched on the tip where she'd used it to scrape the metal.

What to do, she thought. If she put it back where it was before, Robert might see the scratches and realise she'd been using it for more than spreading peanut butter. If she hid it, he might notice it missing and suspect she was up to something. In the end she plunged it into the peanut butter to mask the scratches and then left it by the remains of the bread. She lay back on the bed and flexed the cramping muscles in her hand and wrist. She was about to resume her task when she heard Robert returning.

Thinking quickly, she decided to try and be neutral in her emotions. She didn't like the way he'd left without a word, it frightened her. Sarah sensed she had to try and win him back a little after screaming at him about Maria. Buy some time. As it turned out, her fears were groundless.

"Hello Sarah." He said. "How are you feeling?"

"Pretty good, Robert. What do you have there?" She asked.

As if in answer, the most wonderful aroma filled the chamber.

"Fish and chips?" She asked hopefully.

Robert placed the newspaper-wrapped parcel on the camp bed and opened it up. The smell is sensational. Sarah dragged out a thick piece of battered fish from under the bed of chips that concealed it. She can't remember food tasting this good.

"Sorry the food isn't warmer, but I had to drive a long way after collecting it from the chippo." Robert said.

"Forget it." Sarah replied with a mouth full of fish. "It tastes smashing to me."

"About before, Sarah." Robert said, a little hesitantly. "I'm sorry for storming off like that when you were upset."

"Hey, don't worry about it." Sarah said, trying to put him at ease. "It was probably my fault anyway."

"It's just that we've waited such a long time for you to arrive, Sarah, and I guess it's a huge occasion for us all."

"For you and me both!" Sarah said in what she hoped sounded like a light-hearted tone.

"Now that you've proved to us beyond all doubt who you are, we can't wait to hear what your instructions are. I'm sort of hoping that we can..."

Robert stopped. Sarah thought he looked like a man in pain. He made a strangled sort of cry and madly rubbed his face and waved his arms around his head as though he was trying to bat something away. After a few seconds of this strange behaviour he appeared to calm down. His face relaxed but his eyes were blank as if he'd just woken from a deep sleep. Sarah was alarmed to see that he'd broken out in a sweat despite the chilly air in the chamber. His face was covered in tiny beads of perspiration and before her eyes she saw dark patches appear on the font of his shirt. How can anyone sweat so much so quickly, she wondered.

"Are you okay?" She asked. "It looked like you had a bit of a turn there for a while."

Robert shook his head, attempting to clear his vision. "I'm fine. Sorry. Where were we? I've sort of forgotten what we were talking about."

Sarah decided to take a chance, to deflect the conversation away from her. She remembered some of what Mathias had told her.

"You were telling me about Rachael Telford." She said.

Robert was confused for a moment. "Was I? I guess so. Yes. Rachael had quite a lot to say about the time we live in. Quite a lot. She was determined to raise women to their proper place within society and in fact she was chosen to foretell the one who would appear in our time to finish her work."

"And what would happen to this person?" Sarah asked.

"Well, when her work was done on earth she'd be taken to heaven to be a bride for Christ. Like the Bible says."

"What is her work, exactly?"

"It's not clear from Rachael's writing what exactly she would do but she prophesied that it would strike a blow for women everywhere, helping to throw off their oppression and proving she was worthy to ride with the Lord on the white stallion."

"And when would the work be done."

"Well that's not really clear either. We just know that a destroyer would be raised up and only by the efforts of the loyal ones would her work be completed before he struck."

"And that's why you've brought me here, so I'd be safe from the destroyer?"

Robert's face beamed. "Yes, Sarah. That's exactly right. I'm so glad you see that now."

"And if the destroyer was successful?" Sarah asked. "What would happen then?"

Robert's smile vanished and he became very still. Sarah imagined she could see anger under the surface and instantly regretted her question, which had obviously touched a nerve.

"That's like asking what if Satan *had* managed to tempt our Lord into turning stones into loaves of bread or throwing himself off the temple to see if God would save him." Robert answered patiently, as though explaining it to a child. "It would be the end of the world, Sarah. Apocalypse."

Robert's eyes glazed over and Sarah feared he might be about to have another strange episode but he managed to bring it under control, like a person who needs to yawn but is able to suppress it at the cost of some facial gymnastics. Robert glanced at his watch.

"I can't stop this time. I've brought you more coffee. Next time we can have a long chat, okay?"

"Sounds good." Sarah replied, relieved.

Robert clapped his hands in delight and bounded up the stairs three at a time. Sarah flopped onto her bed, exhausted from maintaining the bizarre conversation and the masquerade of appearing friendly to someone whose eyes she wanted to gouge out.

CHAPTER 16

David glanced at the digital clock on his bedside table. The little green numbers gave him no comfort. He was on the verge of making a doctor's appointment to get some sort of medication to help him sleep, he couldn't go on much longer like this. Two thirty in the morning and he was wide-awake.

That peculiar time in the early morning when your mind's at a low ebb. The time when your confidence is at rock bottom and you wonder if you have any talent at all, wonder whether you're out of your depth. Outside he could hear the soft hiss of falling rain. Under normal circumstances the sound of the rain was almost guaranteed to send him back to sleep but these circumstances were anything but normal. In his mind he replayed the conversations that he'd had with Mathias. Revisited his interviews with witnesses at the hospital, searching for something missed, a subtle nuance that might cast a comment in a new light.

His initial feeling of triumph when Mathias had shown his true colours had been torpedoed by the catastrophe of the dead officer and the escape. The good news was they now at least knew who they were looking for, they had a name and a face at last. The bad news was that their man had turned out to be an intelligent and resourceful killer. A Special Forces soldier who had been trained to evade capture, to kill silently, and to operate alone. With the self doubt that middle of the night introspection brings, David wasn't sure they were any better off than when they were flailing about in ignorance.

The investigation had obviously switched focus as soon as the police knew their man. While they had underestimated him once, they wouldn't let it happen again. David had initially toyed with the possibility that the diversion, which allowed Mathias to escape, had been planned. Perhaps Peter Boulton had done a deal with Mathias in exchange for having Harrison killed. After spending a couple of hours with Peter who was being assessed in a psychiatric facility he abandoned that idea. The poor bugger had just been an almighty mess. Devastated that he had actually hurt an innocent person (who, it was expected, would make a full recovery) Peter was now determined to get his life back together. David hoped he'd receive a compassionate sentence when he went up before the beak.

He didn't have the same forgiveness for Mathias. Natalie's prediction that if Mathias found who he was looking for he might simply disappear, was never far from his thoughts. Also her puzzlement at the method of Sarah's abduction was nagging at the edge of his mind. He'd come to rely on her judgement and she'd been correct more often than not. She was right to point out that the M.O. didn't fit with the earlier murders but he didn't have a theory to reconcile it right now. It was like a toothache in his mind. He could live with it but it wasn't going away and he couldn't forget it.

His thoughts turning to Natalie, he asked himself why he was still lying in the bed alone. She'd certainly sent out enough signals and they had spent many very pleasurable hours together. It was time to take the relationship to the next level, he knew. But this was always the bit he feared. It made him feel like a randy teenager all over again. He sort of wished they could fast forward past the awkwardness of the first time with its uncertainty and fumbles and move on to the comfortable relaxed phase that followed. Jesus, you're a funny bugger, Orbost, he told himself. Punching his pillow into a new shape he rolled over and tried to will himself to think about nothing, hoping that sleep might rescue him from his brooding.

* * *

As David finally managed to fall asleep in the early hours of the morning, Mathias had once again completed a reconnaissance of

Maggie's flat. He was dismayed but not entirely surprised to see that the police presence had been increased. They appeared to be covering all approaches and after observing the pattern of lights at the windows he suspected that an officer might even be stationed inside. Melting into the shadows he had slipped away without detection. He had to find a way to speak with Maggie. The car was a high risk option. At his previous meeting with Maggie they had worked out a fall-back strategy involving a phone box but that was sub-optimal as well.

Mathias liked to read people's faces when they spoke with him. He trusted their faces more than the words coming out of their mouth. This morning he'd surveilled the entrance to Maggie's work from a new vantage point, not wanting to be seen twice in the same spot. He cursed under his breath as he saw Maggie arrive in a Police car that dropped her right outside the main entrance. The car waited until she was inside the building before moving off.

They were presenting him with a challenge. Mathias was well aware that under the constant watch of the police, it wouldn't be long before they had turned Maggie away from him. It was just basic psychology. After a couple of days of this she'd have sufficient doubt in her mind that she might even agree to lure him into a trap. He had to act decisively if he was to find out where Robert was holding Sarah.

* * *

Robert too was having difficulties with the increased police presence. His movements were being monitored in case he was attempting to contact Mathias. He had told them about some research he was doing into an ancient religious order. The research and the time pressure of turning it into a formal thesis made it necessary for him to travel to the library at the University at Edinburgh every couple of days. Maggie had looked at him strangely when they had spoken with the police but to her credit hadn't contradicted him and he was known at the library from previous trips so he thought he'd managed to pull it off. On the way he could spend only a limited amount of time with Sarah, as he knew they were checking to see if he arrived at the other end. The long trip was a bugger too. His only hope was that either Mathias would be recaptured or the Police would ease off when they realised he wasn't presenting a problem for them. He wasn't sure how long that would take; the police were really focussed on finding Mathias. When he spoke with them he sensed a quiet but potent determination. Surely it could only be a few days, he thought.

* * *

Sarah sat back and massaged her aching arm and hand before returning to her task. Her palm bled where the blister had burst and the skin had worn through. Even with her handkerchief wrapped around the metal handle of the knife it was still painful and laborious work. With a squeal of triumph she removes the last tough corner of carpet from the inside of the manacle. She held the carpet strip in her hand, its back still sticky with glue residue. Such a small piece for all the work that it took to liberate it from the metal. She decides that whoever made the glue should use her case as a testimonial for their product. She imagines the headline; 'Desperate prison woman takes five hours to remove small piece of carpet stuck with Brand X Megaglue.'

The moment of truth has arrived. She wriggles the manacle to the best position on her foot and then tries to slide it over her heel. It won't go. The glue still adhering to the inside of the metal is sticking to her foot. She pushes and grunts but it simply won't go far enough. Unless she tears her skin off with it, she will not be slipping it over her heel. She picks up the knife again, wincing as it naturally falls into the damaged part of her palm and struggles to scrape the glue away. After a few minutes she gives up, her efforts are simply moving the glue around. So near and yet so far. She uses the knife as a sort of shoe-horn but only succeeds in cutting her heel. She re-examines the blade and is surprised to discover that her scraping has sharpened the end of the blade to the extent that it might actually cut something. Or someone, she reminds herself.

Sarah scans the dimly lit chamber looking for inspiration. Her eyes settle on the jar of peanut butter. An idea leaps into her mind and she snatches it from the improvised table. Plunging her index finger into the creamy substance, she smears it over the heel of her foot. She spreads some inside the manacle as well for good measure, offering a silent prayer of thanks that it's the smooth variety and not the one with chunks of peanut. Sarah takes a deep breath and pushes. The manacle moves further than before but again stops. The upper edge of the metal is now cutting painfully into the top of her foot. She pushes again and it moves a quarter of an inch farther down her heel but increases its pressure on the top.

Her anger escalates at getting only this far after so much effort. It's infuriating to be so close. She decides that this thing is coming off, end of story. Sarah grips the manacle and pushes down hard. She feels the sharp edge of the metal slicing into the top of her foot and in response she pushes even harder. A scream of pain echoes around the chamber as the manacle slides over her heel, the metal edge tearing a sizeable chunk of flesh from the top of her foot. Slippery with the peanut butter mixed with her own blood, the manacle falls out of her hand and hits the floor with a satisfying clunk.

For a moment Sarah stares down at it lying there at the side of the bed, gazes at the blood trickling down her ankle which only seconds before seemed to irreversibly anchor her to this place and her fate. Then it hits her. She is free. With a shriek, she leaps into the air, ignoring her bleeding foot. It feels so good to be mobile, no longer tied up like someone's dog. She dances a little jig in the ancient space. Then, like a fist in her chest, she is returned to reality by the severity of her surroundings. She has to get out of here before Robert returns.

Hurriedly she pulls on her shoe and sock, slides the now-sharp knife into the back pocket of her jeans and ventures up the stairs. It seemed weird to be able to go beyond the eighth step and she has a moment of apprehension as she realises she doesn't know her way out. How hard can it be? She asks herself as she continues up the steps. She checks her watch, it's eight thirty, should be light by now.

When Sarah arrives at the top of the stone staircase, it is almost totally dark. The feeble light from her chamber doesn't penetrate this far. She stands very still and listens. She can hear rain falling. With her hands against the wall she moves around the room in which she's found herself. As she progresses along the walls she realises that passages lead off in at least two other directions. For one terrible moment she can't remember where the steps are. She concentrates all of her energy on bringing her breathing under control, willing herself to calm down, breathe deliberately, count them in and then out. Sarah retraces her steps and senses the top of the stairs with her toe. Looking down she can make out the almost imperceptible light from her chamber. It suddenly occurs to her that it might actually be eight thirty at night and not the morning as she'd first thought. Perhaps she'd lost track of the time. That would explain how she could hear the rain but yet there was no light. She trudges down the stone steps and sits heavily on the bed.

Without a torch, she will never find her way out tonight. In fact there exists a real danger that she will become lost, the place is obviously larger than she'd imagined. Without a torch she couldn't even hide from Robert. Her heart sinks as she realises that she's stuck here for another night.

Panic flares as the realisation dawns that Robert might return before morning. She rips off her shoe and sock, wincing as the sock comes away, tearing the congealing blood from the wound on her foot. She thrusts her foot into the sticky manacle. It won't go. With mounting horror she realises a fundamental truth; just because she has pulled it off, it doesn't necessarily follow that it will go back on the same way. Desperately she examines the geometry of her foot, the way the heel is shaped in relation to her ankle. She knows it's hopeless. She will never get the manacle back over her heel. Not with a bathtub full of peanut butter. Sarah is in trouble. Whichever way she looks at it, she can't risk Robert finding her like this, can't risk that he'll be angry with her for trying to escape. He is too big, too strong. And what is even more worrying, she was starting to think that he was too mentally unstable.

* * *

Mathias waits in the shadows of the laneway at the back of Maggie's flat. Dressed in a black tracksuit and beanie he is almost invisible. He thinks back to his prearranged phone call with Maggie earlier in the evening. Something had been wrong, he could hear it in her voice. She no longer fully believed him. The police had managed to turn her more quickly than he had estimated. When he'd questioned her about Robert's movements she was evasive, vague. He knew she was lying. He was troubled by Robert's trips to Edinburgh; this was something to be sorted out sooner than later. He had to make Robert tell him. Once again he was being forced into taking drastic action to uncover the truth, to complete his part of the drama. A drama in which he could no more deny his role than could Sarah. Earlier in the evening he'd retrieved certain items that he'd stowed in a deposit box in anticipation of this day. With any luck the whole thing ought to be over in the next twenty four hours.

He remains absolutely still; the only sign of movement is the occasional blink of his eyes. After ten minutes he hears the click of a lighter and sees the reflected glow of a cigarette. Mathias knew if you waited long enough they always gave themselves away. The man was approximately twenty feet to his left, sitting in a folding chair in Maggie's tiny garden with his back against the fence about four feet in from the gate. Obviously using the break in the rain as an opportunity to sit outside and smoke. Stealing along the cobbled lane on the outside of his soles, Mathias moves as silently as a shadow until he is standing right behind the man. He can hear the officer's breathing on the other side of the fence. Hears a tiny asthmatic wheeze as the man takes a drag on his cigarette and draws the smoke deep into his lungs.

Mathias takes a small pebble from his jacket pocket and flips it down the laneway, making a furtive scuttling noise. The man on the other side of the fence stops breathing. Listens. Mathias hears the creak of the chair as he stands, senses him move to the fence and then pause. Mathias flicks another pebble at the opposite wall as he unsheathes a Gerber hunting knife with a black anodised eight-inch blade. He crouches so he's well below the top edge of the wooden fence while staying as close as possible to it. Mathias looks up and waits. Two hands appear above him from the other side of the fence and then a chin as the man uses the top of the fence to pull himself up for a look.

With explosive speed, Mathias uses the power in his legs and arms simultaneously to drive the blade of the knife upwards through the soft skin of the man's jaw, through his tongue and the roof of his mouth and deep into his brain. The power of the blow lifts the policeman off the ground and for a short while his feet jerk and spasm as Mathias bears his weight on the hilt of the knife. The man twitches for a few seconds more and then his body relaxes. No sound escapes his lips. Mathias holds him there a moment longer and then allows him to slump down against the fence. He steps through the gate, removes his knife and wipes it on the officer's sleeve before propping him back in his folding chair as if asleep. He crosses quickly to the back door and retrieves the key that he knows Maggie keeps under the third potted plant from the left. Unlocking the door he steps inside.

There is no sign of an officer in the flat but upstairs he can hear a bath filling. He takes the steps three at a time. He finds Maggie in her bedroom, her dressing gown wrapped around her, laying out her clothes for the morning. Robert is nowhere to be seen. Mathias crosses the bedroom in two strides and grabs Maggie from behind as she begins to turn. His powerful right hand clamps her mouth shut and her arms are pinned by her sides.

"Are there police in the house?" He hisses. "Shake or nod your head. Lie to me and I'll break your neck."

He feels the muscles in her neck attempt to move her head from side to side. Negative.

"Is Robert here?" Negative again.

"I'm going to take my hand away, if you scream it will be the last sound you ever make. Understand?" Maggie nods as vigorously as she can.

Mathias allows his hands to fall away and turns her around to face him. Her dressing gown gapes open revealing one of her heavy breasts and she quickly gathers it tightly around her. Her mouth opens in surprise as she recognises Mathias. He is the last person she expects to be behind the cruel voice and rough hands. She sits down on the bed, not speaking, her eyes wide.

"I'm sorry to be rough with you but I don't have much time. Where is Robert?"

She starts to tell him that Robert hasn't come home tonight and she isn't sure where he is but Mathias slaps her hard, almost knocking her off the bed. Maggie is terrified. It was like some evil force had taken control of Mathias's body. Outwardly she recognised him as the man she knew and respected but he was behaving like a monster. She would never have believed he could strike a woman, let alone her, his friend. Tears of hurt and confusion rolled down her face.

"Look at me." Mathias said, his voice like splintering glass. Robert has been going to Edinburgh, we know that. On the way to Edinburgh there is place, a special place. I'd like you to tell me if by some chance Robert knows about it."

Maggie can't meet his eyes and he knew. His place. Betrayal.

"How did he find out?" Mathias asks, his voice chilling in its complete lack of emotion. Maggie is so petrified she doesn't know if she can speak. She feels a warm trickle down her leg as she loses control of her bladder.

"He... he followed you there once." She whispered.

"When?"

"A long time ago I think. Before we met. When he was younger he said. He wanted to know where you were going, thought you might have discovered something valuable in the hills."

"Did he take you there?" Mathias asked, his eyes never leaving Maggie's face.

Maggie shook her head energetically. "He wouldn't, he swore me to secrecy. Robert just wanted to know what was there in case anything happened to you." A tear flew off and landed on Mathias's cheek. He ignored it. "I've never told anyone. It was his little secret."

"Not even the police?" He asked.

"No, I haven't thought about it in years. Why? Is it important?" She sobbed, burying her head in her hands.

"And did you let Robert know that you had told me he'd started going to Edinburgh again in the last few days?"

Maggie just nodded her head, unable to raise her eyes.

"How did he react?"

"He looked very frightened." Maggie whispered, not raising her head.

"And since then he hasn't come home?"

Maggie shook her head, her body shaking as she sobbed, tears dripping onto the bedroom carpet.

Silently Mathias reached into the black canvas shoulder bag he was carrying and pulled out the silenced .22 calibre Ruger Mk II semiautomatic pistol.

"And in those days two will be raised up, one to protect and one to destroy." Mathias whispered.

As Maggie cradled her head in her hands, her body trembling, he touched the suppressor to the front of her head. Before she had a chance to react he pulled the trigger. There was a small pop, not much louder than a book falling over on a bookshelf and Maggie fell back on the bed. Out of habit more than necessity, Mathias picked up the ejected shell casing still hot from the pistol and dropped it into his pocket. He went downstairs, slipped out of the back door and melted into the night.

CHAPTER 17

Sarah was becoming desperate. She tried every possibility she could think of in an attempt to hide the fact that she was no longer attached to the cable. Her problem was that the manacle was so damn big and bulky it was hard to conceal. She tried sitting on the bed with it under her legs but she could only last a couple of minutes before the sensation of it cutting into her was more than she could endure, leaving her rubbing her ankle in pain.

"Shit!" She said aloud, throwing the manacle to the floor. It was like the stupid thing was destined to be her undoing, even now when she had the bloody thing off. She couldn't disguise it and with no torch she couldn't hide. That didn't leave many options. Suddenly Maria's face floated into her mind and she fought to hold back the tears. She felt the pressure of the knife, still in the back pocket of her jeans and, unbidden, the seed of an idea sent out a tentative shoot into her consciousness. Maybe simply running away from this man isn't enough, she thought. Maybe that's way too easy for him. As she considered this radical idea, a determination that she'd never known began to take over her mind, bulldozing doubts before it. She started to think not in terms of *could* I, but instead, *how* could I.

Sarah looked around, weighing her options. Her eyes fell on the manacle at her feet, the symbol of her captivity. She picked it up and walked to the stone staircase that led down to her chamber. It was steep, each step small, as though designed for tiny feet. The point where the steps disappeared into the tunnel that led toward the upper chamber was well above head height and the side of the staircase opposite the wall had no handrail, as would be the case in modern buildings. A misstep to the side could result in a fall of about ten feet. Sarah walked up the first few steps, her hands exploring the intricate carvings and shapes set into the wall. Retrieving the manacle, she dropped it behind a kind of stone lattice that had been cut into the wall next to the fifth step.

The steel cable slipped down beside the lattice and she was able to hook the manacle over a small stone animal. Effectively the cable was now solidly anchored to the side of the step, the manacle hidden in shadow. Sarah laid the cable along the step, brushing some of the dust to cover it. In the angle formed by two steps the cable was well hidden.

She walked to the other end of the cable still secured to the wall and yanked it hard. Raising a small cloud of dust, the cable sprang from its resting position and snapped taught about two feet above the fifth step. Pulled at the right time, someone coming down the steps would be tripped and, with nothing to hold on to, might fall down the rest of the steps to the stone floor. She took the knife from her pocket. Thrust into someone's eye, or neck, it could be lethal. It could work.

She climbed back to the cable and tucked it into position against the crack of the step. Walking to a point a few steps above the cable she checked her work. Unlikely anyone would notice the trap. The stairs were so small and steep that she had to concentrate herself to avoid falling. The question is, could she pull on the cable at the right moment? Timing would be everything. She picked her way down the steps, intending to have another dry run and suddenly the decision was taken out of her hands. Above her she heard the sound of Robert returning. He sounded panicked, yelling her name even before he got to the top of the stairs. Shouting something about having to move. To pack up and move.

Sarah had no time to prepare herself. With her heart pounding she ran back to the wall and grabbed the cable with both hands. Now or never, she thought. Do or die. Robert came down the stairs quickly, agitated, speaking in a hurry. She heard his voice getting louder. Saw the light of his torch dancing crazily around the walls, animating the stone faces that stared down at her. Abruptly his legs came into view.

Blue jeans, wet at the bottom. White trainers. Almost in slow motion she saw him lift his left leg to take another step. She pulled on the cable with all her strength.

The effect was far more devastating then she'd hoped. The cable snagged Robert's leg and his forward momentum was irresistible. He tried to grab the wall but only succeeded in tearing off a fingernail and unbalancing himself even more. He began falling sideways, over the edge of the steps. He lost his grip on the torch he was carrying and it fell, bouncing down the steps, the light stabbing randomly into the gloom. The cable was wrenched out of Sarah's hands as much of Robert's weight was transferred to the wire. The force pulled Sarah forward and before she could put her hands out to protect herself she smashed into the stone wall, her forehead skidding off, driving grit under the skin.

Robert continued to pitch forward, instinctively shooting out his right hand to protect himself. His arm snapped above the wrist as it contacted the edge of the step, spinning him around. With an obscene crunch, the small of his back collided with the bottom two steps, his arms flailing at his sides. Sarah gasped in horror as, for an instant, his back was bent at a grotesque angle. He appeared to bounce off the edge of the steps, land face down on the stone floor in a cloud of dust before rolling onto his back.

The chamber is silent. Grey dust clouds the air. Sarah rubs her head where she'd collided with the wall and is relieved to find only a bad graze. Already a lump was rising above her eye. She pulls the knife from her pocket and advances on Robert's motionless form. Her heart races and she's panting. The act of stabbing someone now takes on an entirely different reality from when she'd rehearsed it in her mind. She bends over him, cautious that he might be simply feigning unconsciousness. Robert opens his eyes. Sarah screams and jumps backwards, holding the knife out in front of her. Robert doesn't move.

His eyes blink once or twice and his chest rises and falls. She sees his gaze follow the cable from the wall across to the steps before returning to her face. A tear rolls down his cheek. Sarah is surprised to feel a pang of guilt. The jubilation she'd expected to experience if her plan was successful simply isn't there. Staring down at the broken man lying at her feet she felt as though she might be sick.

"Sarah." Robert whispers. He seemed to be having trouble getting enough air.

"Sarah, I can't move." He said. A second tear tracked through the fine dust settling on his face. "Why, Sarah? Why did you do it?"

"You killed Maria." Sarah said. "You chained me up like a dog."

Robert closes his eyes for a couple of seconds. "I didn't kill Maria." He said. "I just had to distract her for a while. To get you away. She's probably home. By now." He closes his eyes again, the effort of speaking was obviously costing him dearly. "I'm sorry you felt. Like a dog."

"I don't believe you." Sarah said. Confused.

"I need to tell you something." He said. "Please, Sarah."

She moved closer to him. "I have a knife." She said, immediately feeling foolish.

"Sarah you have to get out. Of here. Get out. Quickly." He gasped, his voice fading.

Sarah knelt by his side. "Why?"

"Mathias is coming. For you. To kill. You." His breath in short bursts now.

"Mathias?" Sarah gasped. "Coming here?"

"Listen to me." Robert said, his eyes blazing. "You have. To move. Run or hide. Not the steps. Just get. Out. Now."

"Why is Mathias coming here?" She asks, attempting to make sense of his words.

"Because. He is. The." He was now struggling to breathe at all. His voice almost inaudible.

"He is the what?" Sarah shouted, seeing him fade before her eyes.

"Destroyer!" Robert hissed. "Run!"

Sarah jumps to her feet and looks desperately around her, fear slowing her mind. She can hear Robert's breath dwindling to intermittent stabs. She spies the torch in the corner of the chamber, still shining, and snatches it up. It's heavy and encased in black rubber. Five tiny but incredibly bright lights cast a broad white beam. She scoops up her bag, stuffing the muesli bars inside because it makes no sense to leave them behind. She crouches next to Robert. He's stopped breathing. She puts her ear to his mouth but hears nothing. His eyes are still open and she supposes that she should close them but she can't bring herself to touch his face. She feels bad about that. She fumbles through his coat pockets and her fingers close around his mobile phone. "Thank God." She whispers.

Sarah steps back, pauses for a moment, so many thoughts whirling around in her head. A dead man lies at her feet. A real man of flesh and blood that only minutes before had been alive and, despite the hatred she'd felt for him, seemed genuine in his wish to protect her. And she, Sarah Nelson, through forethought and action had ended his life. Had killed sweet Maggie's boyfriend. She felt hot bile rise into her throat, her body began to shake. Her legs became rubbery and she sat on the edge of the bed, her eyes never leaving Robert's broken body. She concentrated on her breathing.

What if he had been telling the truth? Extremely weird and unorthodox in his methods, sure. But if he'd been truthful and if he hadn't hurt Maria, then she'd just killed a disturbed but otherwise innocent man. A man who saw himself as her protector. And she had planned in advance to do exactly that. To kill him, to stab him in the eye with the knife if she had to. It sounded like murder to her. Sarah felt the crushing weight of the enormity and irreversibility of what she'd done. And if Robert was right, Mathias was coming right now to kill her. Was she supposed to murder him too? Just in case Robert was telling the truth?

In that moment she decided that she couldn't do it. She wouldn't do it. She wouldn't attempt something that might have such ruinous consequences again without absolute certainty that Mathias meant her harm. For all she knew Robert might have been lying to the end and Mathias could be her rescuer. No, what she'd done she couldn't undo but she wouldn't end another man's life like this. Gasping for breath on a cold stone floor. She couldn't live with it. She wasn't even sure she could live with what she'd already done.

The decision made, she felt her resolve returning. She had to escape. If Mathias is a killer, the police would catch him eventually. Her only priority was to get out of this place and hide from Mathias until she was sure he meant her no harm. She'd deal with Robert's death when this nightmare was over. She'd tell the truth about what she'd feared, drugged and tied up in this place as well as what she'd done and she'd live with the consequences. That's how it would be.

Not the steps, he'd said. She looked around the chamber; saw the electricity wire snaking off into the darkness. As good a path as any, she thinks.

* * *

The area around Maggie's flat was cordoned off with police tape. Tied to fences and signposts it formed a perimeter encircling more than a dozen men and women. Neighbours stood together in small groups, watching, speculating. Educated by years of television crime, the police tape evoked simultaneous feelings of curiosity, dread and insecurity in the minds of the onlookers. On the other side of the tape the faces of the officers were grim, businesslike, determined. Once again they had been made to feel inadequate. Made to feel that they'd failed in their duty to serve and protect. Particularly to protect.

Once more they had underestimated this man, for there was no doubt in any of their minds who's hand was behind this carnage. And another of their brethren had been killed. No, *killed* wasn't the right word to describe his death, for them the word was too impersonal to adequately capture what had happened here. Maggie had been killed. Executed. Their man had been *Slaughtered*. This time a man close to his retirement, a family man well liked and known to most. A man not unlike any of them. This same thought passed through the minds of almost every person working the scene, like a small zephyr of wind that whispered in their ear before gliding to the next person.

* * *

As the police made their grisly discoveries, Mathias arrived at his special place. A place that he'd assumed was known only to him. He had made the drive practically on autopilot as his mind calculated and weighed the options available and the possible scenarios that might develop. He still struggled to understand how Robert had managed to follow him to this place undetected. Even more amazing was how he had been able to find the entrance to the upper chamber. In his mind, there was only one explanation. Robert must have observed his car leave the road, must have pulled over and then walked to the top of one of the surrounding hills. It would have been pure luck for him to see Mathias leave the chamber. The number of gullies and hills was too great for it to be otherwise. Once the spot was pinpointed, Robert would have scrambled down and hunted until he found the entrance.

Begrudgingly Mathias had to admit that it was quite a feat. In the army, Robert had been a medic and Mathias wouldn't have credited him with the skills to pull this off. No matter, Robert's betrayal would cost him his life and then knowledge of the tomb would once again be secure.

Mathias stopped his vehicle in one of the several spots that he employed when coming here. Robert's car was fifty yards away in full view, the white paint almost luminous in the weak moonlight. He considered his options. He could wait for the pair to return, pick them off with the rifle hidden in his car as they hurried along. Too noisy, he decided. He also didn't like the idea of someone else controlling the timing. If it was daylight when they arrived back at the car things became more complicated.

He would do what he did best; take the fight to the enemy, get in close, strike hard and then disappear. Mathias walked to Robert's car and tried the door handle. Unlocked. Sometimes it was just too easy. He popped the bonnet and, working quickly by the light of a tiny torch held in his mouth, removed a pair of cables forming part of the electrical system, rolling them up and slipping them into his coat pocket. He eased the bonnet closed, shouldered his canvas bag and began walking.

* * *

Sarah followed the cable as it snaked along the wall. It led her to a passageway that angled left, her torch unable to penetrate to the far end. She felt uneasy at leaving the familiar surroundings of what she'd come to think of as the prison chamber. The ceiling of the narrow passageway was arched and at the point where it left the chamber, small stone creatures reached out with twisted claws, attempting to snag the hair of anyone passing beneath them. She ducked her head to avoid getting too close to their horrid little hands. As she walked down the passageway, her feet raising fine clouds of dust, the noise from the generator grew louder. Archways on both sides provided access to small rooms.

The same menacing creatures clustered above each doorway seemingly to discourage entry. She shone her torch into the first one she passed. The centre of the chamber contained what she guessed to be a large stone sarcophagus. Children prayed at either end and a knight in full armour lay on top, his hands clasped prayerfully. Sarah hurried past, not really wanting to know what the other rooms held.

Sarah estimated the length of the passageway to be about fifty yards. The final archway led to a small chamber, which housed the generator and the end of the electricity cable. It was much louder in here. Next to the generator stood fuel cans, five red and three green. The sort of cans that wannabe four-wheel-drivers clamped to the back of their trucks along with shovels and jacks that looked as though they could lift an airliner.

Sarah examined the machine. Where the electrical cable connected, a black switch in the centre of a yellow plastic panel appeared to be the only control. She took hold of it and twisted it to the right. The noise stopped and the lights died. While the light had been comforting, the drone of the generator could mask the sound of someone approaching and she didn't want Mathias sneaking up on her. She shone the torch over the machine, looking for a way to disable it permanently. It appeared to be well protected and solid. She noticed a small plastic toolbox next to the fuel cans and, flipping it open, spotted a set of wire cutters with red plastic-coated handles.

She found what she assumed to be a wire on the side of the machine and cut through it easily. Fuel began running out in a small trickle causing Sarah to step back hurriedly. It wasn't what she had expected but she figured that the bleeding machine was mortally wounded anyway. She tossed the wire cutters back into the toolbox and began to retrace her steps.

Sarah was about to step back into the prison chamber when she heard footsteps at the head of the stairs. She froze. She heard the sound of someone coming down the steps. Without daring to breath she backed into the passageway and slipped into the first room she came to. She almost screamed as one of the grotesques brushed her head with its evil little monkey claw. She clicked off the torch and pressed her back to the wall, closing her eyes.

Mathias walked halfway down the steps. Robert's body came into view as did the tripwire. A smile played at his lips as he reconstructed the chain of events. Sarah had saved him some effort and done a pretty good job of it too. He wouldn't have thought she had the bottle to go for this sort of thing. He was impressed. He walked down the remaining steps and placed his hand on Robert's face. Cool. He figured Sarah could have had anything up to a couple of hours to hide. He looked around the chamber and didn't see the torch he was certain Robert would have carried. Knowing Robert it would be some newfangled long life LED torch where the batteries lasted for days, he thought. Sarah would have it now.

"Sarah!" He yelled. The word probed the passageways and chambers before returning to him in an echo.

"I know you're in here. I've come to take you home. You've already dealt with the killer so you're safe now. Let's go."

Sarah was torn. Who to believe. Part of her wanted to run to Mathias and throw herself into his arms. Let him rescue her. But she wasn't sure. What if Robert had been telling the truth? The more she considered it the more unlikely it seemed for a dying man to be telling lies. What was to be gained? And before she'd tripped him he was agitated, he knew Mathias was coming. But on the other hand, if he *was* a killer he would have wanted to flee with her, particularly if he thought his hiding place had been discovered. And he had said earlier that he'd killed Maria, hadn't he? She couldn't remember his exact words.

"Come on Sarah! Let's get you home. Your mum and dad are sick with worry."

Suddenly she was sure. If he knew where she was and had come to rescue her, not knowing Robert was dead, why hadn't he told the police? Why wasn't a detective calling her? Surely they would have the place covered, knowing they had a killer trapped inside with a hostage? She decided to stay put.

Mathias walked back up and sat on the top step. He flicked the beam of his torch back and forth across Robert's foot that was just visible to him. Weighed his options. He was certain that Sarah was inside somewhere. He'd spent countless nights attempting to map this place and even he hadn't managed to explore all of it. It was massive and labyrinthine. He also knew that the probability of him finding Sarah down there was certainly much lower than the probability that the police helicopters would find his or Robert's vehicles once dawn broke.

He made a decision. His best option given limited choices. It wasn't ideal as it didn't give him the certainty that his professionalism usually required. It also saddened him in a way. This place had served him well for almost two decades and on more occasions than the police with their plodding methods and facile processes would ever know. In fact it was being led to this place that had confirmed his calling. He had been guided, not to a church but to a tomb. It had struck him as an almost pure truth with its sublime simplicity. His military training, really his whole life had been building up to that moment in time when he accepted without question the path he would follow. He was well aware that the voice that energised and motivated him was not God's. There always had to be two sides and even as a boy he'd been more comfortable in the dark.

But, sad or not, his decision was the only thing that made sense and you had to admit, Mathias thought to himself, it had a certain irony to it. And anyway, whichever way you added it up, when this was over he would have to leave this place forever. He knew there were other groups following Rachael's teachings, he'd communicated with them often over the years, always on the alert. Maybe it's time for a change of scenery, he told himself. He'd even heard of a small group in New Zealand. A warm climate would be a welcome relief. He turned his mind back to the task at hand. His greatest accomplishment so far.

There was only one way in and out. Years ago he'd been surprised to realise this but if there was another entrance he hadn't been able to find it despite hundreds of hours spent searching. He unzipped his canvas bag and removed a piece of kit that he'd assembled for use as a diversion in his assault on Maggie's flat but hadn't needed due to the inadequacy of the officer on watch. A vague smell of marzipan filled the tiny upper chamber. Moving slowly and deliberately, he placed the device above the stone lintel holding back the earth over the tiny entrance. A small sliding switch armed the device. No tell-tale lights blinked, no numbers began counting down, the situation inside the entranceway simply escalated from risky to very dangerous. Ducking through the hole he emerged outside where a light drizzle had begun to fall.

Mathias worked his way down the gully for about fifty yards before pulling a small black object from the bag on his shoulder. A remote trigger, it looked like a cross between a garage door opener and a walkie-talkie. He extended the metal antenna, switched the unit on and pressed a single button. There was a deep rumble underground and the earth trembled with the power of the blast. Part of the hill collapsed and boulders bounced down the slope filling in a portion of the steep gully. The area was sufficiently remote that the sound would draw little attention. Once the dust settled anyone observing the hill would assume a small landslide brought on by the winter rains.

Mathias retracted the antenna and slipped the trigger back into his bag before his final task, ensuring the disappearance of the vehicles.

CHAPTER 18

The percussive thump of the explosion slams into Sarah's body, driving the breath from her lungs. Despite being some distance from the source of the blast she is battered to her knees by the shock wave inside the chamber. The air is thick with choking and blinding dust and something is wrong with her hearing, it's like she has her head underwater. In the distance she can hear a bell ringing, like a fire alarm. It takes a few moments for her to realise that the ringing is coming from inside her head. Coughing and spitting, she pulls her coat over her head and makes a kind of tent for her face.

She curls up and lays on the cold stone floor, her breath coming in short bursts, her mouth gritty with the taste of stone dust and decay. For what seemed to Sarah like hours but was only about twenty minutes she lays motionless on the hard surface, waiting for the ringing in her ears to subside, concentrating on her breathing, doing nothing to stir the fine particles. The dust gradually settles over her huddled form. After a few minutes she is indistinguishable from the statues and monuments around her.

* * *

A massive manhunt is now underway. Roadblocks are in place across Northumbria. The problem facing the authorities is that this most North-easterly of England's extremities constituted a vast area overlaid with moorland, ruins, castles and wilderness. Hadrian's Wall, built by the Romans in about 120 AD snaked through the rugged treeless hills and served as a constant reminder of the landscape's antiquity. Evidence of Viking savagery can be found up and down the coast. A man has lots of places to hide in country like this.

The remainder of Mathias's group, confused and frightened have been moved temporarily to safer locations. Robert simply hasn't returned and grave fears are held for his safety.

Police helicopters and fixed wing aircraft patrol the skies at all times and copies of Mathias's head shot have been circulated to stations, tourist attractions, car rental depots, airports, boat hiring businesses, shops, libraries, really anywhere people are likely to gather. An unprecedented reward has been posted for information leading to his apprehension. A grim faced Chief Constable has appeared on television, urging people to be on the alert for anything out of the ordinary and not to pick up hitchhikers under any circumstances.

Farmers in isolated areas are warned to keep their barns and sheds secured and to report immediately any incidence of stolen food, vehicles or broken locks. Long meetings are held with Special Forces personnel and the killer's training is dissected and analysed in an attempt to predict where he might go or what methods he might employ to evade capture. While keen to help, the general consensus of the SAS trainers, much to the anger and frustration of the detectives, is that if he didn't want to be found he wouldn't be found. End of story.

* * *

His slippered feet propped up on the coffee table; David sat alone and in darkness. Occasionally sipping from the cup of tea he cradles against his chest, his mind actively scanning the conversations he's had with Mathias. Thinking back to the control that he demonstrated, how only once or twice he allowed a small chink in the facade. There was something that gnawed at David from their last interview. He thought back to the moment when Mathias had closed his eyes, had gone blank. He knew that some certainty, some sort of realisation had struck him at that point. He ran the conversation back and forth in his mind as if forwarding and reversing a tape recording, trying to nail down something that might provide a clue. Mathias had been protesting that he hadn't abducted Sarah. Pointing out how different the M.O. was.

No that wasn't quite right. He was pointing out the stupidity of not giving himself an alibi. The police knew the M.O. was different, Mathias as the killer also knew but he was too smart to say so. Instead he banged on about how stupid he would have to be, allowing his face to be seen, snatching her in a public place and so on. Then, in answer to David's taunt, he reminded them that he hadn't stuck his religious views down anyone's neck. Then he stopped. That was the point at which something hit him. David took a sip of his tea, sensing he was close to something but not knowing what it was.

An inept abduction, and Mathias's religious views. That was the significant pairing. Something linking the two, or connected with both. These two factors had been joined in some way by Mathias. Suddenly David sat upright, his tea sloshing into his lap. What if he had been telling the truth? It *was* a stupid and risky abduction from the killer's perspective. Messy and amateurish, not worthy of a professional, but it *did* have a religious connection. It wasn't Mathias but it *was* someone with the same religious views. Someone known to Sarah. Someone whose physical description matched Mathias. David began recalling the interviews he'd conducted with other members of Mathias's group, and immediately it hit him. Robert!

David leapt to his feet and grabbed the phone, his tea forgotten, punching in Walter's number despite the lateness of the hour.

* * *

Sarah cautiously poked her head out from under the coat. Tiny avalanches of stone dust cascaded like grey liquid from her shoulders as she slowly eased herself upright. Her throat was scratchy and dry; her nose caked with the fine powder that blanketed her underground world. She could taste the ancient stone at the back of her throat.

Switching on the torch, she was glad to see that most of the heavy dust had settled. What remained hung like a fog in the air. Everything in the chamber appeared as before.

She climbed gingerly to her feet, wincing at the pain in her knee. She couldn't remember how she'd injured it, there was a blank page in her memory from just before the blast until she was on the ground sheltering under her coat and trying not to choke to death. She flexed her leg a couple of times and winced, sore but manageable. She did need some painkillers though.

Sarah poured the dust from her handbag and remembered with alarm that she now had none of her medication left and only three painkillers. She flexed the leg again and decided to put up with it for the time being, conserve the painkillers. Not having her medication frightened her. The prospect of having to manage without it for an extended period was unnerving. She'd been on medication of one sort or another since puberty and she wasn't sure what would happen if she suddenly stopped. She knew it couldn't be good. The last thing she needed in this place was to start hearing voices. The thought added new urgency to her plight.

Sarah made her way back to the chamber in which she had been imprisoned and was stunned at the transformation. Her torch illuminated the fine dust particles still suspended in the air, adding an otherworldly glow to the scene. Not only was everything covered in dust, giving the impression that it had been turned to stone, but a vast pile of dark brown earth had tumbled down the steps, partially filling the chamber. Only Robert's head and shoulders were visible from under the mound. The stairs themselves were totally buried. It would be impossible to enter or exit from that way again.

Conscious of her thirst she began pushing earth from the top of her stone table and managed to rescue the thermos, dented and filthy but intact. The peanut butter was a write-off however, the glass jar having smashed into small pieces. She didn't even attempt to look for the remainder of the bread. Sarah brushed the thermos clean and wiped the cup on her sleeve. It was about half full with lukewarm coffee. She used the first mouthful as a rinse, spitting it out into the dust where it immediately turned into little balls of mud. She drank half of what was left in one huge draught. She desperately wanted the rest but she forced herself to put the stopper back and replace the lid.

With a flash of inspiration she ran to the bucket of water next to the bird bath. It was now a soup of stone dust and earth. The disappointment of losing the water was crushing. She dragged the blanket from the bed, taking care to disturb the dust as little as possible and wrapped it around her shoulders before taking stock of her position. Six muesli bars, a quarter of a thermos of coffee, three painkillers, one blanket. And a mobile phone! Her spirits leapt as she realised that she still had Robert's phone in her pocket.

Hurriedly she switched it on, watching the tiny display by the light of the torch. Relieved to find that Robert didn't have a PIN number enabled, she waited for the phone to complete its power-up sequence. The first indicator to appear was the battery, almost full! Then the signal. Nothing. Not even one little bar. She supposed it wasn't surprising considering how far underground she must be. For one mad second she wanted to hurl the stupid phone across the chamber. Instead she closed her eyes and counted to ten. When I get out of this place I'll use this damn phone to call for help, she promised herself. With a sigh she turned it off to conserve the batteries and shoved it back into her pocket. Sitting down on the bed she turned off the torch for the same reason while she thought about her next course of action.

The chamber was absolutely dark. Not the kind of dark that exists in cities where streetlights and windows always provide low-level illumination. The darkness in the chamber was total, the blackness all-consuming, oppressive. Sarah had never in her life experienced such an incredible absence of light. It was as though a great weight was pressing down on her. She was gripped by an almost overwhelming urge to snap the torch back on. To verify that she still existed. As was her habit when stressed, she closed her eyes and concentrated on her breathing. In, count. Out, count.

A seemingly dislocated scent came to her. The smell of the sea. Concentrating, she wasn't sure if she'd really smelled it anew or simply remembered the smell. Sitting very still she thought she could almost hear the waves although her hearing was still somewhat deadened from the blast so she couldn't be sure. It certainly sounded like the sea. She pushed the distraction aside and forced herself to concentrate on her current situation. Her immediate problem was that she didn't know the real intent behind the cave-in. Was Mathias attempting to bury her in here forever or was he simply blocking an escape route so he could approach from another direction and trap her? She had no way of knowing. What she *did* know however, was that before the explosion she had felt a breeze that must have been coming from outside. She knew also that if she stayed in this spot she would die. Her torch would fade and then the blackness would take her. She didn't know if her mind was strong enough to endure that. Nobody knew she was here and she couldn't dig her way out. Sarah clicked the torch back on and decided to keep moving.

* * *

Mathias deliberated over the inconvenience presented by the two vehicles. Either vehicle was problematic as the police were certain to be looking for both. Their proximity to the tomb was also undesirable. Fortunately he knew the area well. After replacing the electrical cables he'd previously removed, and with a modicum of careful driving he was able to line Robert's vehicle up about fifty yards back from the edge of a rocky outcrop.

The North Sea surged and boiled a hundred feet below. After lowering all of the windows he located a suitable stick and wedged the accelerator to the floor before reaching his arm in through the window and flicking the automatic gear selector into drive. The car raced to the edge of the cliff and then disappeared, the engine screaming as it plummeted, its wheels struggling pointlessly for a hold on the cold night air. After retrieving his Bergen and other essential items he repeated the process with his own vehicle.

Mathias walked to the edge of the cliff and looked down. It was still several hours before dawn but sufficient light was cast by the watery moon for him to be confident both vehicles had sunk like stones. If it pained him at all to send his perfectly serviceable car to a watery grave, it didn't show on his face. He had long ago come to regard possessions as transitory. He couldn't risk driving the car and as he intended to leave the country anyway he had no further use for the vehicle. Standing on the edge of the bluff, the wind buffeting his body, he felt calm, content.

His work here was finished, time to move on. Mathias was looking forward to the freedom of a long hike with no deadlines or fixed timetable. It was time to go. In the last couple of years he'd begun to feel restless, his job routine and unchallenging, his companions dull and uninspiring. And now he had performed his primary service of neutralising The Redeemer he really could allow himself some time to relocate. It would be good to get away, to stretch himself physically, to blow the cobwebs from his mind. He could reach his destination with only minimum human contact and easily avoiding large cities. Not utilising stolen cars, main roads or ferries made for a more relaxed and leisurely pace and didn't draw attention. If it took a few weeks for him to make the trip, even better. Mathias knew well the eroding effect that time has on human vigilance.

After ensuring that the surface of the sea held no signs of oil leaks or other debris, he shouldered his heavy bergen and began a hike that he planned would take him to one of the remote fishing ports in the north east of the country, not far south of the Orkneys. Life was good.

* * *

Sarah stood at the far side of the prison chamber, her back to the blocked entrance and Robert's body. To her left, a passageway led to the disabled generator and the dust shadow left by her prostrate form on the stone floor. With the gift of clarity that hindsight bestows she regretted killing the machine. Its warm light and familiar drone would be comforting if she had to return to this room. Briefly she toyed with the possibility of a repair attempt. Her problem was that she had no way of knowing how much power remained in the torch batteries. The difference between dying lost in this underground labyrinth of decay and finding a way out pivoted on those batteries. She decided she couldn't waste them farting around with a machine about which she didn't have the first idea.

Sarah stepped out of the prison chamber and into a small and oddly shaped room where the entrances to three passageways stood facing her. These were obviously major passageways; they were higher and wider than the one leading to the generator. The room is shaped like a large wedge. She'd entered at the point of the wedge and a broad curved wall stood opposite her with the three passages spaced equally across its width. The archway above each passage was adorned with a collection of bizarre and misshapen forms. She studied them, hoping they would provide a clue to the destination of each passage. As she expected, her torch couldn't penetrate the passageways to any great depth.

The first archway featured a collection of skulls, some wearing hats, some with hairpieces made from snakes or scorpions. Sarah didn't know what they signified but she didn't like the look of them.

The second passageway was even more disturbing. Its archway contained a stone shelf on which an intricately carved set of scales had been set. The kind of scales that weigh one thing against another in shallow bowls, the scales of justice. In the left bowl, a dove sat on a nest, its feathers carefully outlined and detailed. Sarah flicked the torch to the other side and instinctively stepped back. Telling herself she was only looking at stone for God's sake, she forced herself closer to examine the object. It's a dead baby. Its abdomen has been eviscerated, liberating its intestines that spill out in a ghastly confusion. The left side of its head appears to have been violently beaten, the eye and cheek destroyed. It was disgusting, she couldn't imagine anyone spending time carving such an obscene object, much less what it was supposed to mean.

It was then that she detected a smell, how it carried to her in the deathly still air she wasn't sure but it appeared to leach out of the passageway identified by the scales. Not the smell of the sea. This was the fetid smell of the earth. The smell of dank, rotting, oozing mud. The kind of smell that coated your tongue, a smell you could taste. And underneath, a particular odour that awakened in Sarah an unpleasant childhood memory.

A walk with her father, a sheep caught in a barbed wire fence. Dead and bloated, tiny white things crawling out of its nose. And the smell that made her cry, her father picking her up in his arms and hurrying away from that place. As she studied the scales, which seemed to weigh peace against horror and obscenity, the carving began to transform before her eyes. Sarah screamed and jumped backwards, the thermos falling from under her arm, the torch almost slipping from her grasp. When she worked up the courage to look again the illusion had gone. For one awful moment, the angle of her torchlight and the design of the carving had revealed a face. A face that materialised from the known objects as they merged to create something new, something dreadful. A face of such awful disfigurement that its features evoked a primal response of loathing and fear.

In a detached way she could see how the components of the scales had formed part of the illusion but she didn't want to look too hard lest the carvings merged again to reveal the mutilated face. Her heart was still thudding in her chest as it was. Sarah wiped a sheen of perspiration from her face. This was a passageway she would not walk down. The stench that drifted from it was almost as revolting as the symbols above it. Sarah refused to contemplate what it might hold.

That left the final archway, its passageway seeming to rise at a slight angle as it disappeared into the gloom. Its adornment was simple and significantly less disturbing than those of the two alternatives. The arch contained a picture, carved into the stone wall. A man lay on his back, his arms clasped over his chest as if he was praying. Not unlike some of the other statues she'd seen reposing on the tops of stone caskets. The man seemed to float on the surface of the water. Underneath, a giant fishlike creature with huge scales and the head of a dragon, its mouth a gaping cavern ringed with fangs, swam upwards, its intention obvious. As she stood before it she was certain that this passageway was the source of both the sounds and the smells of the ocean that she'd detected earlier. Relieved that she'd been given an apparently benign option following her revulsion at the other two possibilities, she wrapped the blanket around her throat like a scarf and set off at a cautious pace along the gently climbing passage.

* * *

The wait for the library to open was torturous for David and Walter. They had spent the early hours of the morning going through Maggie's interview notes. They had confirmed Robert's trips to the library at the university in Edinburgh but had to wait until staff arrived before calling. David punched the button for the speakerphone after getting the senior person on the line and introducing himself and the reason for their inquiry.

"As I told your colleagues the other day, he visited us several times over the last little while." The University Librarian said.

"And had he visited the library before that, perhaps months or years ago?" David asked.

"Well, we do get lots of visitors, Inspector so obviously I'm not going to remember every time he arrived, but one of my staff distinctly recalls assisting him with quite a difficult reference enquiry at one stage. It would have been a couple of years back at least. She managed to find some material in the archives that interested him greatly. He then returned several times to study it, often staying until closing time."

"And when he visited last week, did he access the same material?"

"Well, interesting that you should ask. Following all of the inquisitiveness that you gentlemen have displayed toward this man, I had a conversation with my staff only yesterday and their recollections were somewhat curious."

"Please go on." David prompted, trying to hide his impatience.

"Well it appears that on these most recent visits he didn't request the original material or any material for that matter. Staff recall him as most preoccupied, constantly scanning the library, looking at his watch regularly and moving from magazines to newspapers to the computers and back. They said he appeared to be very unsettled, as though he needed to kill time, as the expression goes. He visited the cafe frequently for hot beverages. When approached and offered assistance he politely but firmly declined it. The general consensus seemed to be that he lacked any sort of purpose related to the library whatsoever. Quite at odds with his previous visits where one could have characterised his deportment as that of an engaged and dedicated amateur absorbed in his research."

"And was he seen making phone calls at any time?"

"Well, of course, Inspector we don't permit the use of portable telephones within our library, but there are telephone cubicles outside the reading areas. I can't say anyone mentioned trips to the telephones, however. I expect they would have done so because two of my more attentive staff members became quite curious regarding his behaviour after several hours had elapsed. We have to be vigilant you see, Inspector, as we do occasionally fall foul of petty theft."

"Yes, I'm sure you do. One final question. Did he meet anyone in the library?" David asked.

"Not that my staff recalled. That was their first impression, you see, that he had arranged to meet someone and they were obviously late for their appointment. But apparently not, by all accounts."

David thanked her for her time and disconnected the call.

"What do you think?" He asked Walter.

"Methinks woe betide the lad upon whose head and shoulders her wrath should descend. Petty theft indeed!" Walter allowed himself a rare chuckle. "I'm also surmising that his trips to the library represented a pretext to go somewhere else. Somewhere else on the way there or back."

"Exactly!" David exclaimed. I'd wager my left nut that he has, or had, Sarah confined somewhere between here and the University. And not too far from the normal route so as to arouse suspicion."

"I should be a bit more circumspect, old chap before wagering what may yet prove to be a useful anatomical component, but essentially I have to agree with you. Unfortunately, we're talking about a monstrously large stretch of country."

"Yes, but it's getting narrower, and that's the point." David said, his finger punching a hole in the air between them.

Walter nodded his encouragement. "Absolutely, old boy. Narrower, just as you say."

* * *

As Sarah makes her way down the long passageway and into the unknown it strikes her that Robert's torch throws out a wonderfully dispersed and soft light but it doesn't project very far. The result is a broadly illuminated area in front of her, spilling across the walls, ceiling and floor, which extends for about fifteen feet but then rapidly fades into darkness beyond. She's reminded of being a passenger in a car driving in thick fog where what's ahead on the road is concealed to the very last moment. It's not a comfortable feeling staring into the blackness and waiting for something, anything, to emerge out of it. Her hand holding the torch begins to ache and she realises she's gripping it much too tightly. She forces herself to relax and swaps the torch to the other hand. Breathe in, count, breathe out, count.

The sound of the ocean is definitely getting louder; there is no mistaking it now. The smell of the sea is wonderful. To Sarah it's the smell of life itself, salt, seaweed, rock pools, and birds. Abruptly the passageway opens out into a massive chamber, at once wonderful and terrifying with its imposing carvings and vaulted ceiling. The ocean sounds reverberate clearly to Sarah now and in parts of the chamber a light mist falls from the ceiling and blackens the enormous stone slabs of the floor.

The centre of the chamber is dominated by a large circular hole about fifteen feet in diameter. Around the edges of the hole, Sarah can see that the stone floor is wet, glistening in her torch beam. She walks to the edge and points the torch into the shaft. The sides are smooth and slick with moisture, like a well. Water can be heard somewhere deep below, gurgling and sucking at the rocks. Suddenly a booming sound causes Sarah to step back and a fine mist shoots vertically from the hole before settling on the stone around the edges. She steps forward again, crouching by the edge. Shining her torch into the abyss is like shining it into the passageway. She sees the sides but the bottom disappears into the darkness.

Sarah turns to the carvings on the walls and began following what appeared to be a story in pictures, a story that unfolded around the room. Men with robes and tall hats like bishops lead a group of slaves who are tied together, their shoulders slumped, heads bowed in submission. The slaves are dragged up onto a platform and are somehow tested; it appeared that snakes were involved. Tiny creatures with spears and branches growing from their heads seem to be delighting in stabbing at the slave's feet whenever they can. Sarah isn't sure what happens to the ones that pass the test, if indeed any did, but the failures are herded toward the well in the centre of the room where the evil little creatures dance crazily as they prod the terrified slaves to the edge of the void. It held no meaning for her. Maybe the wretched souls are thrown into the hole for the giant dragon-fish to eat, she thinks. Who can know, violence and religion always seemed to go hand in glove.

Disappointed that the passageway hadn't led her anywhere useful, she sat on the stone ledge which ran the entire length of one wall. Her stomach rumbled as a reminder that she hadn't eaten for a while. She looks at her watch and is saddened to see that the glass has been broken and one of the little hands is missing. The watch had been a gift from her parents on her thirtieth birthday. Sarah wanted to cry. Shaking her head, she pulls a muesli bar from her bag and tears off the wrapper, screwing it up and flicking it across the floor where it topples into the hole and is gone.

Switching off the torch she sat in the darkness and ate her meagre breakfast, washing it down with the few remaining mouthfuls of cold coffee from the thermos. She flirted with eating another before deciding against it.

The sounds of the sea began to calm Sarah's agitated mind, providing the first real connection to the world of the living she'd experienced in what felt like weeks. She closed her eyes and listened to the wonderful music of life as it filtered through the cracks in the rocks. Weariness slowly embraced her tired and bruised body, her head began to droop. She pulled her coat tightly around herself and curled up on the floor, her head resting on an outstretched arm, intending to rest for a few minutes before setting off again. Sleep found her within seconds.

CHAPTER 19

Walter's pessimism appears justified as the pair contemplate a map of the area between the station house and Edinburgh. With his finger Walter traces out the most direct route, tapping at various points to indicate remote areas or potential hiding places.

"Unfortunately, old man it's a real needle-in-a-haystack quest I'm afraid." He said. "With so many men spread out looking for the killer there's scant resources to be applied in the search for Sarah. Particularly as we have no actual proof she's in this area at all."

"I know she is, Walter. Just like I knew Mathias was the hub of this whole thing. We just have to find a way to narrow this down. You can see now why Mathias couldn't leave Maggie alive." David said.

"He thought she might have information that would prove useful to us in pinpointing Sarah's location."

"He couldn't risk it... Shit!" David cursed his own stupidity.

"What is it?" Walter asked.

David didn't answer, he simply dragged the telephone across the desk and dumped it on top of the map they had been poring over. Hitting the redial button, he had the University Librarian on the phone within a couple of minutes.

"Yes, Inspector." She said, her forced patience transmitted clearly. "How may I be of service?"

"You said that when Robert visited some time ago he found some material that excited him, kept him there until closing hours." David said.

"Actually, *we* found it for him but yes, go on."

"What was the material?" David asked.

"As I said, it related to some ancient religious order, I believe. I'm not aware of the detail, Inspector, it was some time ago you understand."

"How quickly can I get my hands on that information?"

"I can fax you a form for you to complete which..."

"No." David interrupted. "Listen to me carefully. We are investigating a series of murders. We have cause to believe that a missing woman's life is in danger and I think the material in question may be of assistance in locating her. I don't want to hear any talk of forms or processes. I want you to find that bloody material and fax it to the number I give you within the hour. Do *you* understand?"

"There is no need for vulgarity, Inspector. As it happens, today is the day the staff member involved takes for her rostered day off but I will certainly leave a note..."

"Listen to me, woman!" David yelled. "I don't care if you have to send a bloody taxi to pick this person up! Get her in there now! If that information isn't on my bloody desk within one hour I'm calling the Vice Chancellor. Do I need to spell it out any more clearly?"

There was a pause on the line. "No, Inspector, you have made yourself perfectly clear. And when this is over the Chief Constable can expect a call from me, you can be sure of that. Now give me your facsimile number and I'll obtain the information you request."

"A bit tough on the old girl." Walter said after David had disconnected the call.

"Bloody librarians." David replied. "I took enough stick from those starchy little buggers when I was a kid. I'm not about to be told what to do by some old fossil now."

Walter smiled. "I'm sure they've mellowed somewhat since then." He said.

"Sure they have, but the really evil ones still lurk in university libraries waiting for some poor sod to fart too loudly so they have an excuse to fry them with the stare of death."

Walter punched David's arm playfully. "And I'm sure that young Master Orbost somehow never managed to master the secret art of the silent but deadly flatulence."

David shook his head, smiling. "No, never did seem to work that one out."

* * *

Sarah forced her eyes open. Still sore from the dust and grit in the air, they had gummed together while she slept. She wiped her eyes on the tail of her shirt, using the cleanest spot she could find. Her body is sore from contact with the cold floor and her neck muscles feel knotted and cramped. Her knee is stiff and it screamed at her when she flexed it. She sat upright and peered at her watch before remembering it had been smashed.

A sudden realisation struck her, she could see! Without the torch she could see around the chamber! The light was very dim but somewhere it was finding a way to filter in. It was like a moonlit night inside the cavernous room. There was no colour but she could definitely detect shapes by the slivery light. The black yawning hole in the centre of the chamber was quite visible against the dimly illuminated floor. Her mind raced, attempting to understand the significance of her finding. Drizzle fell from above soaking approximately half of the chamber's floor.

Acting on a hunch she ran to the wall nearest to the wet area and discovered trough-like stone receptacles extending a couple of feet out from the wall. She felt with her hand and was delighted to discover the troughs full to the brim with rainwater. She scooped some out. The water was freezing but it tasted wonderful. Dropping to her knees she drank greedily from the stone trough. Switching on the torch, more troughs were revealed, side by side around almost half of the chamber. All full. She grabbed the thermos and rinsed it in the adjacent trough before refilling it from the first and capping it tightly. Here was one problem solved, she thought. Even without food, Sarah knew she could survive several weeks now she had access to water.

Sarah gazed around the chamber, delighted by the simple pleasure of being able to see without the aid of the torch. Even if it looked like night time, it was still wonderful. Sarah had another thought. She pulled Robert's mobile from her coat pocket and turned it on, the screen dazzlingly bright in the subdued light. She literally jumped for joy as she saw two small bars of signal creep up the left hand side of the display, like two tiny black ants on the screen. Weak but useable. She had a moment of panic as one bar suddenly disappeared. She moved her position slightly and found she could make it come back. A foot or so either way seemed to make a big difference. Who to call? It came to her immediately. She had to know. She dialled Maria's mobile.

Sarah burst into tears when Maria's subdued voice greeted her. Maria too was overcome with emotion and the two babbled out the details of their last few days including Maria's ordeal of waking in a hotel room in Paris with no money, no passport, no clothes, and no idea how she came to be there. Sarah was so emotional that she couldn't think logically.

Maria took over, noting down Sarah's number displayed on her own phone. She told Sarah to hang up and that she would call her parents and then the police and the police would call her back with a plan. Never mind that Sarah had no idea where she was, the police would figure it out. Sarah didn't want to sever the connection to her friend but Maria wisely insisted. Already she was thinking of the gut wrenching possibility of the phone battery becoming exhausted before the police figured out where Sarah was. Or before someone came to harm her.

Maria hung up and Sarah continued to stand in the same spot, the best-reception spot, tears pouring down her face, adding their tiny contribution to the dampness of the stone slabs beneath her feet.

* * *

Mathias leaned back against the damp earth. Providing shelter and concealment, the massive boulder above him had been forced from the hillside when the land was young. Its uneven surface bore the scars of centuries. He sipped at his tea and gazed out at the frigid waters of the North Sea. He recalled one of his instructors telling him that in midwinter, a normally clothed man would last about four minutes in that stretch of water before losing consciousness. He could believe it.

In the distance, giant container ships ploughed through the grey waves with unrelenting determination, their decks loaded with containers housing cars and machinery and televisions. The accoutrements of modern life. From this distance the ships looked like children's toys with their rows of coloured metal boxes stacked up three and four high. Mathias never did understand how the ships stayed upright; they seemed to be so top-heavy with all that cargo. He imagined that he could sit in this spot permanently and at no time would he be able to look at the sea without seeing at least one ship heading North or South. It was a highway of ships.

He was reminded of how good it felt to be leaving this behind, setting out for a place with wide open spaces, and blue water instead of grey. A work-mate had once told him about a beach somewhere on the east coast of Africa that he'd visited. He said you could sit all day with a pair of binoculars and not manage to spot another person, let alone a ship. That sounded like the place to be.

His thoughts returned to the last few days, to the people he had killed. He felt no real remorse for his actions, he knew that it had been necessary and that he'd simply performed a service. Inevitably some people would be casualties. His analysis was limited to reviewing his decisions, were they tactically correct, had he left any loose ends, made any errors. It was the same process he had used following a mission.

You couldn't be second guessing your assignment, you simply performed, reviewed, and then put the individuals out of your mind, or at least you tried to. You didn't choose the assignment and therefore you couldn't ultimately be responsible. Even if someone was killed in error, it represented an operational or tactical mistake not a crime. These things happen on complex missions.

This was something Mathias had missed when adjusting to civilian life, the unambiguous nature of his former role. One day you're on a mission, someone tries to stop you and he gets a double tap to the chest for his trouble. The next day you're a civilian, you shove some idiot who gets in your face in a pub and they want to charge you with assault. It wasn't that he wanted to go around killing people but these days it seemed like simply yelling at someone could land a man in hot water. It felt like another world. He figured it was no surprise that the writings of Rachael Telford reached out to him. He found her black and white language refreshing. The clarity of good versus evil, protector against destroyer. It was clear and simple, had a purity he loved.

He was disappointed about Robert, though. The betrayal stung but it was also a shame he'd chosen to pitch himself as an adversary. There had been times when Mathias toyed with the idea of them working together. It would have been nice not to have to operate alone every time. But, Robert had cast his lot and there was no turning back now.

He drained the last of his tea, folded up his tiny MSR stove and stowed it in the bergen along with his titanium mug. In one smooth action he swung the heavy pack onto his shoulder and continued his way North, a tiny speck in a rugged and ancient landscape.

* * *

David, Walter, and several other officers huddle over the pages, snatching them eagerly from the fax machine as it squeezed them out at an irritatingly parsimonious rate. David scanned the small text that comprised several extracts from a very old book, judging by the style and the typeface. To David's eye it was an almost impenetrable hash of mumbo-jumbo and ecclesiastical terminology. For a while David suspected that it would prove to be a blind alley. They persevered with the tiny script and eventually found something that initially looked promising.

On one of the final pages to be laboriously ground out of the machine there was a description that related to a specific place. The description was filled with expressions such as Men of the dammed, and Sin before the Holy Spirit, and Everlasting Disgrace. A pen-and-ink drawing showed what appeared to be a room in which living men could be entombed, literally bricked into a specially constructed wall designed for that purpose alone. The room had the appearance of a horse stable with multiple bays lined up side by side. The grisly idea seemed to be that a wall was constructed across one of the bays leaving just enough room for the unfortunate fellow to stand behind it, essentially becoming trapped for all time when the final stones were mortared in place. This act of interment would reduce the depth of the bay by about three feet leaving room for several more wretched souls to be entombed until the bay was full.

The drawing showed the room complete, all of the bays filled with miserable creatures left to die a sort of death David didn't even want to think about.

"Bloody 'ell." One of the detectives said. "Is that what I think it is?"

"Pretty damn grim, all right." David agreed.

"I'd have to be dead before I let them buggers brick me into that hole." Said another.

"You'd bloody well want to be dead, I reckon." Replied his companion.

Walter looked up from the document. "Actually I think those chaps went willingly." He said.

"No bloody way!"

"Afraid so. I remember reading it somewhere. It seems that members of a particular group of religious hermits were so terminally Holy that they ended their lives voluntarily by being bricked alive into a room adjoining the church. Sort of the ultimate sacrifice for the cause. Barking mad, if you ask me."

Around the room heads were shaking in disbelief.

"And we think the poor girl's trapped inside this house of horrors?" Someone said.

"We believe she might be." Walter replied.

"God help her, then."

The phone rang, David picked it up, listened for a moment, made a note on the edge of the map, the fax from the library forgotten.

"Bingo!" He shouted. Every head in the room turned to him.

* * *

Sarah is cold and wet. The place she occupies as she waits for the phone to ring experiences intermittent bouts of falling mist which clings to her eyelashes and slowly wets her hair. Water drips from her nose and chin making tiny plinking noises on the stone floor. It felt like she'd been standing in this spot for hours. How long can they take? She wonders. Sarah didn't dare to move in case the mobile phone signal is lost and she can't get it back. She doesn't know how the phone works but it makes sense to her that it's probably easier for the thing to stay in touch than to get in touch in the first place. Maybe it didn't work like that at all but she wasn't willing to test it right now. She swapped the phone to her other hand and thrust the wet and freezing one into her coat pocket to thaw out.

When the phone rings it startles her and she fumbles. The smooth plastic case almost slips through her numb fingers. She grips it tightly with both hands, unwilling to contemplate the prospect of it smashing if it fell to the stone floor.

"Hello?" Her voice sounds strange to her as it reverberates around the walls of the vast chamber. She hears a cheer on the other end of the phone; obviously a number of people are listening in.

"Sarah, this is Detective Inspector David Orbost and we are so delighted to hear your voice." A wave of relief sweeps over Sarah. Talking to someone who would take charge at last. Someone who knew what to do.

"Thank you." She said, her voice unsteady.

"Are you injured in any way?" David asked.

"No, I'm fine. A few cuts and bruises but mostly just cold and hungry."

"Can you tell us where you are?"

" I don't know. Underground in some huge tomb somewhere. I remember we drove North before I blacked out"

"Okay, we'll come back to that later. I'm assuming that Robert Shipton brought you to this place against your will, is that correct?"

Sarah realised she hadn't even known his surname. "That's right."

"Is he in there with you still?" David asked.

Sarah thought about that question for a moment. The awful weight it carried. The question she'd been dreading. The enormous importance of her answer, standing now at the crossroads, a decision point that she'd thought about so often during the last forty eight hours.

"Are you still there, Sarah?" David's voice brought her back.

"He's dead." She said, hearing the words for the first time as though spoken by someone else. This time a pause at the other end of the line.

"Dead how?"

"I killed him." There it was. She felt naked and exposed. No going back now. "My leg was tied to a wire. I managed to get it off. I put it across the stairs and he fell. I tripped him. I think his neck broke. I saw him die. He was talking to me."

The tears began pouring from Sarah's eyes, her words tumbling out faster and faster. Something deep inside her mind began to tear and she thought she might faint.

"Sarah, listen to me." David's voice, calm, controlled, in charge. "Nobody will blame you for Shipton's death. I think you're incredibly brave for what you've done. Kidnapping is a serious crime in this country and he brought it on himself. If you hadn't done what you did you might not be alive to have this conversation."

Sarah didn't quite believe that but it was nice to hear a policeman say it.

"He said he'd killed Maria." She said, her control returning. "I couldn't let him get away with that."

"He lied. She's alive and well and I've just spoken to her but obviously you know that now. Sarah, we need to work out where you are. Are you able to see any landmarks?"

"No. I'm under the ground but I'm near the edge of the sea. I can hear the waves and sometimes birds but I can't see anything at all."

"Okay. How much charge do you have left in the battery of your phone?"

"It's Robert's phone." She said. Somehow that seemed important. "Hang on." Sarah looked at the little ant-like bars and was shocked to see that one had disappeared already. "About three quarters I think."

"Right. I'm going to hang up now. We need to think and I don't want to flatten the battery. I'll call you back soon and we'll work out a plan. Is that okay?"

"Okay." Sarah managed.

"And Sarah." David added. "We *will* find you, don't you doubt that for one minute."

Sarah could stand no longer. After David hung up she dropped to the floor. After a few minutes rest she struggled back to her feet and sat on her ledge out of the falling mist. She glanced at the phone, both of the little signal-ants had gone. She figured that she could rest for a while. He wouldn't call back immediately and she needed to sit down. She reached into her bag and ate another of the Muesli bars. Now half of the packet was empty. You better find me soon, she thought.

As she rolled the wrapper into a ball and flipped it across the floor into the hole, something occurred to her. A memory from nowhere. Eric used to have a setting on his phone that displayed which cell he was connected to. The cells had names. Place names! She fumbled with the tiny keys, calling up the menu. So many options. She found something that sounded right, selected the 'yes' answer and backed out of the menu. Hurriedly she took up her position again and waited. Just when she thought it was hopeless a new line of text appeared on the display: ST ABBS HD.

"Yes!" She yelled, punching the air in triumph.

This was too important to wait for the phone call. She called emergency, told them who she was, got the message through to the policeman, and then disconnected. All within a minute. Good work, Sarah. That's what he'd said. And now for the first time she began to allow herself to believe that they actually *would* find her. Now they had a fighting chance.

CHAPTER 20

The news injected fresh hope into the team gathered around the map on David's desk. A constable poked his head around the corner.

"Five miles, Guv'." He said. David nodded his thanks.

David took a pencil and counted out the squares on the map before making a mark. He then did the same in the opposite direction.

"Okay. The phone people reckon she has to be within five miles of the tower on top of the hill at St Abbs Head. Because there isn't full coverage up there we can't triangulate her position any more accurately. But, we know she's next to the sea so..."

"That gives us ten miles of shoreline as our search zone." One of the others said, completing David's sentence for him.

They were silent as they considered what that meant. Their exultation at having narrowed it down began to evaporate as they realised that it wasn't nearly enough. One of their number had already been dispatched to check whether any underground tombs were known to exist in the search area. He would soon return with a negative report.

"How long could she last under there?"

"Well if she has water, she might go for a few weeks." David replied. "But that mobile phone will be lucky to last three days. Once we've lost touch with her. Well..." He didn't need to finish his thought. Heads nodded around the room, the men solemn.

David's head snapped up. "I have an idea. It might be risky but it could work." All eyes were fixed on him, expectant, hopeful.

* * *

Sarah passed the time by experimenting with the phone, testing where the signal was and wasn't available. She discovered an area about six feet in diameter on the opposite side of the hole where the signal was equally strong. The advantage of the new spot was that it was out of the rain and it was dry. She moved her meagre possessions across and folded the blanket to form a cushion. At least she could sit down now and stay out of the numbing drizzle.

Sarah thought about what the policeman had said. How he thought she was very brave. It *was* a pretty brave thing she'd done wasn't it? She asked herself. Now that the police had characterised Robert's actions as a serious crime she allowed herself to think again about what she'd actually done. Not just what she did to Robert, but what she'd done for herself. She'd set a trap and killed a man who had kidnapped her. A man twice her size. Sarah the warrior. It didn't work.

Her mind constantly returned to the fact that she believed he meant her no harm. But what if she hadn't done it, what if she hadn't managed to detach herself from the wire, what then? Sarah forced herself to imagine the consequences. She would have been tied up, Mathias would have come and then what? She'd seen Mathias scare off *two* men in the alley that night when they went to Maggie's flat. One of the men was at least as big as Robert and he'd been knocked out cold. For the first time since she'd been able to put the pieces in place she realised that she'd actually saved her own life by killing Robert. Had she still been chained up, Mathias would have killed them both. So Robert would have been dead anyway but now, because of what she'd done, she at least had a fighting chance. It was true.

She probed at this new realisation from several angles but she couldn't fault it. With hindsight, she was only alive right now because she had managed to escape and also stopped Robert from restraining her again. Maybe there would have been other ways to achieve those two objectives but she couldn't think of any. She knew she was rationalising but it felt as though at least part of the weight of culpability for his death had been lifted from her shoulders. Her spirits began to brighten.

She was startled out of her thoughts by the telephone. She made a mental note to turn the volume of the ringer down. It wasn't as though the phone had to compete with anything else and it had nearly given her a heart attack twice now. She answered the call.

"How you doing, Sarah?" David asked.

"Oh, you know, just chillin'." She said. Sarah heard laughter in the background.

"Good for you. Now listen up. You said you can hear the birds. Can you see any part of the sky?"

"No, but weak light gets in here somehow, although I can't see where."

"Great. Do you have anything to burn? Papers, books wood, that sort of thing. And something to light it with."

Sarah thought for a moment. "I've got a packet of toilet rolls." She said. "And some petrol from the generator." She added

"You have a generator down there?" David asked.

"Well, I sabotaged it when I ran from Mathias but there's cans of fuel left."

There was a silence on the end of the line. "Did you say Mathias?" David asked.

"Yes, he let off an explosion that buried me in here in the first place. Because I wouldn't answer him when he called me. He pretended he was going to rescue me but I didn't believe him." Sarah said.

"You did very well not to reveal your position, Sarah, in fact that caution probably saved your life. How long ago was this?"

"I'm not sure. I got knocked down when the explosion went off and smashed my watch. But I think it was sometime last night." In the background she could hear men moving and shouting into other telephones.

"That's great, Sarah. That really helps us. Back to the toilet rolls. Do you have any matches or a lighter?"

"No, I don't smoke"

"Was Shipton a smoker?" David asked.

Sarah thought back to her time in Robert's car. She remembered a pack of cigarettes on the dashboard, remembered hoping he wouldn't smoke them while she was in the car.

"Yes he was." She said confidently.

"Excellent. That means he probably has a lighter on him. What we want you to do is to get the lighter and the fuel if you can, but for God's sake be careful with it, and make a small fire with the toilet rolls and anything else you have that will burn. We want you to make some smoke, Sarah. We'll have spotter planes in the air. We'll have to be careful but if we get it right, the smoke will show us where you are down there. If the light can get in then the smoke will be able to escape."

* * *

David checked his watch. In two hours it would be dark and the smoke would be useless. He and Sarah had agreed that she would prepare everything and then call him before lighting the fire. They had three choppers on standby including one from the local emergency rescue squadron. He tapped his fingers restlessly, waiting for her call. After she'd positively placed Mathias in the area within the last eighteen hours, they had tightened the net, contracting most of their resources within what they estimated to be the limits of his movement. The police were confident that he wasn't using his car or they would have spotted it. A stolen car was a possibility but they doubted that too. One of the advantages of being in a rural area was that the number of roads is reduced and they had been watching them all. Their hopes were high that they now had him encircled. David desperately hoped they had what it would take to stop him if he attempted to breach their perimeter.

"She's got guts, you have to give her that." David said. Waiting by the phone.

"And then some." Walter Replied. "Shipton was quite a big chap I'm told."

"He was a big guy, that's for sure. A bodybuilder, I think. Amazing that she managed to pull it off. And she must have realised that if she didn't succeed he'd probably kill her. Takes balls to roll that dice." David said.

"Indeed. Let's hope her nerve holds for a little longer. I can't bear the thought of losing her when we're this close."

* * *

Sarah had cringed when David suggested retrieving Robert's lighter. Not only did she not want to leave her current location with its proximity to the outside world, she didn't want to go back and rummage through the dead man's pockets. But he was right; the plan sounded like it could work. She recalled Robert's notebook sitting on the folding chair, another thing to burn but then she dismissed the idea when she remembered that the chair was now crushed under tons of dirt. Sarah turned the phone off and left it with her bag, the thermos and the blanket. She needed only the torch and she had things to carry back. It was unnerving, walking away from her connection to the outside world, walking back into the darkness toward the graves but she scurried along the passageway, eager to get it over with.

Sarah emerged back into her old chamber, immediately turned right and followed the wire to where the generator was located. Everything was quiet now, the machine's main artery had been severed and the bleeding reduced to an occasional drip. There was little of the leaked fuel remaining, which surprised Sarah until she thought about how quickly it could evaporate. She tapped on the cans until she discovered a full one, the hollow sounds of the empty fuel cans booming around the walls in the absolute silence of the chamber. When she attempted to lift the full can her arm felt as though it would be wrenched from its socket. She kept tapping until she discovered a can that seemed to be about a third full. She hurried back to the chamber with it and set it down near the birdbath. In the silence she could hear the fuel sloshing back and forth inside the steel can as it settled.

Sarah moved toward Robert's body. Fine dust covered his open eyes and made her cringe. She wished she'd had the courage to close them earlier. Ironic, she thought, courage to kill but not to touch. Her immediate problem was that only his head and shoulders protruded from the pile of earth. She needed to clear a sizeable amount of dirt to get to his pockets. Staring at him, Sarah had the idea of taking his jacket as well to burn on the fire. The damp cloth would generate lots of smoke. It's not like he needs it anymore she told herself. She took the bucket, now filled with sludge and tossed the contents into the corner of the chamber. She then set the torch on the camp bed and began scooping the soil away with the bucket.

It was hard work and Sarah's back soon began to protest. The difficulty was that as she pulled the soil away, little avalanches continually spilled down to fill the void. It took her thirty minutes before she saw the bottom of his jacket. As it was, one arm was still buried almost to the shoulder. She put the bucket down and flexed her back. Trying not to touch his cold body, she unzipped the coat and attempted to slide his arm out of the sleeve. It wouldn't budge.

With difficulty she could bend his free arm a little at the shoulder but his elbow was locked solid. Rigour-mortis. She chided herself for not thinking of that before. Stupid. The jacket wouldn't be adding its contribution to her signal fire. She sat down on the bed in disgust, intending to rest for a minute. The torch bounced as she sat on the flimsy camp bed, wobbled slightly on the edge and then fell the twelve inches to the floor. The light flickered off and Sarah was plunged into darkness.

* * *

Ten miles away, Mathias detected activity. In the distance he could see helicopters patrolling. Through his binoculars he'd observed dozens of police vehicles moving north of his position. From here on he would be able to travel only at night. He was sheltered in what he guessed was the ruins of a pillbox of some sort. The roof had long since collapsed but thick brambles had grown over one corner providing a moderately dry and sheltered if somewhat cramped space sufficient to conceal a man who wasn't afraid to push his way in. He fully expected the search aircraft to work their way up the coast and over his position and this current location would shield him well from their prying eyes. It felt great to be back in the field again.

The discomforts didn't worry him at all, he felt alive and all of his senses were working overtime. Mathias loved the smell of the earth, the scent of foxes and rabbits. In the military, he had enjoyed every one of his training missions, regardless of the weather or the conditions. In fact the more miserable the better, it made the whole thing easier. Not many people liked standing out in the rain with the wind lashing at their face, peering into the darkness. He had embarrassed more than one instructor on training exercises by materialising out of thin air during a raging storm.

By moving at night, hiding during the day and using his night vision scope he was quite confident of his ability to detect and evade the clumsy efforts of the locals. Particularly if the bad weather kept up. One thing though had cast a small shadow over his confident outlook. Through his binoculars he'd spotted a couple of military wagons moving north. If they were using his own kind to come after him then he would need to be very careful indeed. It wouldn't be the first time this sort of thing had occurred but it certainly raised the stakes. If nothing else, it'll make the game interesting he thought, smiling to himself.

CHAPTER 21

Sarah lunges for the torch and manages to grab it before it rolls away from her. She desperately thumbed the switch but without results. Her panic rising, she bangs the torch on the palm of her hand. The light flicked on and then immediately off again, a flash of light imprinted on her retinas. She forces herself to slow down, closes her eyes and manages to rise above the panic that had bubbled almost to the surface.

When her hands stop shaking, she puts her knees together to ensure she doesn't drop any small parts and begins dismantling the torch, working by feel alone. She discovers that, for some strange reason, it's actually easier to do when she closes her eyes. She unscrews the base and removes the batteries, rubs the contacts on her jeans and slips them back into the steel tube. She then unscrews the front of the torch and feels several parts become loose in her hands. She carefully replaces them in the same order and then tries the switch. Nothing. The torch is dead.

Sarah cursed the torch, her situation, Mathias, Robert and the world in general. How could the fucking thing bounce all the way down the stone steps when Robert tripped and then break by rolling off the bed and dropping a foot to the floor? When she was practically hoarse from yelling into the darkness, her anger remained alive, its edge was still keen. She told herself that with or without the torch she still had to do what she came for and she wasn't about to let some pissy little setback stop her. Stuffing the broken torch back into her coat pocket she drops to her knees and feels her way toward Robert's corpse. Her fingers contact the skin on his face; she thought she'd touched his eye and her hand instinctively retracts. She tries again, a little to the right this time and locates his shoulder. Sarah slips her hand inside his jacket. His body is cold, his dead flesh springy to the touch. Just like touching a big Christmas ham, she tells herself.

Sarah carefully works her hands into every pocket she can find. She transfers a folding knife to her own pocket. Inside his jacket she finds a thick envelope, turns it around in her hands trying to guess what it could be, heavy, flexible. Some sort of paperwork maybe. She zips it into her jacket; something else to burn. She ignores his keys, his loose change, and his wallet. She crawls back to the bed. He is carrying no cigarettes and no lighter. Sarah recalled the rush he'd been in as he bounded down the steps. Must have left them in the car. Sarah won't be able to light the fire after all. She felt the panic and despair attempt to claw its way to the surface again, wanting to take control, to send her screaming and running into the darkness where her mind would crack open and she'd be lost forever.

Sarah simply won't allow that to happen. Summoning her anger again she absolutely refuses to be stopped, despite her worsening circumstances. The fucking police will have to find another way! She tells herself.

"Do I have to do every fucking thing myself?" She yells into the darkness. What more was she supposed to do? She'd already killed a man, survived an explosion and cave-in, found her way to a place where *she* could contact *them*. It's about time they did some fucking work for a change! Sarah screams in frustration, adrenalin flooding her system, pushing her on. She stands up and, arms stretched out before her, works her way around the chamber. She feels the ring in the wall where her cable was secured, the opening that led to the generator. She continues feeling along the next wall, her fingers loosening small fragments of stone, which tumble to the floor with tiny scuttling sounds. Eventually she arrives at the entrance to the wedge shaped chamber containing the three passageways and the arches she'd forced herself to inspect previously.

Sarah's confidence is abruptly shattered. Her legs fail her and she sits down heavily. Her stomach is gripped by a wave of nausea and for a few minutes she simply curls into a foetal position, her breathing rapid and shallow in the absolute darkness.

Sarah can't remember which of the three passageways leads her back.

* * *

Activity was frantic around David and Walter's desk. When Sarah hadn't called back as expected they were despairing. David's mind struggled with the possibilities, he dreaded the thought that maybe she'd had an accident with the fuel, that his plan had caused her some sort of harm. David had ordered the helicopters into the air anyway in case Sarah had started the fire but hadn't been able to call. While they hadn't seen any smoke, one of the chopper pilots reported a ground disturbance in the Northern half of their search area. It looked like a small landslide. They were now trying to determine who owned the land. A uniformed officer rushed over to David's desk.

"It's gonna take some time. Sir." He said. "There's seems to be some confusion about the title. They're telling me that it goes back a long way though. Very old they reckon."

"Great thanks, keep on it, mate. Max!" David called across the room. "Come over here. Get some earth-moving gear to this place on the map. Make sure they bring a big back-hoe or whatever they call it over here, you know, for digging holes. Tell them to get as close as they can and standby for my call. If we can't find the land owner we crash the fences and sort it out later"

David looked at his watch. Thirty minutes of useful daylight left.

* * *

Sarah struggled to her feet. She felt beaten. It took all of her determination to stop herself simply crawling back to the bed and giving up. At every turn she seemed to have obstacles thrown in her path. She pummelled her mind into concentrating on this new problem. Sarah shuddered as she remembered the face which now hung somewhere above her. She raises her hands in an attempt to feel the stonework at the entrance to the passage but it's out of reach. She does her best to recall what she'd seen earlier by the torch light but it remained just inaccessible to her. The shock of seeing the face was all she could remember, swamping the detail in her mind. She couldn't think of any other option but to try them in turn. She felt a trickle of sweat run down the centre of her back despite the chill conditions. She desperately didn't want to do this.

Sarah held her arms out like a sleepwalker and began moving down the centre passageway. Her entire body trembled and she felt sick with dread at what she might walk up to. Sarah had never felt more afraid in her entire life. She had walked about thirty yards when she thought she heard a sound. A small scuffing noise. As if someone (or something) had allowed its foot to brush against the dusty stone floor. She stood motionless, every nerve in her body was screaming. Then a smell floated to her. Sarah's senses were straining to compensate for her useless eyes.

The air in this passageway was deathly still and yet Sarah was almost certain that the smell was carried on a gentle air current. The sort of air displacement caused by something moving. The smell was fetid and thick with rot, with festering decomposition. She was gripped by an overwhelming fear. A fear so powerful that she suspected she could lose her sanity altogether. She began to walk backwards. The noise again, following her. She quickened the pace, she could sense that only a thread held her mind together. She extended her right arm and held it to the wall so she would know when she emerged back into the prison chamber. Her fingers bumped and skidded over the medieval stonework.

Suddenly the wall disappeared and her hand contacted something crisp and brittle, like old sticks wrapped in ancient paper. The thing crumbled under her fingers and collapsed with a dry rattle, releasing an ancient stench of decay. Sarah snapped. She spun on her heel and ran in a blind panic, her single thought to get out. She hurtled down the stone passageway no longer caring where she was running to, her one thought to escape the stinking evil that shuffled through the darkness. She didn't realise she was screaming until her feet were pulled out from under her and she slammed face down into the pile of earth inside the prison chamber, her mouth and eyes filling with the damp soil. She struggled back up feeling Robert's body move under her feet, she must have pressed her knee into his stomach and he made an obscene wet burping sound. She stepped away, spitting and coughing, the dark earth clinging to her lips. She staggered back to the archways.

"Fuck you!" She shrieked into the blackness, her eyes pouring from the irritation of the dirt.

"Fuck you!" She was wild with frustration and anger, way beyond caring, she simply wanted this to end. She was no longer frightened of what lay in the dark, somehow she'd gone beyond that point, her anger pushing her toward madness.

"You stay out of my fucking way if you know what's good for you!" Sarah screamed.

She felt her way to the right hand passageway and began walking briskly, one hand held outstretched, no longer caring about what might be waiting in front of her.

"Stay the fuck away from me!" She shrieked into the darkness ahead.

After a few minutes and through eyes rimmed with filth she saw the weakest suggestion of light. Her nose was caked in dirt so she could smell nothing but she knew she'd picked the right passage this time. Sarah emerged into what she'd named the water chamber. The mist was still falling in the last of the light and she turned her face toward it. Sarah went to one of the stone troughs and splashed the icy water over her face, her skin tingled from the cold and her exertions, her system still pumped full of adrenalin. She unrolled the blanket and used it to wipe at her dripping face. *Now* she felt like a warrior. *Now* she was fucking invincible.

She grabbed the phone and made the connection, her other hand on her hip, her entire body charged with aggression.

"He doesn't have any fucking matches." She said. "What's next?"

There was a slight pause before David answered. "Are you all right Sarah?" He asked

"My torch died. I've been rummaging about here in total darkness looking for matches in the pockets of a dead man and trying not to get lost in this evil fucking haunted house! I'm tired of this ride and I want to get off..." Her voice began to break.

"Okay Sarah, it's going to be fine. Just hold on, I think we're nearly there. We've made some progress and I think we've got you pinpointed, here's how we'll make certain." David waved his arm to someone across the room who snatched up the phone.

"We're going to fly the helicopter low along the edge of the cliffs where we think you are. If you can hear birds you'll hear it easily. When it gets near you it will get louder until it passes by and then it will get quieter again. You just need to tell me when it's at its loudest. Okay?"

"Yes. Thank you. Sorry for shouting at you."

"Hey, don't worry about it. With what you've been..."

"I hear it!" Sarah interrupted. "I can hear it already!"

The noise of the helicopter built to such a thunderous intensity that Sarah was certain it must be only a few yards above her. Conversation was impossible but it didn't matter as everyone could hear the noise of the chopper on the speakerphone. David punched the air.

"Sarah we know where you are. Stay put and we'll get some machinery in there. We're going to dig you out from the site of the landslide so stay away from that area until I come and get you."

"Will you be here, I mean you personally?" Sarah asked.

"I'm heading to my car now. You'll hear my voice Sarah, and you'll know you're okay."

Sarah sank to her knees and sobbed with relief.

* * *

Mathias's concern was steadily increasing. The helicopters that he'd heard earlier hadn't passed overhead, as he'd expected. They seemed to be searching the area very close to where he'd left Sarah.

Perhaps they've discovered the cars, he'd thought at first. It's difficult to plunge a vehicle into water without it leaving a trace. Any decent oil slick can be spotted from the air if the water isn't too rough. That's more than likely what it is, he'd assumed.

Now he wasn't so sure. He'd risked a small excursion to high ground as the light was fading and seen heavy equipment being moved in. He was confident now that they had found Sarah and intended to dig her out. What he didn't know was whether she was dead or alive. This he would have to determine. One thing was for sure: while he would have to remain patient, his work here might not yet be complete. He fought back the anger and frustration that this thought provoked in him and cautioned himself to wait. While he couldn't wait around here too long, he certainly could bide his time somewhere else.

*　*　*

David had called Sarah three times during the last few hours. The first time from his car to tell her that everything was on its way. The next to comfort her while the workers were delayed waiting for lights to be set up and an engineer to arrive. The last time to tell her that the machines were digging. He didn't actually need to tell her that, she could hear them at the other end of the passage and the ground vibrated as the large machines tore at the earth.

Sarah collected her things and sat in the darkness at the end of the long passageway. Abruptly, the sound of the digging grew in intensity and light flooded the chamber at the far end of the passage. She heard men yelling and the sound of large engines. She wanted to run toward them but David had told her to wait until she heard his voice, so she knew it was safe for her to come out. The intensity of the lights increased and she could hear banging and hammering, the sound of men working. The archway at the other end of the passageway was a brilliant white. Sitting in the gloom, her eyes couldn't penetrate the brightly lit chamber. She waited patiently, wondering what they were doing out there.

A figure appeared at the end of the passageway, framed by the bright lights behind.

"Sarah, it's me, David." The figure yelled.

Suddenly Sarah was on her feet and running, ignoring the pain in her knee. She ran the length of the passage and threw herself into David's arms, sobbing and kissing him and unable to speak for emotion. From David's perspective, the sight of Sarah charging out of the darkness had been disconcerting to say the least. She was totally filthy, only her blue eyes visible against a black mask of a face, dirt flying from her hair as she ran. As she hugged David his own tears began to flow and at that moment he felt that if he never accomplished another thing in his life, it wouldn't matter.

David gently disentangled himself from her embrace and began leading her toward the gaping hole in the side of the hill. Lights began to blind Sarah, men were whistling and people cheering. David felt her go limp and caught her before she fell. The image of him stepping out of the chamber with Sarah unconscious in his arms, tears streaming down his face, would make the front page of every newspaper in the country the next morning and would win prizes for the photographer all around the world.

CHAPTER 22

David sits on the edge of the hospital bed while Walter takes a position by the window. The room is packed full of flowers, every horizontal surface is covered with them and Sarah is now giving them away to other patients as her room will simply not hold any more. Letters and cards pour in from all over the country and many from other parts of the world. Each day Sarah's father brings a sack of mail and each day it seems to get bigger. Sarah is in a private hospital and under strict police guard. This is her fourth day and she's becoming restless, eager to have her life back.

Even with cuts and bruises to her face and a bandaged knee and head, Sarah looks a million times better than she did after collapsing into his arms, David thinks. He bends and gives her a peck on the cheek.

"How you feeling?" He asks.

"Pretty good really, all things being considered. They want to do some more tests tomorrow, something about an enlarged spleen from the explosion, I think. They also seem worried about my foot, the cut is infected and because the place is so old and full of bodies they want to keep an eye on it. I think they've got more of my blood in their lab than I've got left in my body. All that said, I'm hoping I can go home soon, though."

"You've been through a lot, it's probably not good to rush things." David counselled.

Sarah is quiet for a moment. "Any news?"

David knew what she meant. Until they catch Mathias, Sarah won't get her life back. They have broken the news to her about Maggie and Rita, and the two dead policeman. Sarah knows that Mathias could come back for her, actually he probably will come back for her, she imagines. The police too are hoping for that, hoping he shows himself long enough for them to capture him. Or kill him; either way is fine by them. Understandably some among their number would prefer the latter.

"No, nothing yet. He's obviously gone to ground for a while. Not surprising with all the publicity generated by your rescue. His face is on the front page of every paper. He'll have to surface eventually and then we'll pick him up."

"Oh by the way," David said, changing the subject, "it turns out that the place you were imprisoned has enormous archaeological significance. It's like nothing the boffins have ever seen before. The BBC intends to shoot a documentary film as they explore it. They'll probably ask you to make an appearance."

"As long as I don't have to go back inside." Sarah said.

"Oh, I'm sure they will have lights set up all over the place. They won't be expecting you to do your Indiana Jones thing again."

"I don't care what they have, there's evil in that place. I felt it. I beat it once but I'm not pushing my luck. I'll never ever go back inside, not as long as I live." Sarah shudders at the thought.

David gives her hand a squeeze. "Nobody can force you to do anything you don't want to, Sarah. If they give you any stick you send 'em to me."

Sarah knew David's comment was well intentioned, he was trying to protect her and he was sweet but the tone implied that she was helpless and that wasn't how she felt at all. After everything she'd been through she felt a twinge of irritation.

"If they give me any stick I won't *need* to send them to you, David." She said.

Sarah smiled but her tone was firm. David realised his faux pas, blushed, started to apologise.

"Don't worry about it." Sarah said, giving him a playful punch on the arm. "It's nice to know you're sticking up for me."

David changed the subject again. "We've also matched a small piece of stone found in the clothing of one of the dead girls to a chamber not far from where you were held. It seems he kept them there for a period before dumping their bodies. It looks as though two of the victims could have even been there at the same time. I guess the place is big enough. Anyway, I just thought you'd like to know. Your efforts in leading us to the place have helped us tie up a lot of loose ends."

"Shucks." Sarah feigned embarrassment. "A girl's gotta do what a girl's gotta do."

Walter handed David a package.

"Do you remember this?" David asked, giving her the bulky envelope.

Sarah took it and turned it around. It was dirty and creased. She looked at David with a blank expression. Shook her head.

"It was in your coat pocket. The pocket was zipped up."

Sarah looked back at the unfamiliar package and it came to her.

"I took it from Robert's jacket! It was pitch black so I didn't get to see it. I was looking for things to burn so I grabbed it before I realised he had nothing to light it with."

"Just as well you didn't burn it, my dear." Walter said, smiling.

"Why? What is it?" Sarah asked.

"It's a gift to you from Shipton. He gave it to you before he died."

Sarah stared at him, a confused expression on her face.

"Open it." David prompted.

The envelope was tough, some sort of woven paper with a button and a string to keep it closed and Sarah struggled with it. Finally she unwound the string in the right direction and stuck her hand inside. With a look of astonishment on her face, she pulled out a thick wad of cash.

"It's money. A huge pile of it. There's a fortune here." She said, peering into the envelope.

"Well, five thousand pounds anyway." David said, smiling.

Sarah stuffed the money back inside the envelope, folded her arms across her chest.

"This isn't my money. I can't take it just like that, it's not right."

Walter sat down on the edge of the bed, opposite David. "Actually Sarah it *is* your money. This will probably come as quite a shock to you, and David and I wanted to be the ones to break it. Several days before Shipton abducted you he went to his solicitor and made a new will."

"Robert had a solicitor?" Sarah exclaimed. "And a will?" This was too weird; she hadn't pegged him for the kind of person who needed either.

"Indeed he did. Shipton's mother died a couple of years back. She owned an old house on the outskirts of London. It had been in Shipton's family for three generations. The house was a little run down but the area has appreciated in value astronomically during the last three decades. Robert inherited it as the only child along with the balance of his father's insurance policy and a few other bits and pieces. He sold the house last year. His new will nominated you as the sole beneficiary. The estate is worth almost half a million pounds."

Sarah's mouth opened and closed. "But I killed him!" She said. "I can't take that money now. How could I?" His generosity from the grave was more than she could bear. Her sense of guilt was still too raw for her to deal with this. She wanted to cry but she fought the tears back.

David's voice is gentle. "Sarah. The money is yours. Not only did Shipton want you to have it, it now legally passes to you. You can't really refuse it. If you feel so strongly about not keeping the money there's nothing to stop you giving some or all of it away. But it *is* yours, or at least it will be once all of the paperwork is processed."

"But... I don't know what to say. This is crazy. Why would he leave it to me?"

"I guess we'll never know what he was thinking. He was

delusional, totally convinced that you were the one foretold according to their nutty religious doctrine. He probably figured you'd use the money to further whatever it is you were supposed to do. When he'd decided to kidnap you he may have reasoned that such a high risk activity merited a new will. Maybe he thought he might be killed in the attempt. Who knows?"

Sarah shook her head. "I don't know what to think."

"Will you let me give you some advice?" David asked. Sarah nodded.

"Don't make any decisions right now. All that happens is you sign a few papers, and when probate is granted an amount of money is deposited into your account. You don't have to *do* anything. It will take a while for the money to come through anyway. When this is all over and you're up and about, you can then decide what to do with it. By the time you get it you'll have had plenty of time to think about what you want to do with it. Buy a house or two, give it to the cat's home, it doesn't matter. You'll decide then."

Sarah nodded. "Okay, that sounds like good advice. Thank you. Shit. Talk about surprises!"

* * *

The men standing on the deck of the prawn trawler *Vivienne II* stamp their feet and clutch steaming mugs of tea in both hands, waiting for the truck. It's mid afternoon and the light is already fading. When the skipper arrives with the provisions for their next trip they should have just enough time to load the boat and get back to their homes for dinner. Tonight will be the last night they spend in their own beds for the best part of two weeks. Fishing in the North Sea is a dangerous job and a tough way to make a living, particularly with the state of the fish stocks lately. The boats are forced to venture ever further and to move more often before their boxes are filled. The men of the *Vivienne II* along with the five hundred other fishermen in Peterhead, the most easterly point on the Scottish mainland, have few other options.

Their small talk is interrupted by George who squeezes his considerable bulk through the wheelhouse door and jabs his finger in their direction. "Okay, which of you smartarses has moved me gear?"

The men look at each other, shoulders shrug. "What you on about Big George?" One of them asks.

"Me gear is gone from me locker. Waterproofs, vest, even me fuckin boots for Christ's sake. Can't put to sea wi'out me gear."

"It's probably away at home ya dozy bugger. Ya hit the sauce so hard on the way back last time I'm surprised you even know where in God's name you left it."

George rubs his head. "It's always in me locker, why would I take it 'ome?" He says, turning to head back inside for another look.

The men simply shake their heads and return to their conversation.

* * *

At the end of that week, Natalie and Walter raised their glasses to the new celebrity. The small crowd in the pub who recognised David from the papers and television news coverage stood and clapped. David rose from his seat and gave them a theatrical little bow. When they had settled down again, Natalie planted a kiss on his cheek.

"You did really well, David. I'm very proud of you." She said.

"Ah well, you know how these things are, it's a team effort. I was just the lucky bunny who got caught in the media splash."

"Actually, old boy, I think you are being overly modest and I should know, I was there too." Walter leaned toward Natalie. "The reality was that, in the end, David led and we all simply followed. David had his picture splashed all over the world because he was out in front the whole time. While the engineer was still agonising about the possibility of more slippage, David was in there and pulling that girl out. That's the way it was."

"That's very kind of you Walter." David said.

"Not at all old chap, and if you don't get a promotion after all this I for one will consume my trilby."

"How is Sarah, David? Is she holding up?" Asked Natalie.

David wobbled his head from side to side to indicate ambiguity. "She's doing as well as can be expected I suppose, she's a gutsy woman. It's sort of hard to tell because her life can't return to normal yet. I don't think she'll really be able to get on with things until he's caught. Wherever he is."

"I hear she's been offered a book deal for her story. Sort of female hero of the decade."

"Yes, she's had a couple of meetings with a ghost-writer since she was discharged and the publisher has offered her a terrific advance. They seem to think the book will go gangbusters and they're mad keen on getting it out as soon as possible. There's talk of selling the film rights to some studio in the United States. She could do quite well out of it."

"That's great. Has she told you what she intends to do with Shipton's money?" Natalie asked.

"I'm not sure she's made up her mind exactly but she reckons she'll give it all away. All except for the money in the envelope. She's going to buy a little car with that. Spoils of war she called it. I think she has in mind some charities to do with helping women with low self esteem or who suffered through a traumatic childhood. That sort of thing."

"That's very noble."

"She's still struggling with the fact that she caused Shipton's death. Maybe this is her way of atoning. Who knows, people are complex."

"And long may they continue to be so." Said Walter, downing the remainder of his scotch and rising to his feet. "And on that note I fear that I must away. Familial duties beckon."

Natalie waited until Walter was out of earshot. "Has the cop-of-the-year got anything planned for the weekend?" she asked.

"To be honest I haven't had time to think much about weekends this last month. Fortunately the responsibility for the manhunt is now being shared with others so I guess I'll have to figure out something to do on my days off."

"If you're up to a long drive I've got a bottle of champagne in my refrigerator at home that's just crying out to be opened." Natalie said.

"I think the time has come to put it out of its misery." Replied David.

* * *

Mathias walks briskly along the dockside in the hammering rain, his waterproof clothing hiding his face and rendering him unremarkable as the trawlers tug at their moorings, the wind driving the rain almost horizontally. Nobody gives him a second glance. While he appears to be simply hurrying along, attempting to keep the rain out of his face, in fact his eyes are rapidly scanning the boats. Searching. He's looking for something specific. An average boat, older rather than newer, not too brightly painted. He's almost at the end of the dock when he sees it. The whitefish trawler *Mary Joan*. She's obviously seen quite a few seasons but looks well maintained. Even better, a glance at the equipment mounted on the tower tells him that she's been refitted with the latest navigational and electronics systems. Ideal for what he has in mind once the time is right

* * *

Time moves quickly for Sarah. The framework for the book is beginning to take shape and she and Maria have just about finished selecting the charities for the distribution of Robert's money. It was such a marvellous feeling to be making so many people happy. The press had somehow discovered what she was doing and she had the editors of women's magazines practically breaking her door down for an interview. The fact that she wanted the money to be given in private only heightened their interest in her. One of the national newspapers ran a phone poll asking readers what they would do with the money if they had been Sarah. Seventy six per cent said they would have kept it as compensation for the horror they had been made to endure. Sarah thought that it was funny how different it felt when it was your life and your decision, when the burden of killing a well-meaning man was on your conscience every day. The papers were full of mental health specialists who provided expert opinion about Robert's illness and assured the public that had he not maintained his control over Sarah the situation could have turned out quite differently.

Sarah had naturally thought a great deal about what transpired inside the prison chamber and she felt that she was making progress toward sorting it out in her mind. She obviously realised that Robert wasn't the killer she'd imagined him to be but she remained convinced that they would both be dead now if it hadn't been for her initiative. David had told her it was as certain as night follows day. She was sure that there would have been no way she could have managed to convince Robert to let her go, Mathias would have located them before they got too far and that would have been the end of them both.

That's how she saw it anyway. So in a sense, Robert sacrificed his life to save hers. That being the case, she figured he'd given her enough already. His money would go out into the world and do a lot of good for other women and she hoped he would have been happy with that. She didn't expect other people to understand it, and clearly seventy six per cent of phone poll respondents didn't, but that was fine too.

Sarah was even beginning to get used to her bodyguards. She liked the routine that they imposed, the order and structure that they brought into her life. There were so many crazy things happening to her that she imagined it would be easy to spin out of control. Just the other day one of them had brought in a magazine with her picture on the cover! She didn't even know it had been taken. She was coming out of the house to visit the psychologist who's been helping her to sort things out and she'd only walked six feet to reach the car provided by the security guys. Somehow they'd managed to snap the photo as she bent to climb into the car. People reckoned it wasn't a bad picture of her. It was a bit scary really, she thought.

They had wanted her to go to a 'safehouse' in the country. A place where she could be kept secret, hidden away from prying eyes. A place where she'd stay indoors and people would bring her food and books to read. She wouldn't be allowed to have any visitors. To Sarah it sounded like prison again and she said no. She didn't want to move back to her parent's house either while there was any suggestion of danger, even though her dad wanted her to. Not that she would have been allowed to do that either without a fight. She refused to be talked around and so in the end the police had compromised.

They had moved her into a special little house rented just for her. It wasn't a bad place but it wasn't home either. This place was easier for them to guard and they had set up a shed in the garden and special equipment surrounding the house so nobody could sneak in at night.

Because her face was so well known from all of the media coverage, it was impossible to conceal her if she wasn't prepared to go into hiding. As part of the deal, she'd had to agree to a condition. A safehouse located deep in the countryside stood empty and waiting. If Mathias was sighted inside Britain or the police discovered intelligence to that effect, she would be immediately whisked away and deposited into this secret place, no arguments. There she would stay until he was caught. Sarah hoped it wouldn't come to that.

Maria had insisted on moving in with Sarah and she'd hooted when the first picture of herself appeared in a magazine. 'Long time companion' was how the magazine described her. Maria figured her chances with men were now even less than zero since they'd all think she was a Lessie. The really great thing was that Sarah had a dog, although she was really only borrowing him. He was a beautiful German Shepherd named Max and he slept on the end of her bed at night. He was so gentle and obedient, an absolute delight. Max had been trained specifically for this sort of job and when anyone came near her he moved in close and watched them like a hawk. She was sure she'd bawl her eyes out when they eventually had to part company but for now she loved him to bits.

* * *

The wind drives spume from the tops of the waves as Mathias

paddles toward the unlit side of the *Mary Joan*. The night is moonless and the boats bob and roll as the wind whines through wires and pipework and railings. Rain pounds the decks and wheelhouses, bouncing in the air and giving the boats a halo of spray as Mathias peers out of the darkness into the floodlights of the dock. The small tender he's stolen is old and rotting; it won't take much to sink it when he's done. With the boat concealing him from the dock, he tosses over his bergen and then pulls himself up, crouching on the aft deck.

CHAPTER 23

The trawler pitches and rolls in the steep and confused waves of the North Sea. The skipper had laboured over the decision to take the boat and his three-man crew to this spot, weighing up the pros and cons. It's almost one hundred and twenty miles from port but he'd had success here previously by taking a risk. The men grumbled at having to steam so far before shooting the nets but it's only the start of the trip and they still have confidence in the skipper to locate a good catch. After hauling their nets, it proves to be a poor start to the trip; some whiting and haddock and a few small cod. Only enough to fill six boxes. They will have to do better than this if everyone is to get a payday at the end.

Below decks, two men stand side by side cleaning the meagre catch, tossing rubbish fish into a stainless steel chute that feeds a large holding bin below. Smaller fish suitable for sale are hand filleted by the men, otherwise they are put thorough the boat's automatic filleting machine and then eventually into boxes where they'll be packed in crushed ice, ready for sale at the fish market. The men give their work little conscious thought as they brace themselves against the constant motion of the sea. Their talk of boats and cars and women is punctuated by laughter and optimism about their next haul.

Their banter is interrupted by a man, dressed in black jeans and pullover who simply steps out from behind the pipework and ducts descending from the upper deck. Rory, the smaller of the two men is the first to see him.

"Christ on a bike! Who the hell are you?"

In response Mathias raises the gun in his right hand and fires a shot into the centre of Rory's forehead, knocking him back against the bulkhead before he collapses like a rag doll, a surprised look fixed on his face.

"Fuck!" Ivar, the larger man shouts, moving quickly to his left. Mathias swings his outstretched arm to the side, tracking the movement and pulls the trigger. Nothing happens. He bangs the gun against the palm of his hand, cocks the hammer and tries again. Nothing. Mathias tosses the gun aside as Ivar steps around the cleaning station, a wickedly sharp filleting knife in his right hand.

"You're a fuckin dead man, pal, no mistake." He growls, the knife held out in front of him.

Mathias is trapped. Unless he attempts to climb across the filleting equipment, Ivar is blocking his only exit. He calculates his options. He must kill the man with the knife. Mathias knows too well that even a mediocre fighter armed with a razor sharp knife is a dangerous opponent. He wills himself to relax, allows his arms to fall to his sides and looks the man in the eyes.

"You sure you want to do this?" He asks.

Ivar blinks, shakes his head as if at the idiocy of the question and lunges, the knife seeking for the centre of Mathias's chest.

Mathias, anticipating this move, pivots to his left, at the same time raising his left arm. As the knife slides past his body, he clamps his left hand over Ivar's wrist. Continuing to turn he pulls Ivar's arm in the direction of the lunge forcing the man off balance while at the same time clamping a hand around his neck, his fingers digging into hard muscle and sinew. Using the man's momentum against him, Mathias pushes Ivar's head down as he continues to turn. Ivar is now totally unbalanced and beyond the point of recovery. With all of his body weight behind it, Mathias slams the man's head into the diamond plate steel of the floor, his knee following a split second later and landing in the centre of Ivar's chest, cracking his sternum. The knife bounces from his grip and Mathias catches it, flips it around in his hand and slams it through the front of Ivar's neck, severing his spine and snapping off the knife's tip against the steel deck.

Mathias stands and steps back, taking in the scene. He looks for the gun and finds it across the room, up against the wall where it's been kicked. Working swiftly, he dismantles it, cursing himself for not thinking about the affect of the salt laden atmosphere. Grabbing a rag out of a bucket hanging from the pipework, he quickly wipes each piece and reassembles the weapon. He racks the slide, points the silenced barrel at Ivar's chest and pulls the trigger. He's rewarded with a pop and a cartridge that skitters across the deck. Mathias unscrews the silencer from the end of the barrel and places it in his pocket. Reaching around, he slides the gun under his belt at the centre of his back.

Having previously familiarised himself with the vessel, Mathias opens a hatch, steps through and makes his way up a narrow set of steel steps, emerging onto the main deck outside of the wheel house. The weather up here is brutal, at least a force seven, Mathias thinks. Through the wheelhouse windows Mathias can see the Skipper and his mate bent over the chart table, animatedly discussing whether to move or shoot the nets here again. Mathias decides on direct action. With the gun in his right hand, he grips the cold handle of the wheelhouse door with his left, twists it and steps swiftly into the warmth inside.

The skipper glances up but before he has time to move, the gun barks twice. As the skipper hits the floor, Mathias places two more shots into the upper body of the mate. Three seconds after opening the door, both men are on the floor and dying. Two more shots and the dying is over.

* * *

After Natalie, Walter and David leave for their homes, Sarah closes and locks the door. It had been a wonderful evening and the first time since she left hospital that the four of them had been together. Natalie had brought a lovely card and a bottle of champagne to celebrate the sale of the film rights to Sarah's book. Her publisher had warned her that this didn't actually mean that a film would be made but the good news was that if the rights expired before the film was started, Sarah could sell them again. Almost sounds too good to be true, Sarah thought. Either way, she was now wealthier than her parents, which was a bit hard to come to grips with. Sarah walks into her bedroom and flops onto the bed, staring up at the ceiling. Max follows shortly and plonks his muzzle on her stomach.

So life was good, but she couldn't shrug the feeling that it was all transitory. One day the men and the cars and even the dog would pack up and move on to some other person in need of protection and she'd go back to her old life. Except she could never do that, too much had happened to change it. Her old life didn't exist and neither did the old Sarah. It would be a new life and she wasn't really sure how it would all work out, but something inside her longed to get on with it.

* * *

Mathias has spent much of the last twenty four hours preparing the boat. As the trawler steamed on autopilot towards a remote part of the Norwegian coast, the first thing he'd done was to locate the electrical panel and disable the on-board AIS transponder so that the boat's movements couldn't be tracked. He then disconnected the three bilge pumps and opened every hatch, inspection port, door, porthole and window that he could find. He also prepared the small runabout stowed above the aft deck roof ensuring that the motor worked and that the fuel tank was full.

For the last three hours he has been running the *Mary Joan* without lights. Peering into the darkness has been tedious and draining but the GPS has finally brought him to the place he needs to be. The shoreline is less than a mile away and provides some relief from the swell but the water here is over four hundred feet deep. He switches the engines off and flicks the main circuit breakers to kill all power to the boat. Silence falls in the wheelhouse leaving only the howl of the wind outside.

Using his scope he takes a last careful look around until he's confident that there is nobody to see him. Mathias works his way outside, bracing against the movement of the boat and launches the runabout, tying it securely to the stern. He then crosses to the emergency fire pump; a completely independent unit that pumps seawater through a gland in the hull and out of a forty foot hose which he has run out and dropped in the mid section of the boat. He hits the automatic start button and the diesel engine throbs into life. Seconds later he can hear the brass end of the hose bumping and banging below decks as it snakes around under the pressure of delivering fifteen thousand gallons per hour.

Mathias has done the calculations in his head and at about eight and a half pounds per gallon, every hour the pump will deliver more than sixty tons of water into the boat. It's certainly not going to stay afloat until daybreak he thinks. He tosses his bergen into the runabout and starts the motor, giving it a few minutes to warm up. He unties himself from the trawler, which already appears to be sitting lower in the water, before pushing off and heading for an inlet with a small sandy beach that he's identified through his night vision scope.

Within the hour, the runabout and motor is hidden in dense scrub and Mathias is disappearing into the cover of the forest. Within the next hour the *Mary Joan* and her four man crew will be resting on the sea floor.

CHAPTER 24

Three months later, Sarah looked out of her kitchen window to see the first sign of green in the tree shading the rear of the house. The winter was finally losing its grip and signs of spring were shouldering their way into the year. The first draft of her book was just about complete and she couldn't wait for it to be published, it was turning out to be so much better than she expected. Sarah still heard from David most weeks and if his transfer to Edinburgh came through she would miss both him and Natalie. They had enjoyed many dinners together and she was very fond of them. Still, it wasn't that far and he assured her that they'd keep in touch.

There had been sporadic sightings of someone fitting Mathias's description in Europe as well as in South America of all places. None of them led anywhere. Sarah knew it was selfish but it was nice to believe he was at least doing his thing in another country, far away from England. She knew she'd never really put him out of her mind until he was in custody but so far she'd been spared the irritation of having to go into hiding. She no longer woke at night to check that Max was still on the bed, somehow time and distance had conspired to dull the keen edge of her fear.

Sarah had been looking forward to this day for quite some time. She was to speak at a dinner in London honouring successful businesswomen from across Great Britain. They were flying her down in a private plane, which was all very exciting. This was her first real trip anywhere since 'The Trouble" as she light-heartedly referred to her experiences. She'd spent hours on her speech and Angela, the ghost-writer working with her on the book, had helped enormously. She said it had just the right blend of suspense and terror. Sarah's publisher had talked her into giving the speech because she said it would be good for the book that was planned for release in the summer.

Whenever she thought about the speech she almost had to pinch herself to prove it was real. So much had happened to her in such a small space of time. The thing she found really surprising was that she actually felt different inside, as though she really *had* changed in a fundamental way. Sarah wasn't sure whether the confidence she now possessed was something she'd gained through her ordeal or whether it was a strength she'd always had but never really believed was hers. She was inclined to think it was the latter and that's what she intended to say in her speech tonight.

Sarah heard the car beep its horn twice, which was her signal to come out. She gave Max a kiss on the head and told him she'd see him tomorrow, promised him that someone would be along to feed him tonight. He appeared to be satisfied with the arrangements. She checked the tiny screen at the front door before opening it. The car was parked in its usual spot, the back door open. The windows were tinted so she couldn't see who her driver was today.

Sarah stepped out cautiously in her heels and made sure she didn't catch her dress in the door as she closed it. The doors locked automatically under the control of the driver. As the car began reversing out of the driveway she arranged her dress so as not to wrinkle it with the seat belt. She looked up as they pulled into the traffic and was surprised to see only the driver. There should have been a bodyguard as well, she never went anywhere without at least two men at her side.

"On your own today?" She asked, not recognising the bearded driver's profile.

"Meet them at airport." He said in a thick European accent. Polish maybe, she thought.

Sarah pulled the cue cards from her bag and began rehearsing her speech as she'd done many times before. Angela had made little marks on the cards, places where she was supposed to look up or gesture or pause for emphasis. The first card had only three words on it.

STOP. BREATHE. SMILE.

Angela's reminder for Sarah to settle down when she got to the podium, take a few seconds to compose herself before speaking. She ran through the outline under her breath.

Sarah was completely engrossed in her speech for almost twenty minutes. She made a few minor changes and underlined several key words. When she thought they should be getting close to the airport at Newcastle Upon Tyne, she looked up for the first time. They were going in the wrong direction, north instead of south. The sea was on her right hand side. They were driving toward Scotland. Sarah began to panic, she might miss the plane, be late for the dinner. She opened her mouth to speak but then she saw the driver's eyes looking at her in the mirror. Startlingly clear blue eyes framed by olive skin. Skin that had darkened and weathered since she saw it last.

"Did you really think I'd just forget about you, Sarah?" He said.

* * *

The first sign of trouble came when Sarah's security didn't make their scheduled radio check. The local constabulary was informed and a pair of officers made a detour to check it out. Not terribly concerned, equipment failure or human error the two possibilities in their minds. They pulled into the driveway of Sarah's rented house and rang the bell. When they didn't receive an answer they strolled around the back. They experienced their first twinge of alarm when they weren't challenged as they made their way around the side of the house. The side gate was unlocked, the padlock lay on the ground. Something wasn't right. The officers retraced their steps and called for backup. The place was way too quiet.

Within a few minutes several cars pulled up. Shortly after, David and a detective sergeant arrived, a magnetic blue light flashing on the roof of their vehicle. The house was surrounded but no one had entered the premises.

"This doesn't look good." David said unnecessarily as they made their way around to the back of the house.

They came across the first officer about twenty feet from the back door. He lay face down behind a bush; a large bloodstain had soaked through his clothes at his lower back. The second lay slumped in his chair inside the guardhouse; his throat cut from ear to ear, his head almost severed. Blood had pooled and congealed in the folds of his trousers, small terraces of gore. Inside the house, Max barked at the strangers, his breath fogging the windows as he tracked their movements.

David glanced at the security monitors in the guardhouse but the screens were dark, it appeared that the power had been cut. There was a frustrating fifteen minute delay as a police dog handler was called to restrain the animal inside. The possibility of finding Sarah dead was a real one and the dog could be expected to be wild with rage. With the dog still alive, David thought it unlikely she was inside at all and his hunch was proved correct when they finally gained access. His experience taught him that dogs like Max would give their life for the person they were assigned to protect.

Reviewing the footage from the internal security cameras they saw an unsuspecting Sarah climb into the car, and close the door. The vehicle then reversed out of the driveway with no sense of urgency. David made a call. Ten minutes later the bodies of two security officers were discovered dumped in a stolen vehicle about a mile away. They had been shot in the head at close range.

Once again the police went into high alert. Details of the security vehicle were rapidly transmitted and helicopters and fixed wing aircraft began searching main roads. David was counting on the one good card they had been dealt. Mathias had made a mistake this time, his knowledge of security protocols and techniques now a few years out of date. The vehicle he had commandeered after killing the security guards had been fitted with tracking devices for exactly this scenario, as had Sarah's bag without her knowledge. David hoped against hope that he wouldn't abandon either of them before they got a fix.

* * *

In the back seat of the car, Sarah's mind at first refused to believe that it was happening again. After all she'd been through and despite the men and machines that toiled around the clock with the single aim of protecting her, here she was. This time her abductor wasn't some pitiful sick man with good intentions; instead he was known to be a killer and a professional into the bargain. She thought about all the times she'd imagined this scenario, what she would say, how she'd respond.

She'd allowed herself to believe in her own publicity a little too much. Sitting here in her new dress and shoes she felt stupid and powerless. Mathias had a way of making you feel feeble, ineffective, a way of sapping your will to fight with one look. His calm and patient manner made his willingness to kill without hesitation seem even more frightening. In some ways it was worse than if he raged and yelled like everyone else. At least that would be human, something unpleasant but certainly understandable, familiar.

Sarah stuffed her cue cards into her bag and was about to zip it shut when Mathias reached back and snatched it from her lap. She watched him drive with his knees while he rummaged inside the bag. Satisfied she didn't have a weapon he reached over and dropped it in her lap. I guess there will be no speech tonight she thought. Sarah stopped herself. Disapproving of that negative and capitulatory thought and becoming irritated with her weakness, she took the cards back out, put them back in order and slipped them into their envelope. On second thoughts, I'll have a use for these when this is over. And I'll add a few more to the pile. See if I don't.

"Where are we going?" She asked.

"Tell me how you got out of the Blundeston tombs" Mathias said, watching her in the mirror.

"They dug me out."

"Yes. I saw the photograph. Brave policeman rescues helpless damsel."

Sarah didn't respond to his taunt.

"How did they know where you were, though?"

"How do you think they knew?" Sarah said, watching the thin slice of Mathias's face she could see in the rear vision mirror.

"Well that's what I can't work out. I know that phones don't work in there. You didn't find another exit because they dug you out of the only one. The only other person who knew about the place is Robert and you managed to kill him. Thanks for that by the way. So how? You tell me."

Sarah decided to take a chance. "I used my powers."

"Is that right? Your powers. And what powers might they be?" He scoffed.

Even though he was pretending to laugh at her, Sarah thought she detected the slightest hint of uncertainty in his voice. When she mentioned her powers she'd felt the vehicle sway slightly as though his hands on the wheel had twitched. He believes this stuff, she had to remember that. She decided to push it, recalling something curious that Robert had said.

"I sent them a picture of where I was, they saw it in their heads. I have The Mastery."

Sarah was thrown forward against the seat belt as Mathias stomped on the brakes. The tyres squealed as he pulled over to the side of the road and stopped the car under a large tree. That touched a nerve, she thought. Leaving the engine running he twisted around in his seat to face her.

"What are you saying?"

Sarah held his gaze, found she could stare into those intense eyes without backing down. If not fear, she definitely could detect hesitation and uncertainty. That was all she needed.

"I learned things about myself in that place. I found strength I didn't know that I had."

"What strength?" Mathias yelled. She hadn't seen him angry before but she couldn't stop now.

"You know the middle passageway? With the scales?" She said.

"Yes, what about it?" His eyes narrowed, she was talking about his secrets now. A muscle twitched in his face.

"I walked that passageway in the dark after my torch died and they left me alone. I heard them moving and I called them out and they fucking well backed off!"

Sarah's faced flushed scarlet as she summoned the feeling of mindless fury she'd experienced, lost in the darkness, rage bordering on madness. Mathias actually recoiled as if she'd slapped his face, his look pure astonishment.

"Bullshit! I don't believe you. You're making it up." He shook his head. "No way you could do that. No way." He turned away from her, couldn't hold her stare.

Mathias fumbled with the gear selector before slamming the car into drive and accelerating hard into the traffic. She saw his shoulders twitch as he fought to settle himself down again, saw him wipe his forehead. She had no idea what it all meant to him but she'd certainly rattled his cage. Her only problem was that she wasn't sure it helped or made her situation worse. But, she had touched a nerve, found a way through his defences and that was no small thing. Now she had to figure out how to use it against him without getting herself killed.

* * *

The stolen security vehicle was located within the hour. Members of the Armed Response Unit converged on a dense stand of trees about half a mile from the main road. The car was only visible from the ground and once a secure perimeter had been established the men moved in. As expected, the vehicle was empty. An examination of the nearby soil revealed that a second car had been parked close by, clearly left in anticipation of the switch.

To confirm what they already knew, the vehicle was dusted for fingerprints. Mathias had obviously been heading north but that could have been a feint. The vehicle's engine was still warm and at most the police were thirty minutes behind them. Roadblocks were thrown up and search aircraft refocussed. A level of desperation was creeping into the police effort, after basking in the glory of Sarah's rescue, it was unthinkable for them to lose her now. The race was on, not only to find Mathias, but also to find Sarah. Alive.

* * *

The press was in a frenzy; Sarah's house a hive of police activity, of crime tape and ambulances, grim men with clipboards and oversized measuring tapes, bodies covered by white sheets and strapped to stretchers as though they might even yet resist their fate. Sarah's speech in London had been cancelled and at an afternoon press conference a very uncomfortable and angry Chief Constable broke the news that she had been abducted.

The situation was turned into a political bludgeon and commentators across the nation were asking what kind of a bungling police force do we have when one man can seemingly come and go at will, evading capture for months at a time and then popping up in the middle of the suburbs, turning the streets into a slaughterhouse. In churches up and down the country people prayed, while family and friends wept for the woman they had lost, then found, and now almost unbearably, lost again.

It was altogether too much for Sarah's father who suffered a mild heart attack and was rushed to hospital. Sarah's mother stayed at his side, the pair united in grief. A mob of journalists and photographers kept a hungry vigil outside the hospital, the public's appetite for detail of the parent's suffering appeared to know no bounds.

* * *

After swapping cars Mathias continued to drive west, away from the coast. They had been wrong to think he didn't know about the tracking device in the security vehicle. He had anticipated it from the beginning. There had been trouble at the switch-over with Sarah refusing to move, slowing him down. He knew what she was trying to do and was so angry he debated simply killing her there and then but thought better of it. He'd risked everything to snatch her the way he did and he didn't want his effort to be wasted. She'd fought hard against him and it had been difficult to move her without doing damage. In the end he grew weary of it and held her down while he stabbed a sedative into her thigh. He'd hoped it wouldn't come to that because the sedation was a risky business. Putting someone to sleep was easy, ensuring they woke up again was the difficult part. Anyway, there it was. She was sleeping on the back seat and he now had time to think.

Mathias was alarmed at how fast Sarah had progressed. That she knew about The Mastery, claimed to have it. She said she'd sent a picture to the minds of the police. What Mathias knew she meant was she'd caused them to have a vision, and they had found her. There was the proof. To cause a vision was evidence of power indeed and there was simply no other way that they could have known where she was.

He fretted that he'd left it too long. Mathias had studied the Bible carefully. He knew that when Jesus was called, he went into the wilderness and fasted in preparation for his ministry. For forty days Satan bided his time, waited to the end, when Jesus would have been almost dead from starvation. Then Satan introduced his first temptation; *'If you are the Son of God, command that these stones become loaves of bread.'* Mathias admired his choice of tactics, an excellent plan under the circumstances. But it failed. Having the benefit of hindsight, Mathias knew *why* it failed. It failed because Satan had left his attempt too late. The forty days of praying and fasting and meditation had strengthened Jesus' mind to the point that he could resist the hunger and therefore the temptation wasn't persuasive enough. The Devil should have struck earlier.

Mathias was determined never to make that mistake. If he suspected he'd found the Redeemer, he would allow only a short time to elapse before killing her, even though above everything else he craved the knowledge that he knew she would have. The Mastery, combined with his military training, would make him invincible. He desperately wanted that knowledge, to gain The Mastery himself, but he dared not allow too much time to pass. He was well aware of the power that the knowledge would confer.

And yet maybe when it really counted he had done exactly that, had allowed too much time to elapse. Fucking Robert's meddling. Perhaps she was just too strong now. For the first time he could remember, the thought triggered an unfamiliar emotion in his mind. Fear.

CHAPTER 25

When Sarah woke she had no comprehension of where she was. Her brain slowly engaged with her senses and she realised she was still sitting even though she was no longer in the car. Her vision cleared and she became aware of her surroundings. She was in a barn. Stone walls, roof trestles swathed in spider webs, old straw over a dirt floor. The place smelled of cow dung. And it was cold. She wasn't wearing her shoes.

Her eyes were sticky from a deep, dreamless sleep and she attempted to wipe them. It was then she understood that she was restrained. Her wrists tied to the chair arms with heavy coarse rope. Rope that smelled of old tractors and kerosene heaters, rope that scratched. She tried to move her legs, they were tied as well. An empty armchair faced her. The chair appeared weirdly dislocated inside the barn; made from leather that had once been shiny and red it was now brown and stained, cracked. Stuffing escaped from splits in the armrests. One of its short stubby legs was missing and had been replaced by two bricks. She shivered, not dressed for night time in the country.

Sarah heard a door creak and Mathias came in, sat down on the chair, crossed his legs, uncrossed them. Agitated. In his hand he held a gun with a disproportionally long barrel, almost a cartoon gun, thought Sarah, although she had no doubt it was real. The beard altered the shape of his face but she remembered him without it, she could clearly recall the line of his jaw. Mathias tapped the end of the barrel against his leg. She saw him stiffen, listening, as though he'd heard a noise outside. Then he seemed to discount it.

"Well, Sarah, here we are." He said, looking around, apparently unsure where to begin.

"What do you want with me?" She asked.

"I want to know about The Mastery." He said.

"What's to know?"

"I want to know how you got it, while you were locked up in the tombs."

"I don't know. It just came." Sarah said, struggling to find a way into his thinking.

Mathias stood up, restless energy compelling him to pace up and down the floor of the barn before resuming his seat. Sarah's eyes tracked him left and right, noting his unusual behaviour. He kicked at something lying on the floor and it spun across the barn before striking the opposite wall. His eyes twitched, he kept shaking his head, muttering under his breath. She'd never seen him like this.

"That's not a good answer, Sarah. I need to know!" He yelled.

"You'll never know. Never!" Sarah shot back. She surprised herself by the strength in her own voice.

Mathias looked at her, she could see desperation in his eyes and she realised a pure and fundamental truth. She had power over him. Although she was tied to a chair and he had a gun, the power rested in her hands. Because he *believed* her, in his heart and mind he believed her. He'd spent so long looking for The Redeemer, now he'd finally decided she was the one, all she had to do was to play that role and the power was hers.

"Why, Sarah? Why will I never know? There has to be a way." He said, falling to his knees before her, his expression pleading, begging.

Sarah's imagination was working rapidly. Cursing the cobwebs that still clung to her mind, she knew she was poised on a razor's edge and she wasn't sure which way this confrontation would flip. She just followed her gut.

"Because you don't really know what fear is. How could you?

You've always been in control, always dominated, intimidated. But if you want to know, you have to get to the point where you are so completely terrified that the fear doesn't matter because you don't care anymore. About anything. Don't care whether you live or die, you just want it to end. You have to completely give yourself over to it. Get to a place beyond fear. Then you come up the other side or you die. If you don't die, then you'll know."

Mathias looked at her, his eyes wide, almost like a child. His body was trembling, this was what he'd waited for, hoped for, dreamed of. A tear escaped his eye, its track leaving a glossy line before disappearing into his beard.

"I have to know, Sarah." He said.

Sarah then said something that she couldn't remember even thinking. She heard it for the first time as it came confidently out of her mouth.

"Give me the gun, Mathias." She said.

He looked at her face and she nodded as if understanding, as if reading his thoughts. "If you want to know, first you have to give me the gun."

Sarah's eyes were locked on his, never wavering, holding him, guiding him, maintaining the connection between them, the connection that had so startled her when they first met. When she'd been a different person.

He reached into his boot and pulled out a short knife. Sarah caught a glimpse of steel as the blade slashed through the rope securing her right hand. She lifted her arm free, slowly clenching and unclenching her fist. Mathias's eyes didn't leave her face for an instant. He appeared to be in a trance. He reversed the gun and handed it to her. The world seemed to compress to this tiny room, all other sounds and sensations ceased. Just the here and now. Mathias, Sarah, the gun.

Sarah took the gun from his hand. She could feel the residual warmth from Mathias's grip. It was heavy, the long barrel wanted to droop forward. She forced it up. She placed the end of the barrel on Mathias's forehead; saw the tiny indentation made by the muzzle on his skin. He closed his eyes, a slight smile on his face. He looked relaxed now, the trembling had stopped, his breathing slowed. He appeared tranquil.

Sarah's finger tightened on the trigger, took up the slack in the mechanism. She knew the power was now hers. His life, her hands. She was distracted by a shape on her right. Sarah's gaze flicked across to a group of men standing just inside the door. Big men, dressed in black body armour, automatic weapons in their hands. They were silent, watching her. David stood with them. Their eyes met and he gave a tiny shake of his head.

Sarah removed the gun from Mathias's forehead, his eyes began to open. He was crashed from the side by two of the men and he sprawled on the hard floor. Instantly four of them were on top of him, holding him down, pressing his face into the cobbled floor, twisting his arms behind his back, handcuffing his arms and feet. They dragged him to his knees. He didn't speak but his eyes locked onto Sarah's face. She was drained. David took the gun out of her hands.

Still bound, Sarah met his stare and held it. Unafraid. Mathias was the first to back down, his eyes dropped to the floor. Humbled, broken.

"Why didn't you kill me?" his voice a whisper. "It would have been better than this."

"Not for me." Sarah said.

As Mathias was led away, David knelt in front of Sarah and untied the ropes, took her cold hands in his.

"Thank you, Sarah." He said.

EPILOGUE

Sarah's book was released in the summer and it exceeded even her publisher's grand expectations. She toured the world promoting it and became one of the most sought after speakers on the after-dinner circuit. Sarah began writing a second book, this one without Angela's help. Her working title was 'Beyond Fear' and she hoped it would inspire women everywhere in the fight to unlock their hidden confidence.

Although asked about it often, she never did speak about that night in the barn. For her it was as though, just for a moment, she'd experienced something to which she had no right. Mastery that one human being should never be able to wield over another. She gave much thought to what would have happened if the police had arrived ten minutes later. In her heart she knew that she would have pulled the trigger. David told her it was better this way. Better that she didn't have to live with his death on her conscience. For Sarah it was almost the same as she had no doubt about what she would have done.

While Robert's death caused her pain, the fact that she would have shot Mathias as he kneeled before her somehow seemed worse. Worse because of the power she wielded over him and to which she almost surrendered. She didn't ever want that feeling to return. It didn't belong to her. It didn't belong to anyone.

Sarah thought that Walter, who alone appeared to understand her reluctance to discuss that night, summed it up perfectly with one of his signature quotations:

"If a man, even fleetingly, should taste of the power of The Divine, far from salvation, and with all certitude, the result to his fellow will be destruction."